AND WE SHALL HAVE SNOW

AND WE SHALL HAVE SNOW

A Roxanne Calloway Mystery

RAYE ANDERSON

Doug Whiteway, Editor

Signature
EDITIONS

Cover design by Doowah Design.
Photo of author by Michael Long.

This book was printed on Ancient Forest Friendly paper.
Printed and bound in Canada by Hignell Book Printing Inc.

We acknowledge the support of the Canada Council for the Arts and the Manitoba Arts Council for our publishing program.

Library and Archives Canada Cataloguing in Publication

Title: And we shall have snow / Raye Anderson.
Names: Anderson, Raye, 1943- author.
Description: Series statement: A Roxanne Calloway mystery
Identifiers: Canadiana (print) 20200184474 |
Canadiana (ebook) 20200184482 |
ISBN 9781773240664 (softcover) | ISBN 9781773240671 (HTML)
Classification: LCC PS8601.N44725 A64 2020 | DDC C813/.6—dc23

Signature Editions
P.O. Box 206, RPO Corydon, Winnipeg, Manitoba, R3M 3S7
www.signature-editions.com

For Rachel, Kirsty and Fiona

1

PANDA AND ANNIE were headed for the dump. It was January, deep in the throes of a Manitoba winter. The temperature hovered around minus thirty-five Celsius, but the sky was an unblemished blue, the air crisp and cold, the snow sparkled, clean and white. It might be freezing outside, but there wasn't a breath of wind. They turned off the highway onto the dump road. It ran straight as a die all the way to the lake, five kilometres beyond, a smudge on the horizon visible through stands of trees, ashy brown and bare, casting cobalt shadows on the snow. Apart from the two of them, not a thing moved in any direction. Animals and people knew better than to venture out on a day like this unless they had to. It looked pretty outside their truck windows, but this cold could be deadly.

Panda and Annie knew how to dress for the weather on days like these. They wore down-filled parkas with hoods edged with fur, scarves to wrap around their faces and knit toques to pull down over their heads so that only their eyes were visible, leather mitts over thinner wool ones, and felt-lined boots with thick socks inside. They wouldn't stay out for long. They wouldn't risk freezing. From the window of his shack beside the entrance gate Archie Huminski, who managed Cullen Dump, waved their big, red Sierra truck through. There was no need for them to show their resident's pass. They were regular visitors.

Panda and Annie lived in the Interlake, named for the land between two large expanses of water, remnants of an enormous prehistoric lake that had dried to form the prairies. One lake lay to the west and the other, just to the east, was so big that it resembled an inland sea smack dab in the middle of Canada. Their house, the one they had built several years before, was out in the country, near Cullen Village, which lay on the shore of that big, frozen lake. There was no garbage pickup service out where they lived, so once every couple of weeks Panda and Annie would load plastic bags containing all their household waste into the back of the truck and do a dump run.

Cullen Village prided itself on being environmentally conscious and was rightly proud of its landfill, which was situated about four kilometres outside of town. Archie kept the place well organized and recycling was encouraged. There was no sewer system in the village. Waste fluids were picked up from holding tanks and carted in "honey trucks" to the sewage lagoon beside the dump, even in the depths of winter. It was far enough away for the residents not to be reminded of its existence whenever the wind blew in their direction, but near enough to allow residents like Panda and Annie to have convenient access.

Now, Panda drove the truck slowly along the snow-packed track that served as a road, past piles of concrete rubble, broken toilets and sinks and heaps of discarded metal waiting to be picked up for scrap. She watched out for debris on the track. It was easy to pick up a nail or a shard of metal, and a flat tire when it was this cold was no fun. Trees, clumped along the perimeter of the site, were festooned with white plastic grocery bags that had snagged on branches on windier days. They passed the turnoff that led to the area where grass cuttings and leaves were deposited in the summer, to decompose into compost. No one went there in winter. That track was buried in undisturbed snow. Beside it was a grey shed with an adjoining cage, where hazardous wastes were left for disposal.

They usually liked to stop at the lumber section. Old, discarded furniture often showed up, even in wintertime. Panda had an eye for antiques and liked to restore old wood. She would search for a well-made chair, a dresser, a table made of solid wood, half buried in the snow. She took such items home, sanded them down, polished them or gave them a fresh coat of paint, then sold them online. Winter was a good time to hunker down and get the work done. On this day, however, she headed straight up the hill. Panda had previously lived in the city. Winnipeg, Manitoba's capital city, lay an hour's drive to the south. Panda had been surprised to discover what "over the hill" really meant, that you drove up a sloping incline, a solid hill built of dirt and garbage, to the top, where you parked and chucked your bags over the cliff-like edge, literally, "over the hill."

"Imagine that," said Panda. "Never occurred to me."

The Cullen Village garbage trucks (there were two) headed dutifully out every Monday morning to retrieve the village's garbage from curbsides and driveways. They brought it to the dump and piled all the trash they collected along the top of the hill, where it remained until Archie got into his big yellow Bobcat and used the front end to shove the whole lot over the edge. He then trundled the machine down a ramp at the side of the hill to the bottom, where he pushed and compressed the garbage into the side of the mound. So the hill grew, even in wintertime. It was fifteen feet high, the only incline as far as the eye could see. By Monday's end the heap of rubbish was usually gone, but this was Tuesday and this week, all of it remained.

Full black plastic bags, interspersed with boxes, bags and smaller white grocery bags that were stuffed to capacity, lay piled along the edge of the hill. Some bags had burst open. There were broken toys, sheets of cardboard, empty bottles, pots, crockery, books and pieces of torn fabric scattered among them. Seagulls swooped overhead, scavenging for anything edible. They were eerily quiet, silenced by the cold. Another truck and a car were parked at the top of the hill. "Look who's here," said Panda, backing her own truck up alongside the others. She understood dump protocol.

"Hi there, Angus. Hi, Jack," she called, hauling her large bulk out of the cab. Annie clambered out on the passenger side. She barely reached Panda's shoulder. Their breath turned into ice crystals as they spoke. "Cold day, eh?"

"How come the Cullen garbage is still here?" asked Annie.

"Archie's Bobcat's broke. We've been trying to help him fix it but it needs a part from Winnipeg."

Angus Smith lived in an old farmhouse at the south end of Cullen Village. He had a large workshop, well equipped with table saws, sanders, an extractor fan and a worktable. Angus played host to a men's group that gathered there each week, to build and fix things and gossip. Currently they were collecting aluminum that they could smelt down and mould into other things. Angus had an inventive mind and had built a small foundry. He also had a fascination with fire.

"That's what comes of living in this damned Frigidaire," said Panda, who often said she wanted to move to British Columbia, to the milder climate of the West Coast. Annie loved the intense stillness of the winter cold. She had no wish to live anywhere else and so far her will prevailed.

"Ha!" said Angus. "See what I've found already." He waved a pair of old brass candlesticks. "Look at these, I'll be able to melt them down just fine." He threw the candlesticks into the back of his grey truck. Jack Sawatsky was one of his best cronies. He was hauling a box of old magazines away from the edge of the hill.

"You want to have a look at these, Panda?" He knew from experience that Panda liked to scan the illustrations, to find ideas as to how she could update old furniture.

"Sure, I'll have a look." She squatted down beside him. "Is Archie going to be able to move all this stuff today?" She watched Annie walking along the edge of the hill, surveying the assorted rubbish.

"He's gone to get his old tractor."

At the entrance to the dump was a sign that said, "No Scavenging." Archie knew what they were up to but he turned a blind eye. He collected items himself, ones with resell value, bikes in decent shape, radios that worked. He got first pick as a perk of the job. He passed them on to a niece who held garage sales in the summer, on the other side of the lake. The pieces he found were stored in a shed. He also stashed logs, enough to feed the wood stove that kept his shack warm and snug on days like this. Angus and Jack were among the handful of men who were sometimes invited to join him on a quiet afternoon for a game of cards. Archie liked company and he liked to talk. "You can tell a lot about folks from what they throw out," he said.

Annie and Panda had never been invited into the all-male world of the dump shack but their presence on the hill itself was tolerated and guys like Angus often passed on an interesting bit of news as they clambered over the plastic bags that littered the area. In a place as isolated as this, in the wintertime, it helped to know what was going on.

The roar of an engine shattered the quiet. Archie drove a red tractor up the hill and used its front end loader to start sending bags crashing over the edge. Panda watched him drive to and fro, then she walked further along the hill. A box of old china caught her eye. She picked up a pink-flowered cup and shook her head. People used to treasure that stuff. Now it was thrown away, useless and unwanted. Last summer she had seen a piano in the lumber area, lying on its back, broken, its keys gaping silently up at the sky. She went back to the Sierra, opened the back gate and hauled out three full garbage bags and a box of rubbish. She tossed them over the hill herself.

It didn't take Archie long to shove all the trash off the top. He was doing a rough job, working fast, just pushing most of the bags over. Annie watched as each load crashed over the edge. Usually he cleared everything, including stray bottles and cans. Archie took pride in doing a good job, leaving the top of the hill clean and flat. That would obviously have to wait until his big loader was fixed. Today, he was only doing what needed to be done. It wasn't long until he swung over to the ramp and was chugging down to the bottom of the hill, his machine belching exhaust fog behind him. Annie was glad to see him, his noise and his fumes, gone. She walked back to where Panda was loading the magazines into the back of the truck. "You taking those home?" Angus and Jack looked like they had finished for the day too. They were walking towards their vehicles.

Archie's voice, coming from the foot of the hill, stopped them.

"Oh, geez!" they heard him yell. "Hey, guys!" Angus, Jack, Panda and Annie went to the edge of the hill and looked over.

"What's up, Archie?" Angus shouted down. Archie had stopped the tractor and was clambering out.

"There's something here!" Archie was approaching a heap of black garbage bags at the foot of the vertical fall, ten or so feet below. "This is bad, real bad."

Angus and Jack skidded down the slippery ramp on foot towards Archie, who was staring at the plastic bags. Panda and Annie followed. They could see that one bag had ruptured on impact. As they drew closer they could see the cause of Archie's alarm.

The bag lay against a pile of metal cans partially covered with snow. Protruding from it was a naked human foot. The pink flesh was glossy and cold, like plastic, startling against the white snow and the black, shiny plastic bag. Clumps of black and white newsprint bulged around it. The toenails were painted turquoise.

Angus reached over into the tractor and turned off the engine. There was a moment of stunned silence, then Panda pulled off her leather mitts and reached into her pocket for her cellphone. "I'm calling 911," she said. Annie stood stock still, watching.

"Wonder where the rest of her is?" said Angus, looking closer. He started poking around among the other bags.

"You shouldn't be doing that, Angus!" Panda said, but then someone answered her call. "We need the police," they heard her say.

"What else is here?" Angus said, still rooting among the bags. Archie joined him. Jack looked on, helpless. Annie still surveyed the scene, grim-faced. Panda was on the phone, giving directions.

"Got something!" cried Angus, throwing down his mitts and seizing another bag.

"You need to leave that alone!" Panda put her phone back in her pocket. "The police are on their way."

It was too late. They all watched as Angus ripped the bag open. He held it up by the bottom corners and what rolled out was a head, severed at the neck. The hair was blonde, almost white. The eyes stared, blue and vacant. The mouth gaped in a silent scream. They could see teeth, a protruding tongue.

Annie's voice cut through the cold. "That," she said, "is Stella Magnusson."

2

"I THOUGHT STELLA was going to Nashville, like she usually does." Roberta Axelsson was stirring a pot of soup, Hubbard squash that she'd grown in her garden when the days were warmer.

Margo Wishart watched from the kitchen table. Everything about Roberta was round and colourful. Her face was rosy, weathered from time spent outdoors, her body was round, even when it was cinched, as now, by an apron. Her jeans were worn and her sweater was an old red hand-knit, worn at the elbows and baggy, the sleeves rolled up. Her head was wreathed in golden curls. Margo doubted that the colour was real, but it didn't matter. Their glow suited Roberta's sunny disposition.

"No. Dublin first, then London and Italy. She was going to fly home from Paris." Sasha Rosenberg stood at the kitchen counter. She was angular and bony in comparison, dressed in dark greys and purples. "Would have been a great trip if she had made it."

Margo had driven Sasha the twelve kilometres north from Cullen Village to Roberta's farmhouse. Sasha pulled a covered dish out of a bag.

"Meatballs. They should probably go in the oven."

"That's a good idea." Roberta reached for the dish. "Annie will probably be late. Panda can't make it. She had to go into Winnipeg to see a client."

Panda worked as an accountant. She had cut back on her business when she moved out to the Interlake, but still balanced the books and did the occasional audit for customers she liked and others that paid well.

Roberta sniffed at the contents of the dish. "Did you cook these yourself, Sasha?"

"Who? Me? You kidding? I dropped by IKEA last time I was in Winnipeg. Picked up a bag."

Roberta looked reproachfully at Sasha over the top of the dish. Roberta believed in natural food and avoided all things processed or preserved. Sasha didn't care. Cooking wasn't her thing.

"I made cheese scones," Margo said. "From scratch. They didn't rise the way they should but they taste okay." She had grown up in Scotland and retained some of her accent. She peered out the window. The weather pundits had labelled this cold spell a "polar vortex." The jet stream, which normally swooshed its way across the northern hemisphere, had stalled, creating a pocket of Arctic air that hovered above the prairies. The temperature hadn't risen above minus twenty since Christmas. Three nights ago the thermometer had gone down to minus fifty. That was unusual even in this part of the world. Margo shivered, thinking of anything or anyone being out there in that freezing cold.

"If Stella was frozen outside in this weather she could have been there for days," she said. She picked up a bundle of cutlery. Soon she was moving around the table laying out forks, knives and spoons.

"Do you think someone left her outside to freeze, deliberately?" Roberta's eyebrows knotted in concern.

"No. The coyotes would have got her," said Sasha.

"She might have been left in a shed," Roberta suggested.

"Or maybe inside somebody's freezer." Margo sank into a chair and wrapped the scarf that was draped around her shoulders a little closer. The kitchen was snug but the thought was chilling. "But can you imagine living with a dead body lying there, right inside your house?"

"Whoever did it chopped her up and sent her to the dump." Sasha parked herself opposite. "Freaky."

"Bodies sometimes do end up in landfills, though." Roberta put the lid back on the soup pot.

"Yes, but not our landfill. Not Cullen Dump." Margo was relatively new to Cullen Village. She still viewed it through honeymoon eyes and hated the idea of her newfound paradise being tainted. "How long was she planning to be away?"

"Until April," Sasha replied. "She would have been home by the beginning of the month, to get ready for StarFest. Guess that's all over now."

Erik, Roberta's husband, strolled in carrying a guitar case. The Axelssons' kitchen was connected to the back door by a corridor lined with coats on hooks. Boots and shoes lay strewn upon racks at the foot of each wall. A basket of slippers stood ready for visitors. Tracking snowy feet into the house was discouraged in Canadian homes. Erik was of Icelandic origin, like many of the inhabitants of the area. He wore his fair hair long, and sported a beard. He looked a bit like an aging Viking.

"What's over?"

"StarFest. It's too bad," Sasha said, poking through the plate of scones and choosing one. "I'm having one of these right now. I'm starving."

"Didn't you make money at it?" Erik was pulling on heavy boots. Sasha made pottery and metal sculptures, tall and angular. Margo thought they looked a bit like Sasha herself. Her job at StarFest had been to run the crafts section, named Constellation Craft Corner.

"I did okay. I guess I'll have to forget about that now." Sasha spread butter on the scone and looked carefully indifferent. Margo knew that Sasha was always broke. She probably needed every cent she earned at StarFest. Roberta had gone to the sink to fill the kettle.

The Stargazer Music Festival happened annually, on a large field behind Stella Magnusson's house, in tents, with a centre stage that attracted crowds each evening. Stella had started the festival seven years before. It had been a success from the beginning and had grown each year. Since it happened at the end of June, on or around the summer solstice, it was seen as a harbinger of summer. Stella had established it with the help of a few friends who contributed their talents. Now it attracted guest artists from all over the country. StarFest, as it had quickly come to be known, had grown into a four-day event. Visitors paid for passes, which sold out, and camped in the surrounding fields. There was plenty of room. Stella owned eighty-six acres. She employed a seasonal staff of four and a squad of volunteers to help but the concept, the programming and the promotion were all unmistakably hers. There was little space left in StarFest now for local performers. It had become a professional event.

"I never had a chance to go," said Margo. She had arrived in Cullen Village during the previous summer. "But it was obviously successful. Who would possibly want to kill Stella?"

Roberta lit the gas under the kettle. It fired up with a loud pop.

Erik zipped up his jacket. "It's clouded over. Not so cold out there. Bet it's going to snow," he said, avoiding answering the question. When Roberta, Margo and Sasha's book group got together, Erik knew to take himself off for the afternoon. The group started with lunch at one. It could go on for hours.

There was a knock at the door. Erik pulled it open and in walked a woman in a smart wool coat. Phyllis Smedley sat down to pull off tall leather boots. Under the coat, the sweater she wore looked like cashmere. It was pink.

"I'm off now." Erik picked up his guitar case. "Don't forget to feed the animals if it gets late."

"Me? Forget?" But Roberta was busy filling up a large, stoneware teapot.

The book group met every six weeks or so. The members had all lived in Winnipeg before moving to the lake. The Interlake towns on the east shore welcomed incomers, even unconventional ones like artists, and an informal art colony had grown along the lakeshore over the years. Now all of the members regarded this place as home, and all of them had links to the art community.

They had decided from the start not to follow any fixed rules or to have an organized discussion about their chosen book. Margo, who was new to the group, had soon come to realize that the book club was just an excuse to get together, to eat and spend an afternoon in each other's company and, in its way, it worked. Somehow the conversation flowed easily all afternoon, sometimes about the book, sometimes not.

"Has anyone talked to Annie and Panda about what happened at the dump?" asked Phyllis, bringing a bowl of potato salad to the table.

"I called," said Roberta. "Got Panda. She says Annie's doing a drawing of the head."

"She is? That is disgusting." Phyllis pursed her lips in distaste. Sasha took the bowl from her and peeled off a layer of shrink-wrap.

"Well, Phyllis, that's what Annie does," she said. "She paints everything."

"And when is she going to get a topic like that again?" added Margo.

"It certainly must have been, well, memorable," Phyllis grudgingly conceded. "George and I saw Stella just last week. We were going to check up on her house while she was away."

"So you must have been among the last to see her."

"I suppose so."

Roberta brought over the large pot of tea. "Help yourselves."

The group met in each other's houses, but Roberta's big farm kitchen was a favourite. The rectangular table, built to feed a large family, could easily seat ten people. The book group liked to put all the food in the middle, help themselves, sprawl around and eat while they talked. They sipped their tea as they waited for Annie to arrive.

Sasha looked across at Phyllis. "Wouldn't you have wanted to photograph her head, if you had been there?" she asked.

Phyllis's eyebrows shot up. "No, I would not," she said. "I was going to be the official photographer for StarFest this year. This is all such a nasty surprise."

"Was Stella going to pay you?" Sasha asked pointedly. "Or were you going to volunteer?"

"Panda's kind of spooked by the drawing." Roberta poured tea into the mugs, most of them handmade pottery. "She says it looks really ugly."

"It can't. Stella was beautiful," Phyllis protested. "She always looked stunning. I took a great photograph of her last year, on the final day of the festival."

"Remember that painting Roger Kato did of her, the one that caused all the fuss?" Sasha said. Phyllis's precision and affluence irritated her. But Margo welcomed the question. She wanted to know more about Stella's background. Roberta and Sasha had the longest history in the community and the memories that went with it. They knew all the backstories. The question was whether they were true or not.

"Oh, god, yes!" said Roberta, spluttering on a mouthful of tea. "Roger. Now there's someone who might have had it in for her." So far, no one had brought up the question of who could have carried out the murder, although that thought was on all their minds.

"Who was Roger?" asked Margo.

"An old boyfriend, painted her nude, kind of like the Goya *Naked Maja*. Years ago. He used to run a little art gallery at Cullen Village, where the ice cream shop is now. Hung the painting right in the middle of a wall. Everyone could tell it was Stella. Some of the villagers took offence, family values, that kind of stuff. They asked him to take it down. It was quite the controversy. Roger sold up not long after and moved back to Winnipeg. I think he lives mostly in Santa Fe these days."

"Oh, well, that would count him out," said Phyllis.

"She was married once, to some guy in L.A. That's where she was living before she moved back here. Guess he couldn't have done it either. Guys really liked Stella." Sasha ate a last bite of scone.

"She certainly looked attractive," said Margo. She had only seen Stella a couple of times. Sasha had told her in the car on the drive up that Stella's father, like Erik's, had been a direct descendant of the Icelanders, thus her white-blonde hair, pale blue eyes and high-cheeked, fine bone structure.

"I guess she wasn't so pretty when they found her," said Sasha. "Wonder how many more body parts they've found." Phyllis looked disgusted again.

"Has anyone heard anything from the police?" Roberta asked. "Panda says the RCMP taped the place off, soon as they got there. She and Annie and a couple of old guys had to wait down at the shack. Once they'd given their statements they were sent home. The dump's been closed ever since, although the guy who runs it is still around. They need him to help them figure out where to dig. There's a bunch of police in white suits out from the city. All the village garbage is being hauled to Fiskar Bay until they're done."

Fiskar Bay was the nearest town, about fifteen kilometres north of Cullen Village. As well as being fiercely proud of its Icelandic heritage, it was also home to the local detachment of the Royal Canadian Mounted Police. The Mounties, who wore dull navy, not traditional red serge, patrolled the highways in large, white Ford sedans.

"That sounds like Annie now." Roberta looked out the window. Sure enough, Annie was manoeuvring her big red truck into a parking spot between Margo's little blue Honda and a snowbank. "She always looks so little to be driving that big tank of a thing."

Soon Annie was seated at the table with them and bowls of soup were being passed around.

"I bought a cake on the way here," she said. "I didn't have time to cook." They were more interested to find out, first hand, what had happened the previous day at the dump. The RCMP sergeant, Bill Gilchrist, had interviewed her and Panda, she said.

"Matt, Panda's nephew, was with him. You know he's a constable in the RCMP? He got transferred to Fiskar Bay in September. We think that's why they got us out of there first, because Panda's related to him." Yes, she had seen the foot. Yes, it was naked. It looked like cold, pink marble and yes, the toenails were painted turquoise. And the head? Annie paused and looked around the table.

"I woke up that first night with the image of Stella's face staring straight at me and I knew I just had to get up and start drawing," she said quietly. "I needed to get it down on paper, then maybe I'd get back to sleep. Panda doesn't like it but she doesn't have to look at it. I'm keeping it in a drawer." For a few seconds all that could be heard was the sound of eating.

"It was definitely Stella?" asked Phyllis.

"Oh, it was her all right."

"Do you think she had been frozen deliberately?" Sasha inquired, chewing on a meatball. "Did someone freeze her first and then cut her up after?"

"That is so sick," Phyllis said with disdain.

"Something like that must have happened," Sasha continued, watching Phyllis for a reaction. "Either she was chopped up first and then frozen or someone froze the whole body and then cut her up after."

"Won't they be able to tell?" Margo asked, genuinely curious.

"Do we have to talk about this while we are eating?" pleaded Phyllis.

Sasha continued, "Roberta, you cut up animals."

Outside the house was the Axelssons' small farm. They had sheep, some goats, chickens and an alpaca. Roberta spun wool and made soaps and lotions from the goats' milk. Slaughter was a natural part of life for her. They sent their larger animals to a small abattoir, but dealt with the chickens themselves. Sometimes they fattened up a pig and had it killed in the fall, to eat during the winter months. Bacon, ham, pork chops and sausages filled two large freezers in a room off the kitchen where they were eating. Some lambs and goats went the same route.

"Could she have been cut up while she was still fresh, like a hunter does a deer?"

Roberta thought for a moment. "Be messy." She had friends who hunted deer and butchered the carcasses themselves. "There would be a lot of blood. And guts." Phyllis took a deep breath and exhaled, loudly. "If she was frozen, you could just use a saw. It would be easier."

"They'll have a forensic team working on it, won't they?" asked Margo, reaching for the potato salad.

"Don't know," said Roberta. "Murder doesn't happen much out here. There was a kid killed in Fiskar Bay a few years back, on a holiday weekend, but that was a gang, out visiting from the city. It wasn't like this. This is local, I suppose."

"So someone we know might have done it?" Phyllis asked. They all paused again. Annie broke the silence.

"I know how we can find out what's going on," she mused aloud. "I'll get Panda to invite her nephew Matt, the one that's the Mountie, for dinner. He'll tell us."

"Isn't he supposed to keep all that RCMP stuff confidential?" Margo asked.

"Yeah," said Annie. "But Panda will get him to tell her."

"I can't believe this!" Phyllis put down her fork. "What's happened to Stella is appalling. Don't you care? Who could have hated her enough to do that to her? She was so popular! She had so many friends."

"Stella had a lot of acquaintances," Roberta said, her voice unusually cool.

"That's right. There were folks that didn't like her much, Phyllis," Sasha added.

"Well, they were probably jealous of her." Phyllis looked from one to the other. "She did everything so well! Who would be angry enough to freeze her and cut up her body and dispose of it at the dump? Look at what she did for Cullen Village. StarFest is marvellous. It's a huge success. And all thanks to Stella."

"Yup," said Sasha, "and it's over."

"You helped run it, didn't you, Sasha? Aren't you on the board?"

"Sure, but we didn't do much. Stella made all the decisions. We just did as we were told. We'll have to have a meeting, I suppose. Figure out how we shut it down."

Margo watched anxiety flicker behind Sasha's eyes. Roberta stood up and began collecting the soup bowls. "Didn't the farmer that lived next door to Stella cause trouble?"

Sasha smiled again. "Oh, him!" she hooted. "He couldn't stand Stella, or StarFest, all the noise, all the people. He hated the arts, at least so Stella said. But you couldn't always believe what Stella said."

Roberta lifted the teapot. "Does anyone want more tea? Will I make another pot? You know, we haven't talked about the book yet."

They pulled out copies of the book they had been reading, a winner of the Giller prize, the top event on the Canadian literary calendar, from a few years back, but their hearts were not in it. Try as they might, Stella Magnusson's death preoccupied them, making it hard for them to talk about anything else. They finished early, put on coats and boots and mittens and headed out into a late afternoon that was already getting dark. Snowflakes were beginning to fall.

Annie was just reaching her truck as Margo backed out. Sasha sat, bundled in the passenger seat, scarf up over her nose, hat pulled down, trying to keep warm. The car hadn't heated up properly yet. Annie waved to Margo to stop and open the window.

"If we get Matt to come for dinner, do you want to come over? Both of you?"

Sasha poked her head out from under her wraps. "Sure, just tell us when!"

"Let us know," Margo agreed, "and I'll bring dessert."

Margo followed Phyllis's red taillights down the long driveway. She saw Erik's headlights come towards her and wait at the road end to let them pass before he headed home. She drove towards the highway that would take them back home to Cullen Village. Sasha was unusually quiet. Stella's murder and the afternoon's conversation had made them uneasy.

"Phyllis really admired Stella," Margo said.

"I can think of a few people who'll be happy to see her gone." Sasha's voice came darkly out from under her wraps. "You couldn't trust Stella, not ever. She was always out for herself."

"Don't go around saying that in public, will you?" said Margo. "People might think it was you that did it." Snowflakes were drifting down. She turned on the wipers. Sasha didn't reply.

"The north wind doth blow, and we shall have snow…" Margo sang to break the silence.

"Don't know that one," muttered Sasha.

"Don't you? Old kid's song. My Scottish granny used to sing it:

> The north wind doth blow,
> And we shall have snow,
> And what will the robin do then?
> Poor thing."

"Canadian robins fly south for the winter," Sasha grouched. "They've got more sense than to stick around."

"Suppose so."

The flakes were coming down thicker. Margo turned up the speed on the wipers. They swatted back and forth, clearing a space on the windshield.

"Going to be a doozer," said Sasha, sitting up to peer through the window. "Bet it's a snow day tomorrow." She sounded almost cheerful at the thought.

3

A MAJOR STORM blew in overnight, a Colorado low that roared up from the American southwest, then looped eastward over the prairies with Cullen Village directly in its path. It brought warmer air, but also carried fifteen to twenty centimetres of snow on its breath. Margo Wishart gazed out of her window. Usually she could see across the lake to the horizon, but not today. When the weather was clear she could see a dark shimmer out where the water met the sky that suggested the opposite shore, but that was an optical illusion, caused by the earth's curve. From where Margo stood, the lake stretched for twenty-six kilometres before it reached land, all of it now covered in a solid layer of ice. The snow came down thick and steady out of a steely sky. When it gusted, she couldn't see a thing. She sipped her coffee and was glad she didn't have to drive into Winnipeg today.

Margo taught a couple of classes a week at the university. Her subject was art history, with women artists as her special area of interest. She had a grant proposal to work on—an idea for an art show about local women like Roberta who created art with textiles—and student essays to mark. This was a great day to get on with it.

Margo had bought her house at Cullen Village in May and moved in at the end of June. Her city friends all thought she was mad. Cullen Village was a fine place to hang out in the summer, when cottagers walked and biked its grassy paths and swam off rickety wooden piers that jutted out into the water for their special convenience, when boats were moored at the marina and the RV park was full of campers. In the evening there was music at the bandstand and the ice cream shop did a steady business. In winter it would be dead, they said. Her children worried that she'd be lonely. But Margo had needed a change. She'd married Rod Buchanan almost forty years ago, when they were students in Edinburgh. Now Rod was dean of education at the same university where she taught and he had found himself madly in love with a student. He'd left her. That old, sad story. She couldn't stand being in the old neighbourhood with its memories, or the sympathetic, and inquisitive, looks she got from people she knew. She had needed to get away, but she still needed to work, so she couldn't go too far. Life at the lake offered a good compromise. So she had insisted that the old family house be sold. Her share had financed buying this place. Just. A lake view came at a price, but so far she hadn't regretted her choice. And it had turned out that the lakeshore buzzed with life during the winter months. She could join a choir, a dance class or do yoga, be out every night if she wanted. There was an active art club at nearby Fiskar Bay, and she was making new friends, like the book group. So far, it had been a good move.

But she wouldn't be going anywhere today. Schools and public offices were closed. Highway travel was not recommended. The villagers were battening down to wait for the storm to blow itself out. Margo didn't mind. Rod had never been home much. Working, he had said. Now she wasn't so sure about that. Nevertheless, she was used to her own company and as long as she was busy she didn't sink into the doldrums. Her laptop lay invitingly on her old wooden desk, one of the few items of furniture she had retrieved from that big, suburban house. She had her books, which lined the walls like old friends, and some favourite paintings hung between them.

This was a little old cottage, renovated and winterized. Small rooms had been opened up into one large space with an open kitchen. A wall of windows looked out over the lake with glass doors in the middle that led onto a deck. In the summer, there was grass that led to a protective berm. On the other side were a rocky shore, a tiny scrap of sandy beach, and the lake. Right now, there was nothing but greyness. She would have lights on all day. The wind raged and howled around corners and through trees. It would probably bring a few branches down before it was done, but, meantime, Margo was warm and safe inside and she had work to do.

She walked through her house, to open the door on the far side. A gust of snow blew in and with it Bob, her long-legged black dog. She pushed the door shut against the wind, grabbed a towel from a peg and rubbed snow off his back and feet. She'd found Bob at the Fiskar Bay Humane Society, shortly after she had arrived at Cullen Village. She'd missed having a dog. He was two or three years old, of unknown pedigree, amiable company and as happy to be home today as she was.

Most mornings, she and Sasha walked together along the snowy roads of Cullen Village. She'd known Sasha for years. They'd first met when Margo had curated an art show that Sasha had helped organize, and they had kept in touch. Winnipeg's arts community was compact. Everybody knew everybody. Watching how Sasha lived at the lake had given Margo the courage to make the move. Now they spent a lot of time together, as did their dogs. Bob and Lenny, Sasha's basset hound, got along just fine.

Margo filled Bob's food bowl. She made a fresh mug of coffee and sat down at her desk. She was still in her pyjamas. She'd work for an hour or so, then maybe get dressed. She opened up a document on her laptop and started to read. The phone rang.

"Hi! Whatya doing?" It was Sasha.

"I was going to get some work done," Margo hinted.

"Me too," said Sasha. "I've got the stove going in the studio. Should be warm enough to get out there soon."

Sasha made most of her income by selling pottery to summer visitors. Mugs and bowls did well. She had converted an outbuilding into a studio. It housed a wheel and a kiln, but also an area where she created her sculptures. There was welding equipment on shelves alongside driftwood, beach glass, interesting stones and objects washed up from the boats that traversed the lake in the summer months. Scrap metal was stacked along one wall. Like Annie and Panda, she sometimes raided the dump for supplies.

"Are you feeling sick today?"

"Me? No." Margo got up from her desk. She might as well abandon any thought of work for now. She didn't really mind. She had all day to get on with it. She flopped down onto a large, comfortable sofa and put her feet up on the coffee table. Bob jumped up beside her. "Why?"

"Phyllis called. She's feeling rotten. Wondered if it was anything we ate yesterday."

"No. Maybe she's coming down with something. Wasn't she sick a couple of weeks ago?"

"She was. But she looked fine yesterday. Maybe it's a bug."

"Or maybe the conversation turned her stomach. You did kind of lay it on. About the murder. You and Roberta."

"Oh well. Can't help it if she's squeamish."

"You didn't exactly like Stella Magnusson, did you?" Margo heard Sasha slurp her coffee.

"Hey, me and Stella go back a long way. We had our ups and downs. That's all. I was still on her StarFest Committee, right? Lots of other people walked out—Roberta for one, but me, I learned to put up with Stella."

"People like Phyllis thought she was great."

"Suppose so. But what would Phyllis know? She just hung around last year and took snaps with that big camera of hers. Stella probably figured out real fast she could use her. Stella could turn on the charm when she wanted. She'd have had Phyllis eating out of her hand in no time. Stella always had a following. Her fandom. She was kind of famous, locally, anyway. Did you ever hear her sing?"

Sasha didn't wait for an answer. "Well, she wasn't all that good, but she had…?" She searched for the right word. "Charisma. That's what Stella had. And the looks. That helped. She always reserved a spot for herself at StarFest, on the last night. People would go nuts when she came out onto that stage. And Stella liked the limelight. She glowed. You can see how Phyllis would enjoy being in her orbit."

"So it wasn't only Phyllis that thought Stella was great?"

"Oh, don't get me wrong. Stella could manage people when it suited her. I happen to think the only person Stella liked was Stella but that's just my opinion. Phyllis does take decent photographs. And she volunteers because she's got the time and the money and she probably thinks it's fun. Stella would have loved that. George helps out, too. He's on the board with me. The treasurer." George Smedley was Phyllis's husband. "I shouldn't talk, I'm just as bad. I sell a lot of my stuff at StarFest and I get to have a say on how the Constellation Craft Corner works, so it suits me too. It made it worthwhile to try to get along with Stella. But she could be pretty full of herself."

Margo thought that comment was ironic coming from Sasha. She could be self-absorbed too. "So what was all that about the farmer next door?"

"John Andreychuk? Well, think about it. He's got cows out in his pasture and suddenly there's all this loud music, not to mention drunken festivalgoers partying next door. And the drugs. He complained to the municipality to try to stop them from giving her a licence. He thought he'd win, apparently. He's an Andreychuk, after all. They're one of the original families that settled out here and he has a lot of land, but it didn't work. The village council put a word in on her behalf, I heard, so they let her carry on. They liked StarFest. It helped put the village on the map. The little village businesses benefitted from it. People would drop over to look at the beach and while they were around they'd spend money at the village shop, eat in the restaurants. Buy ice cream. The RV park's always booked solid weeks in advance. And the noise and the traffic are far enough away not to be a nuisance to the cottagers. So Stella got her licence and she didn't care if she annoyed the Andreychuks. She just ignored them."

Margo wondered about that. She had learned already that in a small place you depended on the goodwill of the people who lived around you. She knew that if this storm left snow too deep for her snowblower to manage, she could call a neighbour who had a tractor and ask him to clear her driveway. She found it interesting that Cullen Village, the surrounding farming community and the artists who had migrated to the area coexisted as well as they did. She had been told that in Fiskar Bay the Icelanders, who fished the lake and had settled along the shore, did not always get along with the settlers, largely of Ukrainian origin like the Andreychuks, who had broken the land and built farms further inland. During the summer she had watched the tensions that arose among her own neighbours, the year-round residents of the village and the summer cottagers, who loved the village but whose interest sometimes rested in preserving tradition rather than in making changes to how things worked or looked. Harmony was only maintained by striking a balance between the needs of one and the demands of the other. Had Stella Magnusson created an imbalance that was serious enough for someone to want to murder her?

"Could the Andreychuks have hated her enough to want to kill her?" Margo asked.

"Oh, who knows? John Andreychuk wasn't the only person Stella stomped on. She didn't look tough, but she was, you know. She knew what she wanted and she made sure she got it. But it's too bad StarFest's over. People like me did well out of it." Sasha sighed. "Oh well. It was a good run while it lasted."

"I guess with this snow they'll have stopped digging up at the dump."

"Heard they got finished yesterday and cleared off back to the city before the storm hit. There's still a couple of cops nosing around at Stella's house."

How did this news get around? Margo had noticed that Cullen Village often seemed to have eyes and ears of its own. "Have you heard anything from Panda and Annie yet about dinner? Will they get snowed in?"

Panda and Annie lived on a road that was further inland and not on a school bus route, so they had to wait until the end of the snow-clearing schedule for it to be dug out.

"Not yet," Sasha replied. "Let you know if I hear anything."

They hung up and went off to their separate, solitary pursuits. Writing and sculpting required time alone, but Margo was glad to have a friend like Sasha that she could count on for company, even if it was only a chat on the phone on a snowy day. Margo liked to tell her friends and relatives how safe she felt in her house by the lake. Now that this murder had happened, she had had a flurry of emails asking if she was okay and her son had called from Vancouver. Was she safe? Had she ever been? She tried to reassure herself. Stella's death had to be about Stella and her lifestyle, her fame and her devoted fans, the people that it seemed she had offended. Her death couldn't sully life in this beautiful, peaceful village, could it? Margo tried to shake the thought and went to her desk. She needed to get some reading done.

Sasha lived three streets over. She'd have to trudge through snow as high as her boot tops to get to her studio. Margo could picture her stomping along, Lenny flopping behind her from footprint to footprint. At least it would be warm and snug once she got inside, with the wood stove on.

Margo remembered a conversation not so long ago. Sasha had been over for supper. They'd eaten spaghetti and finished a bottle of wine. Sasha had told her that she was worried that Stella was going to close down the Constellation Craft Corner at StarFest, so she could turn it into a second stage for new songwriters.

Margo was just getting used to having to live on less money than she was used to. She didn't know how artists like Sasha survived on what they made. "George Smedley told me Stella had even chosen a name for it. The Pleiades Platform." Sasha had drunk more than Margo that night. Maybe she didn't remember telling her. Margo reached for the phone. She should check up on Phyllis before she got busy.

George answered. "She's gone back to bed," he said. "I'm just making her a cup of peppermint tea to settle her stomach."

"Can I talk to her?" Margo asked.

"I don't think that's wise, dear. She needs time to rest and recover. Don't worry. She'll be back to herself in no time. It's a miserable day, isn't it? I'll tell her you called." And he hung up. Margo stared at the phone. Who did George Smedley think he was, calling her "dear"? She opened up the laptop again. Bob snuggled down at her feet, and she got to work.

4

IT WAS THE following evening. Margo drove between snow-banks that formed ghostly canyons in the headlights. The moon was bright, the night full of shadows. A layer of snow remained on the road surface, but twin tracks shone, shiny and slick, where a few cars had already travelled. She and Sasha were on their way to dinner at Panda and Annie's house. She turned onto a long, narrow driveway. The big wooden A-frame where Panda and Annie lived stood off the roadway, surrounded by trees, in a secluded spot. They parked beside a large garage with a workshop beside it. The big red Sierra was parked outside but there was no sign of another car. Matt Stavros hadn't arrived yet.

Annie met them at the door, small and neat, her hair fastened up on top of her head. Panda was behind the kitchen counter, a tea towel tied around her waist. She waved a large metal spoon. "Hi, Margo. Hi, Sasha."

"What's for dinner?" Sasha asked, peeling off the outer layers of clothes. "Smells good."

"I'm making Matt's favourite. Greek lemon chicken and potatoes."

"You won this time, did you?"

"Gotta butter him up, right? Anyway, he likes my cooking best."

There was an ongoing battle between Panda and Annie as to who would cook when they had guests. Panda loved to feed people, and Annie had grown up in the restaurant trade. Her parents were of Chinese origin. Her great-grandfather had arrived in Canada over a hundred years before to work on building the Canadian

Pacific Railway. Many Chinese men had died doing that work but he had survived. He had stayed and set up a restaurant in Virden, a small Manitoba town near the border with Saskatchewan. Because of a head tax that restricted further immigration from China to Canada, it had taken him a long time to find a bride, but eventually he had been able to bring one over from his homeland, and now his descendants ran that same restaurant.

Annie had grown up in the kitchen. She knew how to make everything on the menu, the ubiquitous Canadian Cantonese cuisine that their customers expected—chow mein, wonton soup, deep-fried battered shrimp in a sweet, slightly sour pink sauce and lemon chicken, the Chinese version—but her mother had also taught her how to make spicy Szechuan food. Today, however, they were going to eat the food that Panda and Matt Stavros had grown up on. The house smelled of garlic and lemon, reminiscent of summer.

Margo studied the large room with its tall, gabled windows along the side opposite the open kitchen. Annie's paintings lined the side walls, large, vivid abstracts that evoked the prairie landscape with the occasional hint of a figure, a watcher. She had gone to have a closer look when the door opened and Matt Stavros appeared, stomping snow off his boots onto the doormat. Annie introduced them.

"Margo, Sasha, this is Constable Stavros, of the Fiskar Bay RCMP."

"Hi, Matt!" Panda came out from behind the kitchen counter to plant a noisy kiss on his cheek. "My nephew. You can tell, eh?" You could. Panda was built just like Matt, tall and square. They had the same olive skin, dark eyes and straight black hair. Margo watched them look at each other and laugh. They sounded alike as well. Matt pulled a bottle of wine from the deep pocket of his parka.

"It's not Greek," he said, before Panda could ask. "It's from B.C."

Soon they were settled at the table. Food was eaten, wine was drunk, and the conversation took its inevitable turn.

"So, Matt, what's been going on at the dump?" Panda asked.

Margo watched Matt smile and put down his fork. He must know perfectly well why Panda had invited him for dinner, she thought. He had probably figured out how much he could tell to keep her happy before he got here. He told them that more body parts had been found, stuffed into black plastic bags, tucked in with scrunched-up newspaper and items of the victim's clothing. Digging at the dump had stopped. Sergeant Donohue from the RCMP Major Crimes Unit was pretty sure they had the whole body. A team from the Forensic Identification Unit had travelled out from the city to carry out the search.

"In the Force we call them 'Ident,'" he said.

"Not 'Forensics'?" asked Margo, surprised. She read a lot of crime fiction and was familiar with the terminology.

"Never. We don't have detectives either. The RCMP is different. The Major Crimes Unit is in charge but the local constables get involved." He described how dirty the work had been, made more difficult because of the intense cold, as they sifted through piles of garbage bags, rotten vegetable peelings, coffee grounds, dirty diapers, looking for the pieces that remained of Stella Magnusson.

Margo remembered watching video footage about a plane crash off the east coast of Canada several years before. The plane and its contents had disintegrated on impact with the surface of the water. Fishermen had gone out in boats, to try to retrieve the debris and what was left of the passengers and crew. That, she thought, would have been worse.

On this search, the bitter cold had meant that at least there had been very little smell. Most of the rubbish had been frozen solid. The constables had taken turns to guard the gate to the landfill from intruders. They could sit in the police car and run the engine to keep themselves warm and the windshield free of frost. Archie kept the wood stove in his shack well stoked. It was snug in there. They had spent twenty minutes digging, taken ten to thaw out, and then gone back at it again. Matt had been happier poking around in the garbage dump with the other police than sitting alone in the car, although he said it was entertaining to watch the villagers drive by, slowing down to peer over, trying to get a look at what was going on. Margo watched Sasha look mildly guilty. She had probably been one of them.

There hadn't been as much trash to sort through as the police had first supposed. Only the garbage from the past two weeks was accessible. The rest had already been compacted and frozen into the hill. If they had needed to get at that it would have been a much bigger operation. They had had a couple of days to search before the snow hit. Stella Magnusson's remains were now in the care of the province's chief medical examiner's office. They'd have to wait for results.

"So you've got all of what's left of her?" Sasha asked.

"We think so."

There was a collective sigh around the table.

"Was there anything unusual at her house?" asked Margo. "Or in her car?"

"We don't know where her car is. It's not in her garage." Matt thought it wouldn't hurt to tell them that. The word would be out soon enough if the car didn't show up. "So if you see it around, give us a call."

"Won't be hard to miss that big yellow thing," Sasha said, pushing her empty plate aside. Stella had driven a distinctive Toyota FJ Cruiser, an SUV with the StarFest logo emblazoned on the back window. It would be easy to spot.

"Are you going to be part of the investigation?" asked Annie. "Will the Fiskar Bay RCMP take it on, or will it be a team from Winnipeg?"

"A bit of both, it looks like," Matt said. "It'll depend on how long it takes and how difficult it is to find out what happened. There's been a sergeant and a corporal out from Winnipeg so far, but it'll help to have some local guys, people that know the lie of the land and the people out here. That kind of cuts me out, though. I'm too new to the area. There are other constables that have been here longer." Matt had arrived in Fiskar Bay in the fall. He'd spent the first three years after leaving the Depot, the RCMP training academy in Regina, in Flin Flon, a northern Manitoba mining town, before he had transferred to Fiskar Bay.

"It's great!" Panda had reported to the book group around the time he had moved. He and Panda were the closest thing they had to family, she said. Margo watched them smile back and forth. They obviously got along. Lucky Panda, she thought.

"Annie's done a drawing of Stella's head." Sasha's voice cut across her thoughts. "Can we have a look?"

"Oh, it's just a sketch," Annie said. "Who would like their glass topped up?" She reached for the wine bottle.

"Come on, Annie. Let's see it. Most of us have never seen a real severed head before." Sasha held out her glass for a refill.

"You don't have to, Annie." Margo had noticed Annie's reluctance and tried to be polite but really she was dying to see it too. Annie put down the bottle and smiled.

"Oh, it's all right. Of course you can have a look." She walked towards the staircase that led upstairs, a tiny little figure, slippers slapping on the floor. Margo would have loved to follow her, to see where the famous Annie Chan worked. The whole upper floor of the house was apparently given over to Annie's studio. Maybe when they got to know each other a bit better she could ask to have a look.

Panda got busy clearing away plates and serving the pie that Margo had brought. Saskatoon. She still had a bag of berries in the freezer. Matt went to help his aunt. Margo noticed that they did differ in one way. While Panda was outgoing and talkative, her nephew was quieter and thought before he spoke. He stood beside Panda at the sink.

"You guys okay, Panda? Can't have been easy, seeing that head fall out of the bag," Margo overheard him say.

"Oh, I'm fine, you know me." Panda shrugged. "Get some ice cream out of the freezer, will you?" She loaded wedges of pie onto plates. She didn't say how Annie was doing.

The drawing was in a folder, protected by a sheet of thin tissue. It was drawn in charcoal, stark black against the white paper. There was a suggestion of the shiny black garbage bag in which the head had been found, of the crushed newsprint that had spilled out of the bag with it. The mouth was coloured crimson. You could almost hear it scream. They passed it around, one to another. Margo looked first at it, then at Annie.

"She looks alive, Annie. It's as if you've caught her as it happened, in the act of being killed, as she's just about to die. She looks terrified. It's not like a dead head at all."

"That's why Annie's so good," said Sasha. "She brings everything she draws to life."

It was true. Annie deserved her reputation as one of Manitoba's best-known artists. You could almost believe that the dead woman was calling out to them, that she was willing someone to find her killer, to discover how and why she had died. Matt Stavros took the life-size drawing between his fingertips.

"Can I take a photo, Annie?" he asked. "It's a much better likeness than the ones we've got at the office. They're all publicity shots from StarFest. This looks more real." Again, Annie hesitated. Margo wasn't surprised. Taking photographs of artists' work was often frowned upon in these days of social media. But Panda intervened.

"Hey, Annie, take a picture of it yourself and email it to Matt. It's just for the police to use."

"Would be great if you could do that, Annie." Matt handed the drawing back.

Annie put it back inside its folder and laid it aside, on a counter. "I'll get it to you by tomorrow." She smiled at Matt as she sat down.

"Now," said Panda, "who wants ice cream on their pie? And Matt, listen up. We've been trying to figure out who might have killed Stella Magnusson." And they told Matt about how the book group had got together and what people had said that afternoon.

"Of course, it's all conjecture," said Margo, who wasn't sure they should be talking to a member of the RCMP about their suspicions.

"Gossip," Sasha said bluntly. "But there's no smoke without fire, right? Do the cops know that Stella was once shagging Roger Kato, the artist?"

"They split up ages ago," Panda chipped in. "But he's moved south, so he couldn't have killed her."

"Well," Sasha confided, "There were always guys hanging around Stella. Not that she was really interested. She just strung them along. Flirted with them, then dropped them. She was married to a filmmaker in L.A. called Freddie Santana. He's quite famous, but their marriage didn't last long. And way back before that she was in a band, her and a bunch of guys. She toured all over the place with them. One of them was Leo Isbister."

"The developer? The one who wants to drain the wetlands north of Fiskar Bay and build there?"

"The same."

Margo watched Matt make a mental note of that.

"Do you have any other suspects?" he prodded.

"Well." Sasha couldn't wait to tell more. "Do you and your buddies know about Andreychuk, the farmer next door to Stella's place? He has a son, Brad, who's no good."

She filled Matt in on what she knew about the Andreychuks. She didn't tell him how much Roberta disliked Stella. She didn't mention that she, herself, was on the StarFest board and her own worries about what would happen to the craft section. But by the time the evening was over, Matt had probably gleaned enough to feel he'd earned his dinner. He'd probably learned as much as he had told. He appeared happy as he got into his car and drove off home in the moonlight.

"Is Panda's real name really Delphia?" asked Margo as she and Sasha took the road east, towards Cullen Village.

"Yeah. Don't ever call her that, though, if you want to get invited back. People joke that she's called Panda because she's Annie's pet bear, but Annie says it's really because everything is black and white with Panda. She's either for you or against you. Great to have as a friend but you wouldn't want to have her as an enemy."

"She does look kind of like a bear though," Margo laughed. Her breath had moistened the scarf that was wrapped around her face.

"They've been together forever, her and Annie. Well, since Annie was in art school. They met at a party. Stella told me the story. They couldn't remember anything about how they met, they were so blotto, but they woke up in the same bed and they've been together ever since."

"How would Stella know that?"

"You'd be surprised how much Stella knew about people. She had lots of parties and she sucked people in. People talk."

"Matt should know that. It's a motive, isn't it? What if someone killed her because she knew something she shouldn't?"

"Maybe. Who knows."

Ten minutes later they reached Cullen Village, back to their own houses and their dogs. The snow was blanketing the village and a wind was beginning to blow from the northwest.

5

CORPORAL ROXANNE CALLOWAY drove along the lakeside road towards Fiskar Bay. It was the scenic route, pretty even in winter, but it wound along the shoreline, a road that took its time. At this rate she wasn't going to make it to the RCMP detachment by 10:00 am, as she had planned. The highway further to the west was fast and straight, but today it was blocked by an accident, a collision between a semi and a car with passengers. There were injuries and the semi was in the ditch. It would take a crane to haul it out. So probably most of the RCMP were busy with that. Roxanne had wanted to debrief with most of them present. Maybe that wasn't going to happen.

She hadn't expected to be assigned to this case. Another corporal had been asked to investigate, but now he was sick, down with pneumonia, probably caught while working at Cullen Dump at minus forty with the flu. So he was off the case and it had defaulted to her. Roxanne couldn't believe her luck. A murder investigation? She hadn't expected this kind of responsibility so soon after transferring to the Manitoba Major Crimes Unit from Saskatchewan. So she'd parked Finn, her son, at her sister's for a couple of days and headed up to the Interlake.

She had spent some time with one of the Fiskar Bay constables, in Winnipeg for the weekend, training to be file coordinator on the case. Constable Izzy McBain had shown up in uniform, a trim figure with blonde hair braided and tucked up above her collar. She had left the day before, Sunday, to head back to Fiskar Bay with a carload of goodies, computer equipment, office supplies, and wearing newly bought street clothes. Her hair had swung behind her in a pony tail.

"All I ever wear off-duty is jeans and an old sweater," she had said. Roxanne thought it was funny how eager young constables were to don the uniform and how soon after they were happy to get out of it. Roxanne had asked Izzy to get an office prepared for them. She hoped the accident hadn't put paid to that. Maybe Constable McBain was now out on the highway, redirecting traffic.

Roxanne had heard about the lake but she hadn't been out here before. She caught glimpses of it through gaps in the trees. It really was huge. She was used to the wide vistas of the prairie, the massive sky, the long horizon where you could see the curve of the earth. The flatlands started east of the Rockies and ended here, in Manitoba. One hour east of Winnipeg, she had been told, you hit the Canadian Shield, solid bedrock and lots of fir trees. She'd have to take Finn for a look someday. And maybe bring him up here for a day at the beach in the summer.

She pulled up in town ten minutes past her deadline. She saw a typical RCMP detachment building, red brick, half of it single, half two-storey. Usually there would be a row of white police cars and trucks, all emblazoned with RCMP insignia, parked outside but today they were reduced to one. She pulled a briefcase from the back seat of her car and marched up to the door.

A shirt-sleeved sergeant, burly and grey-haired, came to greet her. Had he been watching out for her? A constable looked out from a doorway behind the counter, obviously sizing her up. A woman in civilian clothes sat behind a computer screen, typing. Roxanne introduced herself to the sergeant. The woman gave her a thin smile. The constable appeared studiously indifferent, but the room buzzed with an undercurrent of interest. A young blonde woman appeared on a staircase at the back of the office.

"You've met Izzy," said Sergeant Bill Gilchrist. "She's got a room set up for you upstairs."

Roxanne was relieved to see that Constable McBain hadn't been sent out to the accident site to direct traffic. She looked at the sergeant. He must be close to sixty, approaching retirement. She hoped he wasn't too much of an old-school cop.

"How many of your constables are out there on the highway, Sergeant?" she asked. "I'd hoped we could get together. They could tell me what they've observed so far and I could provide you with an update from Winnipeg. Get us all up to speed."

"No problem," said Bill Gilchrist. "Accident's all cleaned up and they're on their way in. Except for one that's still at the hospital taking down statements. You can go upstairs and see what Izzy's been up to. Glad the MCU's paying for all that gear she's got. Wouldn't want her having to raid Kathy's supply cupboard." The woman at the computer—evidently Kathy—raised an eyebrow but carried on typing. "You can go up and have a look and I'll get all the guys into the lunchroom as soon as they're all back."

Roxanne was halfway up the stairs when she heard a low male voice. "There they go, up to the henhouse." She glanced over the banister. The constable had turned back into his office. Bill Gilchrist shrugged, as if to say: what am I supposed to do? Guys will be guys. The woman at the computer kept her eyes on the screen, but the corners of her mouth turned down in a disapproving curve.

"Hey, Kenny!" Izzy McBain called to the disappearing back of the constable. "How come you're not sucking up to the corporal? Thought you wanted the other MCU job?"

Constable Ken Roach ignored her. Bill Gilchrist laughed. "You behave yourself, Izzy," he said. It was no secret that another of the Fiskar Bay constables was to be detailed to the murder investigation. It was one of the reasons Roxanne wanted to see them all together. She had to make a recommendation by the end of the day.

Izzy had done a decent job of setting up the office. Two big tables were pushed together in the centre with chairs ranged around them. There was a computer station in one corner and a large whiteboard fastened to a wall. Supplies were laid out on shelves: paper, toner, Post-it notes, pens and markers. A telephone sat in one corner, a desk in another. "That's for you, Corporal," said Izzy. "We can change it if you like."

"It's fine. Who's the woman downstairs? The civilian at the computer?"

"Kathy Isfeld. Been here forever. She really runs the show. Sergeant Bill wouldn't have a clue what to do without her."

Izzy had provided a coat rack and a tray for boots. Under her coat, Roxanne was wearing a crisp white shirt, a black V-neck sweater and black pants. It wasn't uniform but it was close. Her hair was reddish, cut short, a sleek cut that hugged her head, easy to manage. She glanced out the window. It looked onto the parking lot. Across the street was a Tim Hortons coffee shop, like those to be found in most prairie towns, once a beloved Canadian franchise, now owned by an international syndicate.

"I didn't set up a coffee machine," said Izzy. "We usually just pick up from the Tim's. Want me to run over and get some?"

"Sure," said Roxanne, reaching for some cash. "I take mine black." She was glad to have a few minutes alone in the room to get a feel for the place that would be the hub of the investigation.

By the time Izzy got back, another two constables had returned from the accident site. Roxanne walked into the lunchroom to find them and their sergeant seated at tables near the back of the room, facing forward, waiting for her to speak, coffee cups in hand. Ken Roach sat back in a chair, arms folded, waiting.

"Let's pull two of these tables together," she said. "There's only going to be five of us. There will be room for all of us around them." The constables reluctantly got to their feet and started moving furniture around. An order was an order and in the RCMP rank was respected, even when the corporal was a skinny redhead in city clothes. She looked more like a business manager than one of them.

"We'll be six," said Sergeant Bill Gilchrist. "Matt Stavros just got in from the hospital."

Izzy was already setting up her laptop on a table. The second constable was introduced as Sam Mendes. He pulled a small notepad out of his pocket. A third watched her through hooded eyes. The door opened. Matt Stavros entered, coffee in hand. He was about six feet, solidly built, olive-skinned, dark-haired. He took a seat next to Izzy.

"Right," said Roxanne. "You should know that I have been appointed as primary investigator on this case. Sergeant Brian Donohue is team commander. I think most of you met him last week, when he was out at the search of the murder site. Brian is working from Winnipeg for now but I'm sure you'll be seeing him out here before long." They noticed that she used the sergeant's first name. "The Ident crews are busy examining evidence and Stella Magnusson's body is in the care of the medical examiner. I am going to be here for a few days conducting interviews." She had booked herself into the Fiskar Bay Hotel online. It was off-season. They had plenty of rooms available. She'd scored a suite, cut-rate.

"Constable McBain here has been appointed as our file coordinator. She is at the centre of this investigation. All reports go to her, and she feeds information back to us as needed, but Izzy also will get out in the field at times. We share responsibilities."

Izzy's spine straightened. Roach and Mendes glanced sideways at each other. There was a day when an officer got on with the job himself. Bill Gilchrist remembered those days very well. Now it was all teamwork. Accountability. Transparency. He sipped his coffee and kept his mouth shut.

"We will need one of you to join the investigative team as support staff," Roxanne continued. "This case is attracting media attention and we need to get results as soon as we can." One or two heads nodded. TV crews had shown up at the dump. Reporters had been hanging around, asking questions. Sergeant Donohue had taken care of them until news of the coming storm had sent them all back to the city. "So let's talk about what we know. Any questions so far?"

"How was she killed?" Sam Mendes raised his pencil, ready to write it all down.

"They're still doing lab tests, but she suffered a blow to the back of the head that caused serious injury."

"There was a wood stove with fire irons at the house, and an axe and a maul in the woodshed." Constable Mendes was flipping back through his notes.

"They've been examined," said Roxanne. "They're clean. The body was frozen and then cut up into several parts, head, both arms and legs, each of which was also severed above the knee. The torso was cut into two parts horizontally across the midsection. The pieces were stuffed into black plastic garbage bags, strong ones, each one padded with newspaper, old copies of the *Winnipeg Free Press* from between December 30 and January 10, the outside pages missing. The ones we found had no prints. Ms. Magnusson's clothing and boots were also stuffed into the bags. Different ones. Two rings had been left on her fingers. Theft does not appear to have been a factor in this murder. We believe the bags were collected by the garbage truck in Cullen Village on Monday, January 22, as part of the regular curbside pickup and deposited at the Cullen landfill site. The truck driver and his assistant noticed nothing unusual."

"She'd been left out at someone's curb for the weekly garbage pickup?" Matt asked.

"Or outside several houses. She had been frozen then cut up, probably with a band saw. That could help us narrow things down."

"The butcher will have one of those," said the sergeant.

"There was that break-in at the school during the holidays, just after New Year. There might be one in the shop there," added Mendes.

"Could be one at Cullen Village." Matt Stavros was leaning forward on his elbows, his coffee between his hands. "There's a men's group gets together once a week to do carpentry in someone's workshop. Want me to find out?"

"You do that, constable. The car was found yesterday, in the long-term parking lot at Winnipeg airport."

"Surveillance cameras?"

"Yes. But the video's not much use. You've seen it, Izzy?"

"Yes, ma'am." Izzy had viewed it in Winnipeg as part of her training. "It was snowing and dark when the SUV was dropped off and it was left at the far end of the lot. The picture's fuzzy. There's just a blur. It looks like it was just one person, though. Someone not very tall."

"The vehicle was locked," Roxanne continued, "but the keys were in the glove box, as were the insurance papers. There was a packed suitcase and a travel bag in the back. Stella Magnusson's wallet was in the side pocket of the bag. All her credit cards appear to be there, with two hundred dollars in cash. There are plane tickets, for Dublin then London, Milan and Paris, and a passport. There's no sign of a cellphone, a tablet or a personal laptop. The vehicle appears to have been wiped clean of all fingerprints. It's still being examined."

"When was it dropped off?" Matt asked.

"Saturday, just after 1:00 am. She was seen the Thursday evening before by a couple called Smedley, so we believe that for now death happened between late Thursday night and Friday, January 19. Probably sometime that Friday, since the car wasn't dropped off until early Saturday morning. Has anyone reported anything suspicious?"

"Not much. No one saw anything or heard anything. A couple and two sons live next door, on a farm. The Andreychuks. There's been some friction between them and the victim before." Mendes again.

"Let's call her by her name—Stella Magnusson," Roxanne said firmly. At least one constable shifted uneasily in his chair. It looked like she was one of those politically correct types.

"We had complaints from both sides, Corporal," said Sergeant Gilchrist. "Stella does this StarFest thing, every year, in June, on her land. Concerts. Big crowds. John Andreychuk's a farmer. Complained about the noise, people tramping over his fields, disturbing his cows and calves. Traffic. Cars parked everywhere. You could see his point. He tried to get her closed down. Didn't work."

"And what did she complain about?"

"She thought he was trying to scare her off, to get her to sell and move out. Said she found a dead fox once, on her doorstep. Got some funny phone calls, hang-ups. A skinned coyote was left, hanging on a tree at the edge of her wood. A cat disappeared. Andreychuk swore blind it wasn't him. That was all about four or five years ago, though. And it stopped. There's been nothing since."

"Brad Andreychuk's a nut case," Constable Mendes contributed. "The oldest son. He's been in a few fights over the years, but no one's pressed charges so we haven't been able to hang anything on him. There's a younger boy at the University in Winnipeg. Stays in the city most of the time. There's nobody much else out there."

"She lived out there by herself?"

"Yep, but she was usually away for about three months in the winter and in the summer she had people around her place a lot of the time. She hired staff for the festival, mostly students. And there's a bunch of volunteers. We've got lists of them, and of board members."

"Make sure Izzy has them all," said Roxanne. Izzy glanced up from her laptop and grinned. Roach rolled his eyes.

Bill Gilchrist leaned forward. He knew local history. "She inherited that place from her uncles, her mother's brothers. Her father was from an old Icelandic family, been around Fiskar Bay from the start, but her mom was Ukrainian. Farmers. The uncles were bachelors, lived out there together all their lives. Nice old guys, but quiet. Kept themselves to themselves. One died right after the other and there was no one else to leave the land to.

Nobody expected Stella Magnusson to move back but she did. It must have been nearly ten years ago."

"She came from here?"

"Oh yeah. Went to Fiskar Bay High School, but she cleared off right after she graduated. Got to be thirty-odd years ago," he added. Izzy had returned to clicking away on her keyboard.

"So she would have been thirty-seven when she came back? That would have made her forty-seven now?" Matt Stavros had done the math fast. "She looked younger than that. My aunt lives out here. Delphia Stavros. She's one of the women who were at the dump when the body was discovered. There's a bunch of artists in the area. According to her and her friends, Stella Magnusson wasn't much liked by some of them. And there had been a lot of guys in Stella's life. It's all just rumour but I'll give you some notes, Izzy." He reached into his pocket and took out his phone. "My aunt's partner is Annie Chan. She paints. She did a drawing of Stella's head."

"*The* Annie Chan? Isn't she famous?" Roxanne was surprised. She didn't know much about art but she recognized the name.

"That's the one." He found the photograph and passed the phone to her.

"Well, look at this. That's amazing." Roxanne held it up so they could see. Except for Izzy, they appeared unimpressed. "We could use a printout, life-size, Izzy." She checked the time. She had learned enough for now. She wanted to get started, to begin to get a sense of how the residents who toughed out the long, cold months here lived. She needed a context in which to place Stella Magnusson and the person who had killed her. "If you hear of anything that can help us, we're right upstairs," she said, closing the meeting.

By the time she was ready to leave, Izzy was putting notes and photographs on the whiteboard.

"Where do I find the Andreychuk farm, Izzy?"

"I'll show you." Izzy went to her laptop and pulled up a map on her screen. "Don't trust GPS out here, ma'am. Doesn't work. You're likely to end up in the middle of a field."

"I've got a better idea," said Roxanne. "How about you drive me? It'll give me a chance to look around."

"Sure! Want me to get a car?" Izzy was already reaching for her parka. It looked like she was itching to get out.

"No. You can drive mine. It's less obvious. I'll see you out there." She handed Izzy the car keys, took her coat and went back downstairs. Bill Gilchrist was in his office. He looked up from his desk as she knocked and entered.

"You guys are going to want Stavros, aren't you?" he said. "It makes sense. He's the smartest of the bunch. Apart from Izzy. I'm not surprised you snagged her. A bit of a whizz on all that techie stuff is our Izzy. And she's local. Knows everybody."

"How come she's here, back where she grew up?" The RCMP didn't encourage its members to work on their home turf and it wasn't considered a good career move.

"Her mom got cancer. Right when Izzy was graduating from the Depot. She came back to help out. Her mom got better. So Izzy's stuck here for now. Do her good to work with you," he said, "but I'll miss having her around down here. She's more fun than Kathy Isfeld."

"I'll tell Sergeant Donohue," she said, wrapping a scarf around her neck. "Do you want to tell Stavros yourself?"

"Sure thing."

Roxanne looked out the front window. She could see exhaust fumes puffing from the back of her car. Izzy was warming it up. She straightened her back. Now the work really began.

6

ROXANNE WATCHED OUT the car window while Izzy McBain drove towards the Andreychuk farm. The road followed the lakeshore, then turned inland, where it ran straight, crossing snow-covered farmland. They passed farmhouses surrounded by trees, stands of spruce and willow planted to break the prairie wind, silos, grain bins, a tiny Ukrainian church with an onion dome, disused and dilapidated, the occasional old barn falling into ruin. There were no signs of life apart from a pair of ravens devouring a bloody, grey-furred mess in the middle of the road. The birds flew up into the trees and watched as they drove by. A sign appeared at the side of the road. Cullen Village Environmental Waste Disposal. The dump. "Want to have a look?" Izzy swung left through a gate and stopped beside Archie Huminski's shack.

Smoke rose vertically from the chimney but there was no sign of Archie. Izzy drove up the hill to the top and parked the car. Fat gulls strutted around, then soared to hover overhead as Roxanne and Izzy got out. Roxanne looked over the edge of the hill. To the right, a green and white tanker truck was discharging waste through a long hose into a sewage lagoon. At the bottom of the hill was the usual debris and white grocery bags flapped everywhere, snagged on twigs, on protruding posts, on scraps of metal. Izzy joined her. She looked down at the heap of waste below.

"Pretty sick, isn't it, sending someone's body off to a place like this," she said.

Roxanne was wishing she'd changed into a winter parka. Her city coat wasn't warm enough out here. "Whoever did it planned it carefully. It's smart. It took a complicated mind to dream it up, don't you think?"

Izzy kicked a stray can over the edge. It bounced to the bottom. "Yes, but it didn't work, did it? We found the body. Maybe whoever did it isn't as smart as they think they are."

"We hope. You're right about it being a bleak place to bury someone, though. Whoever did it must have hated her." Roxanne pulled her collar up, then shoved her gloved hands deep into her pockets. "Let's go."

By the time they climbed back into the car, a truck had pulled in. Archie Huminski got out.

"Hey, Izzy McBain, where's the uniform?" He was a gnome of a man with a weathered, wrinkled face. He reached in the window to shake Roxanne's hand. His was large and firm.

"Major Crimes, eh? Tell you what, I'll put the kettle on and you ladies can come have a cup of coffee. Get warmed up."

Izzy turned off the engine. Roxanne realized that refusing wasn't going to be an option. She followed Izzy into the shack. A wood stove in the corner kept it warm. They loosened their coats. Roxanne made a point of not removing hers. She didn't intend to stay long.

"You can have tea or instant." Archie lifted mugs down from a shelf. They didn't look too clean. Roxanne pretended not to notice. The kettle simmered on the stove.

"You girls going to visit the Andreychuks next?"

"Maybe," said Izzy.

So, Roxanne wondered, did the locals, like the police at the detachment, have Brad Andreychuk pegged as the most likely suspect? Archie's next words confirmed it.

"That Bradley's a bad one. Has been ever since he was a kid. Used to see him out there on the farm, riding around on a quad taking pot shots at squirrels when he can't have been more than twelve."

"Did he know Stella Magnusson?" Roxanne asked.

"Sure. His dad tried to get her to sell up and move. You guys know all about that, right? Stella didn't leave though. Toughed it out, gotta say that for her. Have a cookie. Chocolate chip. The missus makes them." He opened a tin and passed it to them. Roxanne thought she'd better take one. They looked okay. Izzy took two.

"Did you know her?"

"Knew who she was. Used to drive in here in that big yellow Toyota like she owned the place. Never stopped to say hello. Thought she was too cool for the likes of me. She didn't come by much these days. Jeremy Andreychuk, Brad's brother, he usually brought her garbage over in the summer. He worked for her at her StarFest thing. Jeremy's not like his brother. He's at the university. Going to be an engineer. Nice lad, Jeremy, always stops and says hello.

"Now, you know George Smedley? He used to hang around Stella's place. You could talk to him. And Angus, him that was here when they found the body, he could maybe tell you something. George'll be at his place this afternoon. Men's group. You could catch him there."

Roxanne made a mental note of that. She finished her coffee as soon as she could and stood up to go. Archie walked them out to the car.

"Stop by, lady. Anytime."

"We got to go inside the dump shack!" Izzy crowed as she drove away. "My mom will be so impressed! It's a guy place. Women never get through the door."

Roxanne pulled out her phone. Matt Stavros could head over to Cullen Village this afternoon and check out this men's group.

It didn't take long to reach the Andreychuk farm. Izzy drove into a driveway surrounded by buildings and trees. There was a large barn, a garage, a Quonset hut, outbuildings, grain bins. The house was single storey, a simple bungalow. Prairie farmers liked to spend their money on their farms, not their houses. And vehicles. Izzy pulled in beside two shiny new trucks and a late-model car. A couple of snowmobiles stood near the house.

The door was opened by a tall, dark-haired man in his mid-twenties. He wore jeans, an old sweater, socks, no shoes.

"Corporal Calloway of the RCMP and Constable McBain," Roxanne announced, flashing her ID. "We need to ask you some questions regarding the remains that were found at the dump."

"Mom!" he hollered. "Police, back again. Hi, Izzy. How come you're not wearing the suit?"

"Hey, Bradley." Izzy looked uncomfortable. Roxanne wondered if she wished that she was back in uniform, with the authority it brought. Brad didn't invite them in. The woman who appeared behind him was large, very large, so wide that Roxanne wondered how she could walk. She appeared no more pleased to see them than her son had been.

"You police have been here already," she said. "We've told you everything we know."

"I'm heading out, Ma," said her son, turning back into the house.

"You need to stay for now." Roxanne put her foot inside the door. She could smell meat cooking, and vegetables. Cabbage.

"It's Mrs. Andreychuk, isn't it?" The woman did not smile. She stood there like a mountain, immoveable. Her husband appeared in the corridor behind her. He was taller and lean, wearing work clothes.

"Better let them in, Maggie."

He led the way into a living room. It was tidy and brown. The furniture was large and rust coloured, the rug in varying shades of taupe, the walls, beige. A large television set occupied a corner. The ceiling was stained nicotine yellow with a large chandelier at the centre. Under the smell of the food there was a whiff of stale cigarette smoke. A few framed family photographs decorated the walls, some black and white, others old, sepia ones.

"Brad, you stick around!" Andreychuk yelled. The son came out of another door that seemed to lead from the kitchen, his jacket already slung on his back. He flopped down into a large armchair and swung one leg over the arm. His father pulled a chair out from below a rectangular wooden table and sat, indicating that Roxanne and Izzy could take the chairs opposite. His wife lowered her gargantuan size onto the sofa. She took up more than half of its width. Roxanne wondered if she could get out of it without help.

"Isabel, how's your mom?" asked the woman on the sofa.

"Doing well, thanks." Izzy remained standing, close to the door. Roxanne took a chair.

"You in charge of this now?" asked John Andreychuk. He reached into his shirt pocket for a pack of cigarettes and a lighter and pulled an ashtray towards himself, then lit one and tossed the pack to his son. He didn't take his eyes off Roxanne. Bradley lit up too.

"I'm leading local investigations, Mr. Andreychuk. Corporal Roxanne Calloway." She heard Brad half humming, whistling through his teeth, "Roxaaaaane." That song, by the Police. She'd heard it before, many times. She ignored him. Izzy didn't.

"Shut it, Brad."

Bradley laughed. *Gotya*, his eyes said. He drew on his cigarette. Roxanne carried on regardless. She was formal. Official. Polite.

"The officers who were here before asked if you had seen anything or anyone suspicious in the days before we discovered Ms. Magnusson's body. I wanted to find out what you knew about her, since you were such close neighbours."

"Did you now. Well, we didn't see much of her. We keep ourselves to ourselves around here." John Andreychuk sat back and folded his arms.

"She wasn't a farmer, like her uncles. They kept cattle like you, didn't they? Did it bother you that she let the farm go? Didn't even rent out her pasture?"

"Nope. Bought her uncles' stock. Got them for a good price. Suited me fine."

Brad and his mother were listening to every word but avoiding looking directly at her or Izzy.

"Would you have liked to buy the land?" Roxanne continued.

"Got plenty of our own, Miss. Ain't we, Bradley."

"But StarFest caused problems for you." It was a statement, not a question.

"Nothing new about that, is there? It's been going on for years now. We learned to live with it." He blew a puff of smoke up towards the ceiling.

"Your other son, Jeremy, he worked there last summer?"

"And the one before. Might as well make a buck out of it." He grinned at her. A look passed between Brad and his mother. They both appeared more alert. The question about Jeremy had caught their attention.

"Does he live in the city?"

"That's right."

"But he was here over Christmas? When, exactly, did he go back?"

"What's this to do with our Jeremy?" The mother interrupted her.

"Just checking, Mrs. Andreychuk. No one mentioned him when the police were here previously." Roxanne kept her voice low. Nonconfrontational. "When did you say he went back to Winnipeg?"

"We didn't. Right after New Year it was, though." Andreychuk answered, stubbing out his cigarette. He peered at her through a smoky haze.

"Did anything unusual happen here around January 19?

"Can't remember. We got asked this already."

"I'd like to hear it for myself."

"That was Friday. We went to Winnipeg," said Maggie emphatically.

"Any special reason?"

"No. The usual. Needed to buy some stuff."

"You could show us some receipts to prove you were there?"

"Look here, what are you doing, checking us out? We've done nothing wrong. If someone had it in for her, it wasn't us. Who's been telling you lies, putting the blame on me and my boys?" Andreychuk got to his feet. His son clambered out of his chair too.

"And you, Bradley, where were you on that day?" Roxanne turned her head but stayed seated.

"Out fishing." It was his turn to grin. He looked a lot like his dad when he did. "The guys will tell you. Got there in the morning, stayed all afternoon. And that night I was in the bar, in Fiskar Bay. Plenty of guys'll tell you about that too, if you ask." Both men loomed over Roxanne. She noticed Izzy's eyebrows rise.

"We'll check for sure," she said, and stood up. They both took their time stepping back. "We'll be going for now. Thanks for your help."

"That's it?" Andreychuk said.

"If there's anything else we'll be in touch." She turned to go. Brad's voice stopped her.

"Hey, missus," he drawled, leaning against the doorframe opposite, his hands in his pockets. "Tell you who you should be talking to instead of us. Erik Axelsson."

"Erik?" said Izzy, stopping in the middle of pulling on her mitts. "You've got to be kidding!"

"You don't know nothin', Izzy McBain." He zipped up his jacket. "He's been hanging around the Magnusson place a lot lately. I've seen his truck parked there, often. Sometimes he's there at night, for hours. Why don't you go and bug him about where he was that Friday?" He turned towards his father. "Reckon I can go now." He slunk off into the kitchen. His father showed Roxanne and Izzy to the door. Maggie remained, huge and still, on her seat.

As they drove away, Roxanne noticed a red glow in the wood beside the barn. Smoke belched up above the treetops.

"Slow down, Izzy." She looked towards a small, metal, domed structure, red light glowing out of the cracks around a small door. Cordwood was stacked beside it.

"An outdoor furnace," said Izzy. "They're using it to heat the barn."

"Don't those things get hot enough to incinerate bone? If Brad and his father had needed to dispose of body parts, wouldn't they have used that, instead of sending them to the dump?"

"Guess so. You can't tell with Brad, though. He's a head case. Always has been."

"You've known him long?"

"Since junior high. He was mean, even then. Used to walk the hallways with his two buddies, Mitch and Billy, like they owned the place. They still hang out together. If that's who's giving him an alibi, ma'am, don't believe a word of it."

"And who is Erik Axelsson?"

"He lives on a farm near Fiskar Bay. Near my parents. His wife's called Roberta. She's his second wife. They're a great couple. They do organic farming, kind of." They were already pulling into Stella Magnusson's driveway. "She's a bit artsy. Erik used to fix cars. Still does sometimes to make ends meet. He's a pretty laid-back kind of guy. I can't see him killing anybody."

Roxanne looked at Stella's house. She saw a restored farmhouse with a peaked roof and a wraparound veranda painted a vibrant teal blue with purple trim. A rectangular building at one side had a sign on the front. THE STARGAZER MUSIC FESTIVAL, ARTISTIC DIRECTOR: STELLA MAGNUSSON. The paint was fresh, the windows appeared new.

"Erik used to sing at StarFest," said Izzy. "But not for years. Him and his pal Mike Little still do a set in the bars sometimes. They're not bad."

"Why did they stop singing here?"

"Dunno. You can ask him. Roberta Axelsson's going to have a fit if he's been messing around with Stella, but I think Brad's just trying to put you off the scent." She got out the car. "Hey, Corporal, I've seen inside the house. How about you go have a look and I'll go for a walk around. Can I have the garage keys? I'll open up the office building for you."

Roxanne unlocked the front door to the house. There were two deadbolts. The shiny silver doorknocker had a star etched into it. Starry wind chimes tinkled softly from the corner of the veranda. She handed the keys to Izzy and watched her head towards the double garage.

Inside, Stella Magnusson's house looked new. Hardwood floors gleamed with polish. Large windows shone. They let in light from the west, facing across the field to woodlands beyond. Walls had been knocked out to open up the space. A black grand piano dominated one corner. The wood stove was a contemporary Norwegian one, tall and tubular with brass fire irons on the hearthstone including a poker, all clean as a whistle, she knew. She'd read the report.

The kitchen had been rebuilt. It was immaculate. Dishes and glasses were neatly stacked in cupboards behind glass doors. The stove and fridge were high-quality stainless steel, as was the dishwasher. The countertops were granite. An espresso maker sat near the sink, the wine rack was well stocked. Stella had hired a cleaning service. They had come in the Saturday after she was supposed to have left on her trip and done a good job. Any evidence of possible wrongdoing was gone, but the cleaners said that they had seen nothing unusual.

Roxanne walked through the bedroom, the bathroom, a home office. Why had Stella kept an office in the house when her business was literally on her doorstep? The star theme was reflected in sparkly light fitments. A dark blue bedcover had a moon at its centre. There were framed pictures on the walls of galaxies and constellations. Books on shelves were about music, travel, biographies of famous singers. A filing cabinet was full of music sheets, systematically filed, alphabetically and by genre. On the walls were signed shots of musicians who had appeared at StarFest. Several were of Stella, one of the earliest a black and white shot of her fronting a band. She looked strikingly beautiful, with a mass of fair hair, big eyes, smiling for the crowd, ridiculously young.

Roxanne went to the window. She could see Izzy crossing the field behind the house towards the woodlands on the far side. She'd found a pair of snowshoes and was lifting her knees as she walked on the surface of the snow, going further afield than Roxanne had expected.

The house had been thoroughly searched by the Ident team. Computers and a personal safe had been taken into Winnipeg. They had obtained warrants to access Stella's email and banking. It must have cost a lot to renovate this house. Where had the money come from? If Stella had a will, it had not turned up yet. Who stood to inherit this place and all the land that went with it?

There were more photographs on the walls throughout the house, most from StarFest. Roxanne could see no family photographs, no shots taken with friends out for dinner, having a good time, on holiday. Had Stella always travelled alone? Everything here related to Stella's professional life. Nothing at all spoke of relationships other than work. The house was beautiful, perfect and silent, unnervingly impersonal.

Roxanne left the house and waded through knee-high snowdrifts to the office building. She could see Izzy returning across the field, the wide, webbed prints of the snowshoes stamped on the surface of the snow. They would soon be blown over. A wind was getting up. Izzy had wrapped a scarf around her face for protection.

Roxanne entered the offices, which had been converted from a large outbuilding. There was a small kitchen and a washroom, but otherwise it was given over to work space. The only sign of unusual activity was the occasional gap where a computer had been removed for examination. It wasn't as tidy or as spotlessly clean as the house, but the Ident technicians had found nothing suspicious. There was a contact list of board members and another of volunteers on a bulletin board. That information would be available to her already, but Roxanne took a photograph anyway. She found a box of old StarFest brochures in a cupboard and helped herself to some. She was flipping through them when she heard banging outside the door. Izzy had removed the snowshoes and was whacking them against the wall to remove the snow.

"I found something. Come see." She led the way over to the garage at the other side of the house. Roxanne followed in her footprints. "There's been a skidoo here. Look, there's a bit of track."

The snow had blown away from the side of the garage. Marks were indented in the snowy ground, largely covered by the recent snowfall but visible in patches where they had blown clear. Izzy pointed to the wood. "See?" she said. "There's a break in the trees."

Roxanne peered across the field. It looked like solid bush on the far side. The sun was sinking towards it, throwing the trees into silhouette, but if she followed the faint line drawn by Izzy's footprints and squinted against the fading sunlight she could see a spot that was darker than the rest.

"A trail?"

"Yup. Probably been there since the days that the old guys lived here, but it's been maintained. There's not much new growth, and the trees are thick enough that the snow hasn't drifted in too much. There are tracks there, Corporal. Someone's been visiting Stella on a skidoo. And guess where it comes from?"

"Andreychuk's farm?"

"Comes out right behind their barn. I tell you, you can't trust a word that Bradley says."

Roxanne's cellphone rang. It was Matt, calling from Cullen Village.

"Hey, Corporal, I'm at Angus Smith's house. There's a bunch of old guys running all over the place saying they can't find Angus Smith. He's supposed to be here. They can't find him anywhere. They say he's gone missing."

7

BY THE TIME Roxanne and Izzy reached Angus Smith's house, Matt had wrangled the men into order. He had them sitting around a table on an enclosed porch while he took down contact information, then sent them on their way, one by one. It was where they smoked when they visited Angus. The large ashtray in the middle of the table filled as they waited. At least four of them had puffed nonstop. There had been eight in all. Worried, they had run all over the house, the barn, the workshop, the yard, looking for Angus. If this was a crime scene, it was hopelessly contaminated.

Roxanne walked over to a fairly new outbuilding, which housed the workshop. It was large. A work table in the middle had stools around it and workbenches on the side. Angus kept the place tidy. Tools hung on hooks. Boxes of nails and screws were ranged on shelves. There was a table saw and a band saw. She called Sergeant Donohue in Winnipeg. He would send someone from the Forensic Identification Unit out first thing in the morning to examine the saws for any sign of bone. He might try to make it out himself.

In the house, Angus's favourite coat hung on a hook by the door, his key ring on another. His winter boots sat side by side at the front door. His truck was parked beside the workshop, an ice auger in the back. Paths had been cleared to the house, to the barn and the workshop. A large snowblower stood alongside the truck.

One of the men was George Smedley. He was listed as the treasurer for the StarFest board of directors. Roxanne turned to Izzy. "Tell him to send us everything he's got, would you? Board minutes. Financial statements." She noticed him looking at them nervously through brown-rimmed glasses before he scurried off to his car. Did he have anything in particular to be nervous about?

Soon, only Jack Sawatsky remained. He put the keys he had to Angus's house on the table. He had been looking after the place while Angus was gone—in the city, he said, staying at his daughter's. Millie, Angus's wife, was in the hospital. She'd fallen and broken her hip just after Christmas. Angus had only come home last weekend, right before they found Stella Magnusson's head and foot at the dump. Jack rattled on, like he couldn't stop talking.

"Angus wants the doctors to send his wife to Fiskar Bay Hospital 'til she gets better, but her daughter wants her to stay in the city. She really wants Angus to sell up, move into an apartment. Like living in a box, Angus says. He'd sooner be dead." Jack's voice petered out as he realized what he had said. Roxanne took the seat opposite him.

Were there other keys? There were. The spare key to the workshop lay under the garbage can outside the door. Any of the guys could go in and finish working on something if they needed to, any time. There was also a key to the house in a drawer in the workshop, in case they needed to use the washroom. Who would know about this? All of the men in the group would.

"We trust each other around here, Corporal," Jack said defensively. "Look, shouldn't we be out there looking for him? We're all willing to come and help. Why are you wasting time sitting around here talking?"

"We need to know where to start looking," Roxanne replied, "if he really is missing." But Jack Sawatsky knew very little that would help them.

"Angus is a great guy," he said before he left. "Nobody ever has a bad word to say about him."

Izzy had called the hospital. Mr. Smith had visited his wife the day before, Sunday, in the early afternoon. They hadn't seen him since.

AT 10:00 THE following morning, Margo Wishart went skating. The Cullen Village skating trail was new. It ran across the surface of the frozen lake from a point north of the village to Cullen Point, at the south end. Two and a half kilometres of pristine ice, a ribbon of aqua blue, gleamed in the winter sunlight.

Sasha had phoned her first thing. She had an unexpected deadline to meet. She'd sold a sculpture. She had to figure out the best way to ship it to Toronto. She sounded too excited to think about anything else. Margo told her to forget about a dog walk, then she looked out at the perfect day and went to find her skates.

Bob, her big, black dog, loped beside her. He stayed alongside where the lake surface had not been cleared and a thin layer of snow gave him some traction. Margo loved to skate, the easy rhythm, the swing and glide, the sound of her blades swishing as they cut across the hard surface. It was so clear that she could see right down into the water, through several feet of ice to the rocks on the lake bottom. The occasional fish swam underneath her. The sky was a cool, pale yellow fading to pink, then to a band of azure. The sun lay to her left, a lemon-coloured ball casting blue shadows. Individual ice crystals on the snow sparkled with rainbow light.

The temperature had risen twenty degrees. Minus ten felt positively balmy after the bitter cold, and she felt warm from the exercise. The shore was to her right. The wooden houses of Cullen Village were painted different colours, tucked among tall green conifers. Look at this, she thought, and we have it all to ourselves right now, me and my dog. That was when she realized Bob was no longer running beside her and glanced back over her shoulder. There he was, way back, standing stock still on the ice. Reluctantly, she dug in her blades and came to a halt.

"Hey, Bob! Come on!" she called. He didn't budge. That was not like him. Like many rescue dogs, he was usually eager to please.

"Bob! Come here, boy!" But he remained still, all four feet planted. He had to have heard her. He pawed at the snowy surface of the ice in front of him. She heard him whine. Slowly, she skated back. He pawed some more, looked straight at her, then lowered his head to the ice once more. He scratched at the surface with both paws like he was trying to dig through. She heard him whimper. She wasn't worried. He had probably just seen a fish under the ice. She speeded up, drew level with him, then skated slowly over the rougher, ungroomed surface.

"What is it Bob? What's up?"

As she got close he came to meet her with a slow wag of his long tail. She reached the place where he had been. He followed beside her, stopped and looked down, where he had scraped a patch clean. Below, through the ice, she could see what appeared to be a large pink fish lying in the water. The pale, dead face of Angus Smith stared back up at her.

POLICE CARS CONVERGED on the spot where Margo stood, her dog at her side, marking the spot where Angus Smith lay. Izzy McBain got there first. "I know how to handle a car on ice," she bragged to Matt Stavros, as she drove out onto the frozen lake. "Did it first when I was fifteen. Used to race with my brothers." Sergeant Gilchrist followed close behind with Constable Roach at his side.

Cullen Village had been alerted by the sound of sirens. The villagers watched from cottage windows along the shore as the RCMP clustered on the ice. Margo and her dog were loaded into a car and Izzy drove her back toward her house. Phones rang throughout the village. Photographs appeared on Instagram, Twitter and Facebook. Worst suspicions were confirmed when old Doctor Gaul's car crawled out onto the lake.

Doc Gaul was old and stooped. Two unusual deaths in less than two weeks had him confounded, but all he had to do was pronounce death. Stavros and Roach cleared away enough of the snow cover to expose the whole body. Angus was naked. There was an obvious wound to his chest.

"It looks like he's been stabbed," said the doctor, "but you'll need to get him out before you know." They called the provincial medical examiner's office. Someone from Winnipeg would be on their way soon, with a refrigerated van.

"He has a lot of body hair. It's snagged on the underside of the ice. That's what's stopping him from drifting away." Angus had a beard, a mat on his chest, and pubic hair. He was entirely exposed. Sergeant Donohue stood beside Roxanne and looked down at the body. They had both been at the Smith house when the call came in. Two members of the Ident team were still there, examining Angus's workshop, including the saws.

"How many men can you spare?" Brian asked Gilchrist. "We need to secure this area as well as the house." The constables were taping off the stretch of land along the shore. Roxanne escorted Doctor Gaul to his car and returned to the others.

"Are those ice-fishing shacks?" Donohue asked. "He could have gone into the water from there." Over to the south at the far side of the point, they could see small rectangular shapes far out on the ice.

"They'll be fishing today," said Izzy.

"We need to get that area cleared too." Roxanne flipped through her phone contacts seeking Jack Sawatsky's number. She remembered the ice auger in Angus Smith's truck. Jack would know if Angus had an ice shack.

"I know who you need to get him out of this." Gilchrist was still looking down at the dead body under the ice. "Peter Flett. Champion ice carver. Lives just north of here. He'll know how to do it. And he's got the gear."

"Call him," said Donohue.

Roxanne got off the phone. "Jack Sawatsky says he'll get a squad from the fishing association to clear everybody off the ice. And he'll show us Angus's shack. Izzy, you're coming with me."

MARGO MADE HERSELF a mug of strong coffee and called Sasha.

"Gee, are you okay? I'll come over."

"No," said Margo. "You get on with what you're doing."

"With this going on? You've got to be kidding."

"I'm fine but I could probably use some company," Margo admitted. "Stay where you are and I'll walk over in a bit."

First she'd drink her coffee, then she'd take a hot, hot shower.

ROXANNE AND IZZY found Jack Sawatsky waiting at the end of the Smith driveway. Police tape surrounded the place. Izzy walked to the house to get Angus's keys.

"How could this happen?" Jack said. "Who would do a thing like that to a good guy like Angus? Does his family know?"

"Someone from headquarters is going to speak to his wife," Roxanne said, glad that she didn't have to do that particular job.

"You follow me." Jack got into a truck parked nearby and led them along the lakeshore to a ramp that accessed the lake. There were only six or seven trucks and a couple of snowmobiles out by the shacks. Jack pulled up alongside one of them and talked to a couple of fishermen, then they drove on. Far over, Roxanne recognized Brad Andreychuk, watching.

Angus's shack was out beyond Cullen Point. The snow around the door had been cleared away.

Izzy unlocked the door. Roxanne had never been inside a fishing shack. There was a single window, which let in some light. She scanned the room. Outside, the shack had had a coat of green paint but inside it was unpainted. A rectangle about fifteen inches by four feet had been cut out of the wooden floor close to one wall to expose the ice underneath. Two large ice holes had been sunk into it. Angus must have enjoyed company while he fished. Four wooden folding chairs were stacked against a wall, cushions heaped beside them. There was a propane heater and a camping stove. A shelving unit held a kettle and a pot, jars of milk powder, sugar and instant coffee. There were mugs, a few plates, and a tray of cutlery including a long, sharp knife. Fishing rods were propped in a corner, a tackle box beside them.

"Someone's been here," said Jack. "The chairs are always left out, not stacked like that. And he'd never chuck the cushions on the floor."

Izzy was crouching down by one of the ice holes. They were big, about fifteen inches wide, with plastic lids. Jack bent down beside her. "No!" she said and reached out a hand to stop him from lifting the lid. Roxanne pulled a pair of latex gloves from her pocket and passed another pair to Izzy. Underneath the lid was a rim of plastic, framing the hole. Its edge extended down about three inches. It was frozen to the ice.

"It's been melted, recently." Izzy examined it. "Looks like someone used hot water to get it off, but it's frozen on again."

The hole must have been widened after the rim was removed. On either side the ice had been drilled away, probably using Angus's ice auger, widening it by about four inches, each side. Izzy shone a flashlight into the hole. The ice went down more than four feet, maybe five.

"Angus was such a skinny little guy," Jack said. Roxanne studied the exposed edges of the ice hole.

"They still had to widen it to squeeze him through." Would traces of skin or hair remain, stuck to the edges? She went outside the shack to phone Sergeant Donohue again. She could see Sawatsky's friends shepherding people off the ice. They were almost all gone.

She left Izzy to keep watch at the shack and got a ride with Jack back to where Angus's body had been found. Vehicles were parked beside the trees at the top of the ramp. A clutch of men stood talking, Archie Huminski among them. There was no sign of Brad Andreychuk any more. Jack slowed down, wound down the window and introduced her.

"We'll keep an eye on things until you're done," one of them said. "Make sure no one gets out there." She thanked him. "We're doing it for Angus," he said and turned back to his friends as if she didn't exist. Archie came over.

"You're going to get the bastard that did this, right, milady?"

"I sure hope so." He reached into the cab and squeezed her hand.

"You come talk to me. Any time."

Jack drove along the road by the lake. The temperature was now minus five with no wind. People were outside, walking dogs on long leashes, stopping to talk and look out over the lake to see what was going on.

Peter Flett, champion carver, was out on the ice. He had brought saws, an auger, a chain saw, ice knives, ropes and poles. He drilled down and started to carve out chunks of ice, which Matt Stavros and Ken Roach lifted and stacked. It was different work than what Peter usually did, carving eagles and polar bears out of giant slabs, but he obviously knew how ice behaved, how to cut it away from the body below without causing further damage.

Margo and Sasha were among those who watched as the day wore on. Peter was at least four feet down by now, a rope tied around his waist. Every now and then, the silence was shattered by the buzz of a chain saw. A large white van had been driven out onto the lake. Two police cars were already there, and the carver's old Ford Ranger.

Margo had recovered from her initial shock. She wanted to see what was happening. She and Sasha had walked to a spot on the shore where they could get a clear view. Their dogs lay at their feet.

"They must be getting close to him," Margo said. "How much ice do you need to still be able to stand on it?"

"Three or four inches would do it."

They watched the ice carver reach down and pass up a large piece. It shone blue and clear in the sunlight. The pile of ice was aquamarine, the surface that had been thinned around the hole slightly translucent.

A big red Sierra truck pulled up on the road behind them. Panda Stavros walked over and patted the dogs. Annie ignored them. All her attention was on the scene on the lake.

"Angus Smith, eh? You're the one that found him, Margo? You okay?" News had travelled fast. Annie walked closer to the shore.

Panda didn't wait for answers. "Nice guy. He was there when we found Stella, you know? People are really pissed off about this. See that Annie? Hope she's not planning to paint this one. She's got that look about her." Another car drove up. George and Phyllis Smedley. "Can't be long until they get him out."

Two of the police walked to the back of the van, opened the doors and lowered a gurney. Ropes were passed to the carver. He fastened them down in the hole and climbed out, then picked up a long pole with a spike on the end. Onlookers could see him reaching down and hear the sound of him chipping at what was left of the ice.

"What is happening?" asked Phyllis. "Two murders in two weeks, right here in Cullen Village?" A truck drove away, off the ice.

"That's Jack Sawatsky's truck," George said. "He and I were there when Angus went missing. I've been asked to help the police with their inquiries," he added, puffing out his chest.

"Angus was there with us at the dump." Panda said, one-upping him. "He's the one who found Stella's head."

Annie had squatted down and taken a pair of binoculars from her pocket. The police were pulling on the ropes. Slowly, carefully, they lifted a sheet of ice up and out of the hole. Under it was Angus Smith, the front of his body still encased in two or three inches of what looked like blue glass. The ice carver chipped around it. What he left was the size of a coffin lid. They laid Angus Smith onto the gurney, lifted him into the back of the white van and closed the door.

They all took a deep breath, almost in unison.

"George made a pot of veggie chili. Why don't you all come over for supper?" said Phyllis.

"Sure." Margo still didn't want to be home alone. "I just need to go put Bob in the house and get the car. Are you coming?" Sasha nodded. Annie had turned back from the scene on the ice. She put the binoculars away.

"We've got leftovers that need eating," said Panda. "Another time, maybe?" She and Annie got into the big red truck and drove away.

"Panda can't stand the stuff that George cooks," said Sasha as she and Margo walked back to their houses, the dogs trotting at their heels. George was a naturopath and a vegan. "She says he's creepy."

OUT ON THE lake, Roxanne talked with the medic from the chief medical examiner's office before he drove off with Angus's frozen body.

"It'll take a while to get a time of death on this one, Corporal," he said, "but we've got other information for you. Stella Magnusson was hit on the head, hard enough to fracture her skull, but it didn't kill her. Afterwards, she was smothered."

Stella had definitely been murdered.

8

THE PEOPLE OF Cullen Village made sure their doors were locked when they went to bed that night. One by one, the house lights went out, apart from coloured bulbs that wound around conifers, making them look Christmassy and bright. Others fringed eavestroughs or twinkled along veranda railings, some blue, some white. Solar lamps capped with snow glowed greenly on driveway posts. The village appeared idyllic, picture perfect.

Bright lamps shone out on the lake, at the place where Angus Smith had been consigned to a cold and watery grave. Figures dressed in white padded in and out of his shack. Two vans stood waiting. The RCMP had sent powerful beams down through the ice hole and spotted a plastic bag resting on the lakebed. A diver had been lowered into the frigid water to retrieve it. He had brought up not one, but two bags.

Over at the Smith house the Ident team worked deep into the night, looking for traces of blood, signs of a scuffle, a knife. They examined Angus's truck minutely, the cab, the wheels, the open bed and everything lying in it, especially the auger. At the workshop, the saws got special attention. They were clean, too clean, said a technician, but still they found what they were looking for, tiny fragments of bone embedded in the teeth of the band saw. They wrapped the saw in plastic and carried it carefully out to their van. In the lab, in Winnipeg, they would seek a DNA match to Stella Magnusson.

By 3:00 am, they were gone. Yellow tape remained around the house and the ice shack. The hole in the surface of the lake had started to freeze over. The pile of ice beside it glowed in the light of a huge full moon, a blue moon in its perigee. Moonlight shone in the windows of the villagers, keeping them awake as they lay in their beds.

Roxanne Calloway also found it hard to sleep. She tossed and turned, thinking about the case. She'd worked the drug unit in Saskatchewan. Murder was a new field for her, one she had wanted. The time she had taken off work to have Finn had slowed her promotion and now she needed to make up for the year she had lost. And she wanted to do well, to make her mark. But she was confronted with what was probably a double murder. Would her bosses want to replace her with someone with more experience? Would she lose this opportunity?

At 6:00 am she gave up on sleep. The temperature outside, according to her phone, had dropped to minus twenty-two. There was hardly any wind. She rose from bed, put on winter running gear, glad she had thought to pack it. She needed to get outdoors, to clear her head. She donned thin wool clothing that would wick moisture away from her body, thermal leggings, wool socks, a cap. She added an outer, windproof layer and winter running shoes. Once she left the side door of the hotel, she pulled on a facemask that allowed her to breathe through her nose and mouth and keep her eyes clear. She didn't get much time to run these days. There was work and there was Finn. But on a job away from home, one where she had time alone to fill, she could maybe get herself back into shape.

The town was deserted. She could run down the centre of the streets, which were unimpeded by piles of snow. Twelve blocks in one direction, six the other, was more than a kilometre, less than a mile. She would run until 7:00 am, then go back to the hotel for a shower and breakfast. A police car crossed an intersection ahead of her. It slowed down. She waved and watched it drive off. She focused on her breathing, her pace, listened to the sound of her feet as they hit tarmac covered with a smooth layer of packed snow. There was a big moon between the houses and the trees, outshining the orange street lamps. She ran from one grey shadow to the next. She could almost sense Jake running beside her, keeping pace with her like he used to. Back before she had Finn they had run together whenever they could. She shook that memory. She didn't believe in ghosts, did she?

By 6:30, cars started to emerge from garages. She had to move onto the sidewalk, where the shovelled surface was less even. There were snowbanks to avoid, and roadside curbs. She jogged on the spot at a corner waiting for a car to pass. She was going to have to rise earlier to do this. Five-thirty would do it. Or she could run later, after midnight.

Brian Donohue had called a meeting for 9:00 am. She had avoided him last night at the hotel. Brian had black Irish good looks. Dark wavy hair, blue eyes, even features. He was cute. The women's washroom rumour mill at headquarters said he was recently divorced, available. There had been envious comments when the word got out that she'd be working this case with him. But Roxanne wasn't going to get herself involved with another RCMP member. Never again. It was too difficult, too painful. Next time, she'd marry a guy with a good, safe desk job. If there ever was a next time.

When she arrived at work, Donohue was standing examining the whiteboard, Sergeant Gilchrist at his side. Annie Chan's drawing of Stella Magnusson's face stared out, joined now by other photos, including one of Angus Smith shrouded in ice. Roxanne joined them. There was a mug shot of Brad Andreychuk, a bruise swelling his cheekbone, a thick and bloody lip.

"We thought we'd got him that time but the other guy wouldn't press charges, even though he landed in hospital," Gilchrist said. "Chickened out."

Izzy walked in carrying a tray of coffees in paper cups and a box of doughnuts. She placed them on the table.

"You do this, Izzy?" asked Gilchrist, pointing a thumb at the board. The Andreychuks' names were stuck up on sticky notes, as were the members of the StarFest board of directors. "You watch too much TV, girl."

"Brought you a coffee, Sarge. Be nice." She grinned at him. He grinned back. "Sugar and cream's in the bag." He helped himself.

"Double double, just how I like it." Gilchrist turned his attention to Roxanne. "You know they're calling you Spiderwoman downstairs? Scared the shit out of Sam Mendes this morning, running down Sixth in the dark with a balaclava over your face."

"You training?" Donohue was searching though the doughnut box.

"Yep," said Roxanne. "If I get in good enough shape I'll try for a half marathon in June." The Manitoba Marathon was run through the streets of Winnipeg each year, on Father's Day. Brian took a chocolate doughnut, with icing, out of the bag. Izzy pulled her phone out of her pocket to read a text.

"Matt's on his way. Might be a bit late."

Gilchrist helped himself to a couple of doughnuts. "One's for Kathy," he said, waving them under Izzy's nose, and clattered downstairs. They found seats around the table.

"Okay," said Brian, taking the lead. "We found blood in the Smith kitchen. It had been cleaned up but there were still traces where the cupboards meet the floor. There were dishes, not many, in the dishwasher, including a sharp kitchen knife from a rack on the counter. The killer may have run the washer to clean the knife. We won't know if it's the weapon until we get the autopsy results for Angus Smith but it's a possibility."

"So this probably wasn't a premeditated murder?" Roxanne asked.

"Maybe. Too early to tell. The bags we fished out of the lake contained indoor clothes, a kitchen towel with traces of blood still on it, and a large bedcover, also stained. We think he was stabbed in the kitchen, rolled in the bedcover and taken out to the lake in the back of his own truck."

The door opened. Matt came in, three or four large books under his arm.

"You're late, Constable," said Brian.

"Sorry, sir."

"I'll catch you up, Matt," said Izzy and passed him a coffee. She flashed him a sympathetic glance. Those two were close, Roxanne thought. If they were a couple, she should have known before they were assigned to this team. Why had Gilchrist not mentioned it? She pulled her attention back to the meeting.

"Are we looking at more than one killer?" asked Matt, sitting down at the table. "That's a lot of lifting for one person."

"Same with Stella Magnusson," said Izzy. "She wasn't big, but she'd be way over a hundred pounds, dead weight."

"And there's also Stella's car," Matt continued. "One person dropped it off at the airport, but how would they get back here without an accomplice? There's no bus service from Winnipeg to the Interlake anymore."

"Assuming it was someone from here." Roxanne sipped her coffee. As usual, she drank it black, no sugar, and she didn't touch the doughnuts. She liked to watch what she ate.

"Had to be someone who knows the village really well." Matt pulled a sugary cruller apart. "Do we know that it's the same killer?"

"If the bone particles we found on the saw are a match to Stella, yes. There's venison in the Smiths' freezer. It's possible Angus used the saw to cut up a deer that he'd hunted. We can't assume he used it to dismember Stella Magnusson's body.

"It's the same kind of mentality, though," Roxanne reasoned.

"How come?" Brian asked. "He was stabbed. She was hit on the head. Now the medical examiner's office is saying she was smothered."

"The disposal of the bodies—it's so complicated," she explained. "Planned. Carefully executed. Difficult. Either of these bodies could have been left out in the woods somewhere and we might not have found them until the spring. Why go to all that trouble?"

"It's smart, but it failed, both times," said Matt.

Roxanne remembered Izzy making the same point at the dump. "Yes, but only through bad luck. If the bag with Stella's foot in it hadn't ruptured she would have been buried in the landfill and we'd be none the wiser. And Angus could have drifted for miles. He'd have been under the ice until the spring."

"He'd have been missed right away, though. He was, already."

Constable Roach appeared at the door. He dropped two large binders on the table.

"For you, McBain. Guy called Smedley left them for you." He glanced around the room, at the whiteboard, the group seated at the table, taking it all in. Roxanne turned to him.

"One of the Andreychuks is supposed to stop by with receipts for us. If he does, let me know. I need to ask him something."

"Brad or the dad?"

"Either."

"Right, ma'am." He looked around the room once more, turned on his heel and left.

"Brad Andreychuk's story about being in the bar the night that Stella died holds," said Matt. "The bartender remembers him being there."

"But it doesn't let him off the hook," Izzy countered. "He could have been out on the ice fishing with his friends all afternoon but he'd still have had to go home before he went to the pub, if his mom and dad were in town. Those beasts of theirs would have had to be fed. He could have taken a skidoo over to Stella's in no time." She described how she had found the path through the woods.

"Has anyone talked to Jeremy Andreychuk?" asked Roxanne. Someone in the city had, Brian reported. Jeremy had been visibly upset to hear about Stella. No one from the family had told him. He'd been in class on Friday, January 19, the day that they believed Stella had been murdered. And he'd worked in a restaurant that evening. Nevertheless, Izzy got to her feet and added his name to the board. She glanced out the window.

"John Andreychuk just pulled up."

Roxanne excused herself and went downstairs. Izzy followed. Andreychuk pushed his way through the front door, stalked to the desk and slapped an envelope down on the counter.

"Corporal wants to see you, John," said the constable on duty. Kathy Isfeld stopped tallying up figures and watched over the top of her reading glasses.

"Does she now." Andreychuk swivelled round to look at Roxanne. "I need those receipts back when you're done with them."

Izzy picked up the envelope. Roxanne opened a door that led into a side office. "In here, Mr. Andreychuk. I need to ask you a question. Won't take long."

He sloped past her and stood waiting, weight balanced on both feet, arms loose by his sides. Izzy stood inside the door and listened.

"What's it about this time?"

"There's a trail runs from behind your barn to Stella Magnusson's place," said Roxanne. His only reaction was to narrow his eyes.

"So? Been there since her uncles lived there. Nobody uses it these days."

"Nobody?"

"You heard me."

"There are snowmobile tracks. Recent ones."

"That right?" He didn't hesitate. Didn't move a muscle. "Must have been folks from her end then. She gets visitors. Why don't you ask them? That all?"

"We're fine for now." He turned to go and saw Izzy.

"Bad business that, about Angus Smith. He was a good guy, Angus."

"I'll copy those receipts and get them back to you," Izzy said. Kathy Isfeld waited until the front door had closed behind him.

"All bark and no bite, John Andreychuk," she said. Her voice scarcely rose above a whisper. "It's his wife, Maggie, that you need to look out for. Bad blood, Maggie. Her and her dad before her. That's where Bradley gets it from." Kathy returned her attention to her ledger. Izzy turned to Roxanne at the foot of the stairs.

"Don't care what Kathy says. John Andreychuk's lying."

"All the Andreychuks are lying. We just need to figure out why. But still. It's too easy, isn't it, to think Brad did it? Too obvious?"

"Suppose so. The guys would love to pin this on him and put him away for once, though." Izzy ran up the stairs, ponytail swinging. And this would all be over and they could get us out of their hair, Roxanne thought as she followed her.

Back up in their office, Donohue was putting his phone back in his pocket.

"I have to get back to the city," he said. "The bosses want a meeting. They're getting a lot of media pressure to get the Magnusson murder solved. Stella's photo's been everywhere. Now that there's another killing it's going to be worse. I'll get back here as soon as I can. Meantime, Roxanne, you're to carry on."

Roxanne breathed a sigh of relief. The investigation was still hers.

"We need to focus on finding Stella Magnusson's killer," Donohue continued. "Assume until we hear otherwise that the bone in the saws from Angus Smith's place is hers. Two murders out here are too much of a coincidence for them not to be linked. If we get Stella's killer, we'll probably have Angus Smith's too."

"Everything we know about Stella so far is related to her work," said Roxanne once Brian had left. She turned to the whiteboard. "We need to interview the board members. Three of them live at Cullen Village—George Smedley, Sasha Rosenberg and Freya Halliday. The last one's a village councillor. Who are these other names?"

Matt joined her at the whiteboard. "I got these from my aunt's friends. Stella was married to Freddie Santana."

"The filmmaker?"

"Yeah, but he's in L.A. And Roger Kato's an old boyfriend, now living in Santa Fe. Leo Isbister's more interesting. He played in a band with Stella in the late eighties but he's been around here lately. He's now a real estate developer and he's planning a development just south of here."

"Really?"

"And he's got a summer cottage between Cullen Village and Fiskar Bay," Izzy said. "On the lakeshore. It's humongous. He must be worth a fortune."

"Okay, we'll check him out too. There's also that guy called Erik Axelsson that Brad Andreychuk says she's been seeing."

"I've got something on him." Matt reached for the books he had brought in with him. They were school yearbooks. "These are from Fiskar Bay High, from the mid-eighties, when Stella Magnusson was a student. That's why I was late. The school secretary took her time." Izzy reached out and touched his back with an easy intimacy that answered Roxanne's question. These two were more than friends.

"But see what she showed me." Matt opened the book for 1987, the year Stella Magnusson would have graduated. One page was marked with a sticky note. "Stella was in a band. There's a photograph."

They examined the shot of four students with guitars. Stella was laughing, big eighties hair, lots of makeup, eyes outlined in black. Behind the group stood a man with shoulder-length blond hair and a beard. Izzy peered closer.

"That's Erik Axelsson," she said. "Geez. He really did look like a Viking back then."

"The secretary's been there for years. She says he used to come in every week. Taught them to play guitar."

"So he knew her back then? We need to talk to him," said Roxanne. "Today."

9

THE AXELSSON FARM had seen better days. The outbuildings needed a fresh lick of paint. Some goats capered around hay bales outside an old rectangular stock barn and Roxanne glimpsed chicken runs at the back. To the right was a double garage. Cars littered the area beside it in various states of disrepair, probably kept for spare parts. The house—one and a half storeys with a sloping roof, a deck to the side, wooden steps leading down from a back door—looked much as it might have done when it was built back in the 1950s. An older Buick and a silver Ford truck were parked in front.

"It looks like they're both home." Roxanne noticed Izzy frown.

"I like Roberta," Izzy had said on the way. Her parents' farm lay just to the east. When her mother had had cancer, Roberta had brought over bottles of goat milk. It had been one of the few things her mother could keep down. Roberta had often stayed to visit. She was a good neighbour. Izzy had probably hoped that Roberta would be out so that they could talk to Erik Axelsson alone. Roxanne wondered if she should have brought Matt along with her instead. She'd thought Izzy's knowledge of the Axelsson household might help but maybe she was too close to them.

The doorbell didn't work. Izzy knocked and walked right in. The kitchen was cheerful and bright. A fire blazed in the wood stove. Warm, woollen cushions padded the chairs and coloured hangings decorated walls and windows. Roberta Axelsson was kneading bread at her large kitchen table.

Erik Axelsson got up from a chair by the wood stove. He wore overalls, thick grey socks and a faded checked shirt. He rubbed his eyes, looking like he'd been wakened from a nap and seemed puzzled to see them, but friendly. "Hi, Izzy. What's up?"

Izzy introduced Roxanne. Roberta eyed her. The corporal who was investigating the murders? Was this an official visit? She waved a floury hand at them.

"Leave your boots on and help yourselves to coffee. It's fresh, I just made a pot."

"This shouldn't take long," said Roxanne, but Izzy was already taking a couple of mugs down from a shelf. She obviously knew her way around the kitchen.

"Roberta makes great coffee. You having some, Erik?"

Roberta kept on kneading the dough.

"I'm okay." Erik indicated another chair by the wood stove. "Have a seat. Make yourselves comfortable."

Roxanne sat. Erik resumed his place, opposite her. This was altogether too relaxed for police business.

"How's your mom doing, Izzy?" Roberta asked. "I made some cheese. Do you want to take some for her?"

"Better not," Izzy replied, fetching a jug of milk from the fridge and sitting at the table. "This is a work call."

Roberta stopped kneading. "What about? We heard you found another body."

"Angus Smith," said Roxanne. "Did you know him?"

Erik stretched out his long legs in front of the stove. The Axelssons looked at each other. Neither reacted. "No," Erik replied. "He's from Cullen Village, right?"

The Axelsson farm was only twelve kilometres north of the village, but the people of the village and those that lived around Fiskar Bay did not always connect. Roxanne changed tack. "Mr. Axelsson, we wondered if you could come into the office. To help us with the Magnusson inquiry."

Izzy flashed a look of surprise at her across the top of her coffee mug.

"Who, me?" Erik Axelsson stopped lounging. He sat up in his chair.

"Well, yes. You lived here when Stella Magnusson came back and started StarFest, right?"

Roberta had gone to the sink to wash her hands. She turned around. "I was there too! I helped set the whole thing up, back in the beginning. Want me to come as well?"

"Hey, Roberta, it's all right. We only need one of you." Izzy put down her mug. "We've got some photographs from StarFest, and also from way back when Stella was still at school here. Erik, you knew her then too, right? We thought you could tell us who some of the other folks in them are."

Not entirely true, thought Roxanne, but it was a story that wouldn't set off alarm bells. Izzy had swung into support seamlessly. Maybe bringing her along had been the right choice after all.

"I wasn't at school with Stella," said Axelsson. "I was older than her."

"But Erik taught Stella to play the guitar." Roberta looked proudly at him. So she had known about that.

"She had a band," Axelsson explained, "and so did I. Me and my buddy Mike and a couple of other guys, we helped those kids out, all of us did. Mike taught the bassist to play. I didn't just teach Stella, I taught their lead guitar too. Look, there's lots of folks around here who were at school with Stella. Shouldn't you be talking to them?"

Roxanne got to her feet. "Well, Mr. Axelsson, you knew her then and again when she came back to live near here. That's useful to us. We think talking with you could be helpful."

"You can talk to me here," said Axelsson, leaning back again in his chair, as if reluctant to go.

"Yeah, Erik, but the photographs are at the office. We can give you a ride." Izzy drained her coffee and stood also. The Axelssons looked uneasy. If Erik was driven to the RCMP detachment office in the back of a police car, the town would notice. There would be talk.

Roberta picked up the smooth ball of dough, put it in a bowl and covered it with a clean cloth. "You'd better go. Erik. Take the truck." She turned to Izzy, concern furrowing her brow. "This won't take long, will it?"

"No, no," said Izzy. "Be back by the time that bread's risen. Why don't you call my mom? She'd love some of that cheese."

Roxanne had reached the door. "Mr. Axelsson, we'll see you back at the detachment." She thanked Roberta for the coffee and went outside. Izzy followed her.

"Well done, Constable," Roxanne said. Izzy stopped dead in her tracks.

"You know what, Corporal, being a cop in your home town is a bitch sometimes. I like those people." She stomped towards the car. "I hate this. I'll text Matt and tell him we're on our way."

"I'll ask him to join me for the interview if you like," said Roxanne, following her.

"Good idea. Why don't you do that." They climbed in, Izzy started the car and they drove off.

NOT LONG AFTER, the phone rang in Margo Wishart's house.

"It's Sasha. You've got to hear this. Roberta just called. The police showed up there this morning, the woman officer that's in charge and Izzy McBain. Erik's had to go into the RCMP office, to answer questions about Stella Magnusson."

Margo was in the middle of marking student papers. This was a great excuse to take a break. "Did they say what it was for?"

"Said it was to look at photographs of Stella. But why couldn't they have brought them there? Why make him go into the office?"

"Don't know. Maybe the photos are on their computer. There's probably nothing much to it."

"Well, yes," said Sasha. "But there might be." And she proceeded to tell Margo how she had seen something, years ago, when

Erik still played at StarFest. Stella and Erik standing together offstage, close together. Too close. And once, a couple of years ago, Sasha had stopped by Stella's place one evening to pick up some paperwork for StarFest, and Erik had been there. "Just leaving!" he'd said. But he'd looked flustered. Stella had just smiled in that enigmatic way of hers and offered no explanation. Sasha had never mentioned it to anyone, least of all Roberta. Had something been going on between the two of them? Did the RCMP suspect him?

"They maybe think Erik's the murderer? Can you see him doing that?"

"He's kind of gutless, but who knows? Maybe it was a crime of passion," Sasha said with relish. "You know Erik used to know Stella, way back? When she was younger? Erik had a band with his pal Mike Little. So did Stella."

"Really? But that must have been years ago. How long?"

"Stella was still in school. Grade twelve, so it was maybe thirty years? Roberta told me all about it when Stella came back here. Erik taught her to play guitar. Stella left Fiskar Bay right after school though, and Erik moved to the city after that."

"How old was Erik then?"

"Oh, I don't know. Late twenties. He got himself a job at a car dealership in town. Then he went to Red River College. Trained to be an auto mechanic and he met his first wife. Kind of settled down."

"Until he met Roberta and left his wife and kids for her.'

"Well, yeah. Too good-looking, Erik. That's his problem. Gets away with blue murder."

"That's not funny, Sasha." But they both laughed anyway. "Maybe we should go over there and keep her company until he gets home."

"I offered already." Roberta had told her she'd be fine. Erik shouldn't be too long. Sasha and Margo decided to wait and see.

"Call me if you hear anything."

"You bet!"

AT THE RCMP detachment office, Erik Axelsson sat across a table from Roxanne and Matt Stavros. They were in a small, grey room, with a window high in the ceiling that did not let in much light. Fluorescent strips shone harshly overhead. A recorder lay on the table humming faintly. A school yearbook was open at the picture of Stella with the members of her band, and Erik.

"Sure, I knew her back then. I knew all those kids. I had a band of my own. Me and the guys, we took them along with us to gigs."

"You said you taught Stella how to play guitar?"

"Well, yeah. Sure I did. We taught the four of them. See him? That's Alex Fletcher. Town councillor, now. Why don't you go ask him about Stella?"

"And the other two?"

"They're long gone. Don't know where they went."

"When Stella moved back, to live near Cullen Village, you were already living here as well?"

"I moved onto the farm with Roberta, my wife, after we got married. We'd been back three or four years before Stella showed up. Nobody expected Stella to come home."

He was lounging again, as much as a plastic straight-backed chair would allow, trying to appear casual. He was still good-looking, but he must be close to sixty, Roxanne thought. Tall, long limbed, hair tied back in a ponytail. But it was going grey and the lines in his face were etched deep.

"You were involved in Stella's music festival, back in the beginning?"

"We both were, me and Roberta. Roberta had a lot to do with getting it up and running. She was on Stella's board, first few years. I just played sometimes. Mike Little and me played as a duo. But StarFest got bigger and we weren't asked back after a while. Didn't really matter. We just played for fun, Mike and me. We still do."

"Did your wife continue with StarFest? After you weren't asked back?"

"Well, no. She stopped when it went all professional. It wasn't just about guys like Mike and me anymore. She liked the whole thing better when it was for the locals. They were never really very close, her and Stella. She thought StarFest was a good idea, back at the beginning, and she could sell the stuff she makes at the craft section. She didn't like what it grew into, so she left. No big deal."

Roxanne could see him getting more comfortable, settling in to the conversation. He'd stared at the tabletop and at the open yearbooks at the beginning, two parallel furrows between his brows. Now he lifted his eyes and made contact. They were pale blue tending towards grey. Nordic eyes. Engaging. He's a charmer, she thought, and he knows it. Does he think he can charm me?

"When did you last see Stella Magnusson?" she asked. He blinked, shrugged, looked away.

"Oh, I don't know. Might have run into her around town. Fiskar Bay's not very big."

"Mr. Axelsson, we have a witness who says that your truck has been seen parked outside Stella Magnusson's house recently." Those eyes met hers again, only for a second. He rubbed his hands on his knees.

"Oh, right. Needed some help with the SUV. It wouldn't start."

"When was that?"

"A while ago. Not sure," he said. He smiled at her. He still had good teeth.

"Our witness says your truck was there not once but several times," said Roxanne.

For a moment he was still, the only sound the whirr of the recorder. "You sure it was mine, Corporal? There's lots of them around here."

Matt nodded his head. Erik was right. He drove a Ford F-250 truck. Even the silver colour was popular.

Roxanne clasped both hands on the table in front of her. "Were you and Stella Magnusson in a relationship, Mr. Axelsson?"

"Hey," he exclaimed, half rising out of his chair. "Me and Stella, we were just friends. That's all. Just friends."

"Please sit down, Mr. Axelsson. You were there at night, our witness tells us, on more than one occasion. For hours. And you were just friends?"

Erik Axelsson sank back into his chair. The look he gave her now was decidedly cooler. "Look, lady, I don't know what you're getting at. Are you trying to pin this murder on me? Forget it. We got along, Stella and me, sure we did, but that's all there was to it. I'm married. I love my wife."

"Where were you on Friday, January 19?"

"I haven't a clue. I'd need to check. Who is this witness? How come you believe whoever it is and not me?" Now his anger was rising. Was it real or was he pretending?

"It's not a matter of whom we believe, Mr. Axelsson. Tell us your whereabouts on those dates and we will probably be fine."

"Maybe I need to be talking to a lawyer?"

"I don't think that's necessary right now. All we are doing is asking questions."

"Well," he said, getting to his feet, "I think I've answered enough of this crap for now. I haven't been charged with anything. I'm free to go, right?"

He was. Roxanne didn't have enough grounds to hold him. He left the room without saying goodbye. Bill Gilchrist came out of his office as Erik strode across the front office and out the door.

"Been beating up on our Erik, have you, Corporal?"

From the window, Roxanne could see Erik get into his truck. "Does he lose his temper much?"

"What, Erik? He's harmless. Was a bit wild they say when he was young but we haven't had any bother from him since he moved back. He's an old hippie. The goat farm thing's a bit stupid, if you ask me. They'll never make money at that, but it's probably more the missus's thing. He's better off sticking to fixing cars. That's what probably keeps them going. He's okay at that, they say. A bit lazy though. Only works when he wants to. He plays the bars sometimes with Mike Little. Doesn't drink."

Kathy Isfeld lifted her head from her work. "Goes to AA," she said. "Never misses. Been going for years."

Upstairs, Izzy McBain also watched Erik rev his truck and back it out, fast, onto the street. Matt entered the room.

"That got him rattled," he said.

"Pleased with yourselves then, are you?"

"Hey, Izzy, you can't let it get personal. This might get results. Want to come over to my place and watch the game tonight?" He was reaching for his coat. "Order in some pizza?"

"No thanks. I've got hockey practice."

Roxanne had come in and had opened her laptop. "They've had a look at Angus Smith's body. He was stabbed with a five-inch blade. It went straight into his heart. And it's a match for the one in Smith's dishwasher. So at least we know how and where that murder happened." She watched Izzy reach for her parka and head off downstairs.

"She okay?"

"Oh," said Matt, "she'll be fine. She'll go chase a hockey puck around the rink and get rid of her bad mood. Then she'll show up at my place and eat all the pizza."

Roxanne watched him get ready to leave too. He and Izzy McBain were a good match. Too bad they were both in the Force, working the same case. She couldn't think of any other constables at Fiskar Bay that she would want to replace either of them, though. She would leave things be.

THREE HOURS LATER, Roxanne was soaking in the tub in her hotel room. She'd phoned her sister and said goodnight to Finn on FaceTime. With a bit of luck she'd get into Winnipeg tomorrow night and have an evening at home with her boy. Then she'd catch up on her emails. Now she could have an early night, set the alarm for 5:30 and have a decent run in the morning.

The phone rang. Matt Stavros. He'd just had a call from his aunt Panda, the one that lived with Annie Chan. Panda wanted to know if they had really hauled Erik Axelsson in for questioning that day.

"How would she know that, Matt?"

"Because she finds out everything. Anyway, she thought we might want to know that Roberta Axelsson showed up at her friend Sasha Rosenberg's house in Cullen Village an hour or so ago, with an overnight bag in her hand. She's walked out on Axelsson. Says he's been screwing Stella Magnusson."

10

"WHAT AM I going to do?" Roberta wailed as she reached for another Kleenex. "I can't just stay here."

"Yes, you can. As long as you like, Roberta." Sasha patted her hand, then glanced across the table at Margo, who was drinking coffee from a hand-thrown pottery mug.

"No, I can't. What about my goats? Erik can't milk a goat to save himself. Who's going to take care of them?" Roberta drooped like a rag doll brought in from the rain.

"You need to talk to a lawyer and find out where you stand," said Sasha.

Margo put down her mug. "I have a niece who does law. She'll know of someone."

"I don't have any money. How am I supposed to pay for a lawyer?"

"Isn't half the farm yours?"

"I don't know. It belonged to Erik's family. I don't even know if we own the land."

Margo caught Sasha's eye again and raised an eyebrow. She found it frustrating when women like Roberta knew so little about their own financial status.

"Erik's the one at fault here, Roberta," Margo said. You shouldn't be the one that has to suffer."

"But I am! I'm the loser all round! That's what's so awful about this." Tears poured down Roberta's face once more. Sasha passed her another tissue.

It was Thursday morning, the first day of February. Roberta had spent the night on Sasha's sofa bed, the one she kept for occasional visitors. Roberta blew her nose.

"How could I have been so stupid?" She scrunched the tissue between her fingers. "Why didn't I see what was going on? You know what? I think I did see, I just didn't want to. I didn't want to believe that he'd fallen for Stella. That he didn't love me anymore."

Margo reached out and touched her shoulder. "You mustn't think that. You and Erik are a great couple. Of course he loves you. This is all Stella's doing."

"Not really." Tears continued to course down Roberta's cheeks. "He liked her. He did. I watched them, years ago, at StarFest. It was a rehearsal, they were doing sound checks, and they were laughing, him and Stella, like no one else was there. Like I wasn't there. There was just the two of them. And you know, I kind of knew, but then I thought, don't be stupid, this is Erik, you can trust Erik. But I guess I was wrong. It must have been going on for years."

"You don't know that for sure. Have some more coffee." Sasha poured another cup.

"It wasn't just that. There were little moments. We'd go to Stella's for meetings, back when StarFest was just getting started. She hadn't fixed up the office yet, so we'd get together in her house. And it looked like Erik belonged there. He was so relaxed, like it was a second home for him. You know, Sasha, when I had that row with her, when I quit StarFest, I don't think I was mad at her because of what she was doing with the festival, I think, now, on a gut level, it was really about her and Erik."

"But she cut Erik out of StarFest too, didn't she?" asked Margo, trying to make sense of all of this.

"Well, yes. And I thought that we were done with Stella, both Erik and me, but I guess that wasn't true. Not really."

There was a knock at the door. Panda and Annie entered. Bob the dog got up from the floor and padded over to greet them.

Sasha's house was tiny and cluttered. The table hardly had enough room around it for four chairs. There was a large, sagging armchair and the sofa, which was covered with a heap of bedding and Lenny, who wagged his tail at them but stayed put. Roberta reached for another tissue and blew her nose loudly. Panda kicked off her boots, hung her parka on a coat stand at the door and flopped into the armchair.

"Are you sure about this, Roberta?" Annie left her boots neatly on a patch of linoleum, avoided Bob the dog and took a seat at the table. "Erik and Stella?"

"Yes! I figured it all out, after he left to go to the police station. It all came back to me. I remembered things. He'd go out, sometimes in the afternoon, more often in the evening. He'd say he was going to practice at Mike's but one night, Alice, Mike's wife, called to see if Mike was at our place and of course he wasn't, and when Erik came home he said he and Mike hadn't gone to his house after all, they'd gone to the pub to talk to someone about a gig, and stupid me, I believed him. I didn't want *not* to believe him. I loved him, I really did."

Margo watched her gather herself together as she told the story. She told it well. Roberta was a bit of a drama queen.

"But he told you? About Stella? He admitted it?" Panda asked.

"Well, yeah. After he got back from talking to the police. He was pretending it was just nothing, but I could tell he was shaken up. I poured him a cup of tea and I just kind of blurted it out. 'Have you been seeing Stella?' I asked him. And he got this evasive look on his face. And I knew. 'You were!' I said. And he got all defensive. Tried to tell me it was nothing. 'You were fucking Stella Magnusson and it was nothing!' I yelled at him. 'How long has this been going on?' And, you know, he didn't know what to say. He just stood there, looking at the floor, shifting from side to side. And that was it. Over, him and me." Roberta paused for breath. She picked up her coffee cup. It was almost empty again. "I need a refill," she said, dehydrated from weeping and talking. "I am so thirsty."

"He's been phoning." Sasha refilled Roberta's mug. "He wants Roberta to go home."

"What will you do, Roberta?" asked Panda, swinging a leg over an arm of the chair.

"I don't know yet." Roberta gulped down the coffee. "But I'm not going back there. I'm not going back to him. He's been lying to me for years. Screwing Stella behind my back." She had stopped crying and sounded like she was beginning to get angry.

"And now she's dead," said Panda.

There was a moment's silence.

"You don't think Erik did it?" she asked.

Roberta shot her an accusing glance.

"Well, he's bound to be a suspect." Panda pointed to a plate of cookies on the table. "Are those oatmeal and raisin?"

"He wouldn't," said Roberta, still challenging her. "He might be stupid enough to mess around with Stella, but he wouldn't kill anyone. Not Erik."

"He's got a bit of a temper on him, Roberta." Sasha passed the cookie plate over to Panda. Bob the dog came to investigate.

"Well, yes. He has. But he's not violent. Not Erik. He just mouths off. He's all talk."

Sasha's phone rang. She moved to answer it.

"Could you go and stay with your daughter in Winnipeg for a while?" said Margo. Sasha's house was too small. She wondered if Roberta was going to end up in her own spare room. She'd need to offer, but would she get any work done with Roberta in the house, in this kind of state?

"I don't know. I haven't talked to her yet. I left a message. That's maybe her now."

Sasha came back with the phone. "Mike Little's wife, for you."

Roberta took it and went off into the next room with it clamped to her ear. The three heads at the table leaned together. Panda clambered out of the chair and came closer to listen.

"This is really bad," said Margo, almost in a whisper. "Do you think the police will arrest him?"

"I still think Roberta should talk to a lawyer and get some advice. Figure out where she stands, legally," said Sasha. She had divorced two husbands already.

"She'll never do it. She's still nuts about the guy."

"What a jerk!"

"What about the farm?"

"She can stay here for now, but there's not much room." Sasha appeared anxious.

Roberta returned. They all went silent, pretending they hadn't been talking about her. "Alice went over and milked the goats. She's offered to look after them. Maybe I should go home."

"Really?" Sasha sat back, surprised. "You said you wouldn't go back to him."

"I'm not. I'm going to kick the bastard out. That's my home. Why should I have to be the one that leaves? He can go find somewhere else to live."

"Is it safe for you to do that?" Margo asked.

"Safe? Me? Erik would never hurt me."

"You don't know that. Someone killed Stella, and Angus Smith. There's a murderer on the loose and, whether you like it or not, Erik will be a suspect."

Roberta sat down again. "I'm starving," she said. "I didn't eat last night."

Panda moved towards the kitchen. "You've got eggs in the fridge, Sasha?" she asked. Soon they could hear her clattering pans around.

"Even if you do persuade him to go, you'd be all on your own, out there in the middle of nowhere," Margo continued.

"So what. You live by yourself, Margo. So does Sasha."

"We're in the village. There are other people around. And Erik might come back," Margo responded. She really was concerned for Roberta's safety.

"Erik's maybe been stupid," Roberta said, "but he's not a murderer."

"You didn't think he would be unfaithful," Panda called from the kitchen. "But he was. With Stella!"

Roberta took a deep breath. "I still want him out. I want my house back. And my goats, and my chickens. It's where I ought to be. I'll be okay. And anyway, there's a shotgun, if I need to protect myself."

"What? You've got a gun?" Margo was incredulous. Panda came through and put a plate of scrambled eggs in front of Roberta.

"Sure, there's a gun. Everybody out here has one. To scare off coyotes," said Roberta.

"Do you know how to use it, Roberta?" asked Annie.

"Don't be ridiculous," Sasha protested. "Nobody is going to be using a gun. If you're going back, I'm coming with you, for the first few nights at least. Me and Lenny." The dog was still dozing on the sofa. Panda sank back into the armchair and rolled her eyes in disbelief. Roberta was devouring the eggs.

"Phone Erik first, and tell him he has to leave," said Margo.

"I need to tell him to his face."

"You are not going alone," Sasha insisted.

"I don't need you there!"

"You need someone. If only to be a witness," Margo said. They all stopped and thought about that.

"Maybe we should all go. We could spell each other off. In pairs. It might be safer that way," said Annie.

"No." Roberta pushed the empty plate away. "Those eggs were good, thanks, Panda."

"You're welcome."

"I've made up my mind. Margo's right. I'll phone him first. No, I'll phone Mike, maybe he'll be able to talk some sense into him."

"Maybe he could go and stay at Mike's house?"

"No way. Alice won't have him. She's pissed off with him too." The phone rang again. "Maybe that's Liz." Liz was Roberta's daughter by her first marriage, the one she had left, fifteen years earlier, to live with Erik. She went back to the bedroom to take the call.

"I hope she goes to Liz's for now," said Margo. "Just until she figures things out.'

"We need to convince her to do that," said Panda.

OVER AT THE Axelsson house, an RCMP car had pulled into the driveway. Erik's silver Ford truck was nowhere to be seen. Roxanne and Matt checked the outbuildings. The chickens had been fed. The goats and the sheep were munching placidly. There was no sign of Erik. That was too bad. Now that it seemed more likely that he actually had been Stella Magnusson's lover, they wanted to talk to him again. Matt tried the front door. It was unlocked.

"What do you think, Corporal?" Roxanne walked past him into the house. "Let's have a quick look." She didn't have a warrant to search, but this was too good an opportunity. "Don't touch anything," she said, just to be on the safe side.

The house phone rang. Roxanne ignored it. They walked from room to room. A mug, almost full of cold tea, milk scum on the surface, sat on the kitchen table. Two loaves of bread rested on a rack on the counter. In the living room a book lay on a side table, turned over at the place where it had last been read. The ash in the wood stove was cold. A big bed in the bedroom was unmade. Roberta's discarded clothes lay on one chair, Erik's on the other. Nothing was disturbed. Everything looked as it might have been when Roberta had stormed out the night before.

"Let's go back to the car and phone the detachment," said Roxanne. "Where does his friend Mike Little live? Who else does he hang out with?" They closed the door behind them and were soon heading back to Fiskar Bay.

BACK AT SASHA'S, progress had been made.

"All right, all right. I'll go to Winnipeg, just for a few days. Stay with Liz."

"Want one of us to drive you in?" Sasha offered.

"No, I can do it. And anyway, I'll need my car."

In less than an hour, Roberta had washed her face, borrowed some makeup to camouflage the red bags under her eyes, brushed her hair and was heading out the door. "Liz never did like Erik," she said. "I think she's kind of glad I've left him."

"What about the goats? And the chickens?" asked Margo.

"I'll call Alice and get her to look after the goats. Erik will feed the rest. They'll be okay." Now that she had made the decision, Roberta couldn't wait to be gone. It wasn't long before her friends watched her drive away.

"They've been married for fifteen years?" asked Margo, as they turned back into the house.

"Something like that. They were both married to other people when they met. Their kids were on the same basketball team. The way Roberta tells it they took one look at each other and that was it. Happily ever after. They left their partners and their kids, everything, and moved out here. It took some time for Liz and her brother to come around, but now Roberta sees them and her grandkids quite often."

"What about Erik's family?"

"I don't know. There was a daughter, around the same age as Liz. I don't know if he ever sees her."

"But he started an affair with Roberta while he was still married to his first wife," said Margo. "What a jerk."

Panda surveyed the room. "Where's Phyllis? How come she's not here?"

"She couldn't make it. She's sick. Throwing up." Sasha went to the kitchen to make more coffee. Panda cleared the dirty dishes from the table and found clean mugs.

"Again?"

"I know. And God knows what that idiot George is giving her to try and cure it."

"He says he's qualified—as a naturopathic doctor," said Margo, sitting back at the table.

"Doctor my foot," Sasha called from the kitchen. "He's a quack. Him and his herbal remedies. Maybe it's him that's making her sick."

"You two should have come for George's chili," Margo laughed. "We got some kind of brown brew to drink with it. You'd have hated it."

"I tipped mine into that aloe plant of his when no one was looking," Sasha said, coming back into the room. "Maybe we should stop by and take her some real food."

"Chicken soup," said Margo.

"Aren't they vegan?" asked Annie.

"She isn't. I cooked her up a plate of sausage and egg over here last week and she gobbled it. Who wants more cookies?" Sasha put another plateful on the table.

Lenny finally got off the sofa and joined Bob. Both dogs looked interested.

ROXANNE AND MATT had not been back long at the RCMP detachment when the front door flew open and Erik Axelsson lurched in, looking the worse for wear. His eyes were red and bleary, his ponytail was undone and his hair hung lank to his shoulders. From where Roxanne stood, behind the counter, she could smell beer.

"You! You meddling bitch!"

"Hey, Erik, stop right there!" Sergeant Gilchrist strode out of his office. Roxanne stood her ground. Izzy stuck her head over the banister to see what was happening. Erik leaned against the counter and pulled some loose papers from his pocket.

"January 19th, eh? Want to know where I was? Here you are!" He picked a scrap of paper from the pile and slammed it down on the countertop. "Fixed a car, all day long. Tricky job. Call this guy.

He'll tell you. I was at his place until almost six." A second piece of paper followed the first. "See this? Receipt. Brake shoes, bought them at the garage. Look here, January 19. Got that, bitch?"

The sergeant moved forward again. Roxanne gestured to him to wait. A third piece of paper joined the other two.

"Receipt for $475. Copy, signed by me. And you want to know what else? It was a Friday. I played a gig that night. People saw me. So I couldn't have killed Stella fuckin' Magnusson and now you can get right off my back. Got that?" He turned, swayed and almost fell.

Matt and the sergeant both moved to grab him. "Hold on there, Erik," said Gilchrist, as Matt reached for Erik's arm. "That's enough."

"Is it, you think? No, it's not." He whipped his arm away and turned back to glare at Roxanne.

"Why don't you check your facts first, you stupid interfering cow, before you go around wrecking people's lives?"

"Let's get some coffee into you, Erik," said the sergeant. Izzy's voice rang out across the room

"Should have thought about that before you screwed Stella Magnusson, Erik. Guys like you piss me right off." She disappeared back upstairs.

"Get him sobered up, Matt," said the sergeant. "And if you don't need him anymore, Corporal, we'll send him home."

Roxanne was leafing through the pieces of paper Erik Axelsson had left scattered on the counter. He had indeed repaired a car on January 19.

"I'll just get Izzy to call and check these, Sergeant. If everything's all right, we'll let him go."

"Too fuckin' right you will," muttered Erik Axelsson. An hour later, he was sent home in a taxi.

Izzy watched him leave from the window of their office upstairs. "They should have made him walk," she said. "Or locked him up for the night. Drunk and disorderly."

His story had checked out. He had worked on a car in the morning of the day Stella Magnusson had died, picked up the brake shoes at noon, had finished the job just before six. Mike Little had been at Erik's house to pick him up by seven. They'd been together right through until 2:00 am. It looked like Erik was in the clear.

Roxanne put on her city coat. She would get to Winnipeg in time to eat with her boy. They'd have a whole evening together. Maybe watch a movie. She watched Izzy pull the sticky note with Erik Axelsson's name on it from the board.

"We need a new lead," Roxanne said. "Can you get me a number for Leo Isbister? I wouldn't mind talking to him while I'm in town."

11

THE HEAD OFFICE of Isbister Homes lay in the south end of
Winnipeg. Roxanne pulled into an industrial park where a two-
storey, glass-fronted building dominated a row of windowless grey
warehouses with loading docks at the front. The parking lot was
full of cars. She found the only remaining space in the visitors'
parking area. J.L. Isbister, otherwise known as Leo, would have
a half hour available at 4:30, his office assistant had conceded on
the phone, only after the words "murder inquiry" had been mentioned. It was exactly 4:28 when Roxanne announced her arrival
at the front desk. A well-groomed receptionist directed her to the
waiting area. Brochures proliferated on countertops and tables,
displaying glossy photographs of Isbister houses and their floor
plans. They promoted the company's latest suburban development.
Isbister Homes seemed to be thriving.

At 4:45 the same brisk young woman ushered Roxanne into
a large office. The man who greeted her was sleek, well-fed and
tanned. His hair was thick and brown, impeccably cut, his suit
tailored to fit, the shirt perfectly collared and cuffed, the shoes
burnished to a dark gloss. The only indication that Leo Isbister
had once enjoyed life as an on-stage performer was a red silk tie
with streaks of orange and purple and the flash of a gold cufflink
as he shook Roxanne's hand.

"Sorry to keep you waiting, Corporal." He appeared more
satisfied than sorry. He did not invite her to sit at his walnut desk,
but indicated a leather chair beside a low table. The pictures on
the walls were all of buildings his company had built. A formal

portrait of a smiling dark-haired woman and two young men who resembled him sat on his desk. It was all conventionally corporate and told Roxanne very little about Leo himself.

"We are investigating the death of Stella Magnusson," she said, getting straight to the point since time was limited.

"Ah, yes." Isbister sat facing her, folding his brows into an expression of concern. Roxanne noticed that his socks had specks of orange and purple to match his tie. "Sad business. I heard about it yesterday. My wife and I have been at our house in Costa Rica the past two weeks. We just got back."

So he would have been away at the time of the murder. Was that the point he was making? That he had an alibi? "We understand that you knew her," she said.

"Well, yes." He relaxed back in his chair and spread himself, a man used to occupying a lot of space. "We were in a band. She sang and I played bass. It only lasted a couple of years and that was a long time ago. Almost thirty years. Why would you want to ask me about that?"

"We're trying to build a picture of Stella Magnusson's life," Roxanne replied, equally smoothly. She smiled. "We hoped you could help us."

"Well, of course, Corporal. Ask away." He steepled his fingers in front of him and regarded her speculatively.

"You have a house in the Interlake. Have you talked to Stella in the years since she moved back there?"

"Sure." He drawled out the word, taking his time. "But not recently. My company sponsors her music festival. Three thousand dollars a year, for old times' sake, that's all. She got in touch with me to set it up but my assistant handles all that now. I just sign the cheque."

"You don't run into her when you're out at the lake?"

"Hey, Corporal, I'm a busy guy. I live a different life from Stella. We didn't move in the same circles any more. Sure, she used to be a girlfriend, but that was back when we were kids. Back when we thought we had talent, we'd hit the big time, make a lot of money, be famous. Didn't happen. So we went our separate ways. Did somebody really cut her up?" He didn't miss a beat as he said it.

"Afraid so," Roxanne responded. "We found body parts at the dump."

"Shocking. Stella was a bit wild back when I knew her, but she didn't deserve that. She was great looking, you know. Stunning." He smiled at the memory.

"How did you meet her?"

"At the lake. Our cottage has been in the family for years, we used to spend our summers out there when I was a kid. Stella was in a group that played the bandstand at Cullen Village one year. She must have still been in school. I was in university and had my own group together by then, so when she showed up in the city a year or so after I knew who she was. She was okay as a singer but nothing great. Looked fantastic, though. All that blonde hair and black leather. People came just to look at her."

"You don't have anything to do with music anymore?"

"Came to my senses. Got a boy though, plays the sax in a jazz band." He waved a hand in the general direction of the family photo. "He just needs a bit of time, then he'll come round. Join me and his brother in the business." He sounded like he had no doubt this would happen, a man used to getting his way. He leaned forward in his seat. "You going to interview all the guys Stella shacked up with, Corporal? It's got to be quite a list."

"Anyone you would suggest?" she countered.

"Don't really know. Used to hear about her on the grapevine for a while after we split so I only know the old stuff. She had something going with a guy at the children's festival, that's where she worked after the band broke up, but he's dead. She only married once that I know of. To Freddie Santana. You know about him?"

"The filmmaker? In L.A.?"

"Stella got into managing bands. She always had a good head for being an agent, that kind of thing. She did a lot of our bookings when we were together. Bet she married Freddie so she could work in the States. She probably wanted to get into Nashville. Or New York. Heard it didn't last long though. Nothing ever did with Stella. I can't believe she's was still doing this StarFest thing. She should have been bored with it long ago." He glanced at his watch. Rolex. "Got to wrap this up, Corporal. I'm due at a meeting downtown at half five." He stood up, reached for a business card from a silver box on his desk and passed it to Roxanne.

"You know, I can't think why she moved back to the Interlake. Stella always sounded like she wanted to play the big time." He shook his head. "Call me if you think I can help you, but frankly, I don't know much. My direct line's on my card. Good luck with your investigation."

She was dismissed. Roxanne didn't mind. She was finished in time to get to her sister's house for supper with Finn.

OVER AT CULLEN Village, Margo and Sasha were ringing the Smedleys' doorbell. George opened the door.

"Why hello!" he said. "This is a surprise!"

"We just thought we'd stop by," said Sasha.

"To visit Phyllis and see if she's feeling any better." Margo stepped up beside her. They both smiled hopeful smiles.

"You'd better come in then." George opened the door wider. Just at that moment, Phyllis appeared at the end of the hallway.

"Margo and Sasha!" she chirruped. "Do come in. I'm afraid we don't have very long. We're driving into Winnipeg to catch a movie and we're going to have a bite to eat first. But we have time for a quick visit, don't we, George?"

George did not appear enthusiastic, Margo thought. Perhaps they should have called ahead. But Sasha had pointed out that if George answered the phone, he might put them off. Margo wondered if Sasha was being unnecessarily negative. George had never shown any signs of being inhospitable. Even now, he had fixed a look of welcome onto his face.

"I'll make a nice pot of rooibos," he said, "Come along in."

"I brought you some homemade chicken soup, Phyllis." Margo pulled a jar from a bag she was carrying. "And Sasha made oatmeal muffins. We thought you might still be sick."

"How lovely!" exclaimed Phyllis. "But I'm so much better. George is such a good cook. He takes very good care of me. I can't eat the soup today. Maybe you should take it home."

Margo felt foolish. Phyllis had obviously recovered, their gifts were unwanted, their visit badly timed.

"We should really go," she said. "Let you get on your way. Keep the soup. You can always freeze it for another time." Sasha gave her a nudge.

"Just what was it that made you sick, Phyllis?" she asked. Phyllis perched on the edge of an armchair.

"Well it's just so strange. I got sick, nauseous, not really throwing up, but queasy. And then there's the palpitations."

Margo and Sasha parked themselves, simultaneously, side by side, on a sofa. George could be heard fussing around in the kitchen.

"Palpitations? You have heart arrhythmia?" Margo leaned forward. "Does this happen often?"

"Only once or twice. Yes, twice, isn't it, George?" George had appeared with a tray. "My silly heart thing. Doesn't hurt or anything, and if I just keep quiet it soon goes away."

"Have you had that checked out?" Margo inquired.

"Phyllis is just fine," her husband responded, laying the tray on a coffee table. "Look at her. The picture of health." He poured the red brew into small china cups. "This is so good for you. Full of anti-oxidants and it will give your immune system a boost."

Sasha rolled her eyes. "You know a lot about that stuff, don't you, George?" she asked innocently.

"'Course he does. George is a brilliant herbalist," said Phyllis. "He knows exactly what to give me when I get sick. Look how quickly I recovered!"

"I do have a degree in naturopathy," George added, sounding knowledgeable. "And I have made a special study of herbs and their healing properties."

"Right," said Sasha.

"How do you qualify as a naturopath?" asked Margo. She was genuinely curious.

"I have a degree from Toronto. It's rigorous training. You have to have seven years of post-secondary education to qualify as a naturopathic doctor."

"You should really be calling him Dr. Smedley." Phyllis beamed at her husband.

"I don't insist." He smiled back at his wife. Sasha and Panda are right, Margo thought. He really is creepy.

"Haven't you seen George's herb garden in the summer!" Phyllis enthused. "So amazing. And many of the plants have beautiful flowers, blue ones, white ones."

"What do you do with them, George?" asked Margo.

"Well, that would be telling," he said. This time his smile was close-lipped.

"I think we should let you get going," said Margo, putting down her cup.

George did not argue with that. In no time at all they found themselves walking back down the Smedleys' path.

"Want to come back to my place?" asked Margo. "I've got faster Internet than you. Let's check out George Smedley. I think you're right. There's something going on here that doesn't quite add up."

ROXANNE WISHED SHE was wearing her parka. A smart wool coat didn't keep out the cold when you were watching four-year-olds practise hockey at an outdoor rink in a Winnipeg suburb on a freezing February night. She stood at the edge of the floodlit oval watching them stagger and slide over the ice, big-headed in their helmets, like overgrown ants. Finn was doing okay, staying upright, occasionally managing to get up some speed. He whacked a passing puck. It spun off his stick and bounced off the boards. He waved to her, delighted with himself. Sometimes he looked so like Jake she could cry. She waved right back.

Her sister Susan had persuaded her to stay the night with them. Finn had nursery school tomorrow, first thing, and Roxanne would need to get back to Fiskar Bay. It made sense, but she would have loved to scoop him up and have him all to herself, at home, for this one night. Next time she'd try for two consecutive nights off. Would that be possible?

Susan and her husband, Roy, were the reason Roxanne had transferred to Manitoba. Susan had offered to take care of Finn, any time. She had a boy the same age and two older kids, so Finn got to spend time with his cousins. His uncle was good with him, next best thing to a dad. Roxanne didn't know how she'd manage to stay in this job without them. The two cousins were out there now, high-fiving each other. Roy had come along too. He stood at her side.

"Is it that Magnusson murder you're working on?"

"Yeah. Double murder now. It's a big case." Roy was a doctor with a family practice. "Can I run something by you? Professional question?"

"Sure," he said. She watched Finn trip and fall. One of the teenagers who helped the coach swooped by and lifted him back onto his feet. He skated off again, perfectly fine.

"The victim in this case was hit first and smothered after. The autopsy report says the impact to her skull was right on the back, where the occipital bone meets the parietal, so she wasn't hit from above. It looks more like a sideways blow."

"Maybe she fell," said Roy. "She could have hit her head against something hard. In which case it might have been an accident."

"But not when someone makes sure she's dead by smothering her after. That makes it murder, for sure. But why would someone do that?"

"The blow probably knocked her out." Roy considered this while still keeping an eye on the rink.

"There's a skull fracture and extensive brain trauma."

"Then she could have gone into a coma. The person often makes a snoring sound with that kind of injury. Still breathing, you know, in and out. Could be that the killer just wanted to stop her making that noise. Maybe it happened in the heat of the moment."

Roxanne tried to remember if she had seen any cushions in the Magnusson house. Of course someone could have used a pillow. The report also said that Stella had eaten dinner. She had died shortly afterwards. Their assumption that the murder had occurred on Friday, January 19, had been right, and now they knew it had happened in the evening. Angus Smith had eaten dinner too, lasagne, so his death had happened at night, too. The knife had gone straight into his heart. There was nothing ambivalent about how he had died.

A whistle blew. Break time, so the kids could go inside for a few minutes and warm up.

"Come on," Roy said. "Let's get you inside. You look frozen."

There was a wooden clubhouse opposite with changing rooms and a cafeteria. She'd go have some hot chocolate with her boy.

IZZY AND MATT were in the Pizza Place at Fiskar Bay, just finishing eating an extra-large pizza, loaded, when Izzy's phone rang.

"Geez, really?" She hung up. "Erik Axelsson showed up at the Andreychuk place not long ago. Got into a fight with Brad. He's badly hurt. An ambulance is on its way. We'd better go."

12

"THEY CONFESSED? BOTH of them?"

"Brad and his dad each say they're the one that did it. Hit Erik on the head with a wrench."

"Together?"

"No. Separately."

"It can't be true. So either one of them is lying or they both are?"

"That's about it."

"This would be funny if it wasn't so serious."

Roxanne's phone had vibrated just as she and her sister were getting the boys ready for bed. Now she stood in the hallway, taking the call out of earshot.

"You're still at Andreychuks'?"

"Me and Izzy. Sam Mendes got here first. He managed to get some photos of Erik where he fell before the medics moved him. It looks like he was hit above the ear. They're radioing the hospital in Winnipeg. He might have a brain bleed."

"Is he conscious?"

"He's not completely out but he isn't coherent either. Doesn't help that he's drunk. Really drunk. We won't be able to talk to him. It's bad. Just a minute."

Roxanne peeked into the kitchen while she waited. Finn and his cousin were goofing around at the kitchen table, waiting for a bedtime drink. He wasn't missing her. Matt's voice crackled on again.

"They're taking him into Winnipeg. Bradley's in the back of a car, giving a statement. He's injured too, something broken. The medics say to take him to the Fiskar Bay hospital. They should be able to handle it there. Erik's truck is still here, in the middle of the yard. Both Andreychuks say he picked a fight with Brad. Was yelling that Brad had shopped him to the police. That Brad was trying to pin Stella's murder on him." Roxanne sat at the foot of the stairs.

"Do you know where Brad was when Erik arrived?"

"In the workshop, at the other side of the yard working on a tractor, he says. He came out with a wrench in his hand, but he says he dropped it when Erik went for him."

"Brad's a lot younger than Erik. And stronger."

"For sure. But he wasn't expecting it when Erik swung the first punch. He says he slipped. The ground's pretty icy in the yard. He fell and landed badly. Did something to his arm. He says Erik jumped on top of him and had him by the throat, screaming that Brad and his father had always had it in for Stella, that Brad must have killed her, that Brad was trying to pin the murder on him. He was squeezing Brad's throat and banging his head on the ground."

"Is he concussed?"

"Maybe. John Andreychuk came out of the house. He ran over and tried to haul Erik off Bradley, and that's where their stories go off in different directions. John says he thought Erik was going to kill Brad. He could see that Bradley was hurt. He couldn't get Erik off, so he picked up the wrench from where it was lying on the ground and whacked him on the back of the head."

"And what does Bradley say?"

"According to him, Erik was distracted by John pulling at him, so Brad was able to roll out from under him. He says Erik got up and started yelling at his dad, accusing him of being in on it all. That everybody knew he wanted to get rid of Stella and take over her land. Then he started shoving him. Brad says he saw Erik raise his hand and make a fist, like he was going to punch his dad, and that's when he grabbed the wrench and hit Erik with it. He says Erik dropped like a stone and when he didn't get up, Brad reckoned he'd better call an ambulance. The old man went back into the house. Brad waited outside."

"So where are they now?"

"Sam is going to take Bradley to the hospital to get that arm and the head checked out. He's got some bruising too. Izzy's in the house with the parents. She taped out the yard and took more photographs."

"And the wrench?"

"It was bagged right away. I'll take the old man to the detachment and get his statement there."

Roxanne couldn't believe it. Who was telling the truth? Was either? She was going to have to head back up that road and try to figure this out. So much for a night off.

"So Brad and his dad haven't talked to each other? They don't know that they've each taken the blame?"

"I don't believe so," Matt replied. "Will we try to keep Brad at the hospital as long as we can?"

"Maybe. Take John in to the detachment and hold him for questioning until I get there. Let's see what happens at the hospital. If you do end up with Brad in the office as well, be sure to keep them apart. Tell Izzy to stay with the mother. Find out which hospital in Winnipeg they're taking Erik to and call Sergeant Donohue. Let him know all of this."

She hung up and turned to see her sister leaning against the far wall, her tilted head asking the question.

"Let's get them to bed and then I'll hit the road."

An hour or so later, she turned on her flashing lights as she drove north out of the city. The road was deserted. She could make up for lost time on the long straight drive north. In the headlights, she could see the ditches filled with snow, rutted snowmobile tracks running along them. The road crews kept the highway clear of snow. Driving fast wasn't a problem. Occasional lights glowed from farmyards and a faint orange glow up ahead indicated Cullen Village. You could see for miles on the flat prairie. The only turn in the road was an S bend that happened halfway and it was there that she saw flashing lights coming from the opposite direction and heard the siren. An ambulance raced past her, probably transporting Erik Axelsson to the hospital in Winnipeg. Since Jake, a siren on an open road always made her shiver.

First stop was the Andreychuk farm. Roxanne parked on the road and pulled her collar up as she crossed a line of police tape. She went into the house. Izzy and Mrs. Andreychuk were in the kitchen, playing cribbage. Maggie sat at the table, mountainous and impassive as ever.

"I saw nothing. I was in the house. Told you guys." She looked at her cards, as if she was annoyed that the game was interrupted.

"But you heard it all?"

"I heard Axelsson yelling. Couldn't hear what he was saying, though." She moved her pegs. She was winning.

"You didn't look out the window?"

"Couldn't see. Truck was in the way. When's my John coming home?"

"We might have to keep him at the detachment overnight, Mrs. Andreychuk."

Maggie lifted her head. Two small eyes, embedded deep in the flesh of her face, peered out.

"Is there someone we can call to come and be with you?" Roxanne asked.

"My boy Jeremy's in the city. He's at the university."

"We'll call him, shall we?"

"There's beasts will need to be fed. My John's done nothing. My Bradley neither. That Erik Axelsson started all this."

"Constable McBain can stay with you."

Izzy barely reacted. She stared straight ahead.

"I'll phone Jeremy," the large woman muttered.

"You do that," said Roxanne. "Here's the phone." She picked up the handset from the house phone and passed it over. Mrs. Andreychuk didn't say thank you.

Izzy reached for her parka and they walked out together into the yard. An orange yard light, high on a pole, illuminated the scene. Roxanne checked Axelsson's truck, still parked where he had left it. The keys were in the ignition.

"The driver's door was wide open when we got here."

The shape of a body was outlined on the frozen ground, marking the spot where Erik Axelsson had fallen, between the truck and the workshop. The Andreychuks had blown the yard clear of snow earlier. A snowbank was piled up on the side closest to the road. A thin layer of packed snow remained on the surface of the ground, polished to a slippery sheen by the vehicles that had driven in and out since the last snowfall. She walked over to the workshop, entered by the side door and switched on the lights. Two snowmobiles and a shiny red tractor were pulled inside the closed doors. Tools and an oilcan lay on the floor beside the tractor.

"Well, it looks like that part of Brad's story holds up," Roxanne said.

A car and two trucks were parked close to the workshop doors. Extension cords ran from the plugs that protruded from their radiators to electrical sockets on the wall. Manitoban cars had block heaters to keep the engines from freezing on nights like this. It was very quiet.

"If Erik doesn't make it, this will be another murder. If it is, this place will have to be searched and checked by the Ident guys. You are going to have to stay, Izzy. Make sure nothing gets touched."

Izzy shrugged, resigned to spending the night in Maggie Andreychuk's company. "Do we still need the brother, then?"

"I want to talk to Jeremy Andreychuk." Roxanne had reached her car. "This is as good a reason to get him out here as any."

"Okay. He can help me feed the cows in the morning." Izzy turned towards the house, then looked back. "How did you get on with Jaws?"

"Who?"

"Isbister. That's what my dad and the guys out here call him."

Roxanne laughed. Her breath froze in the cold air. "He didn't say much. He has an alibi. He was in Costa Rica."

"Figures." Izzy went back towards the house.

Twelve minutes later, Roxanne pulled up outside the emergency entrance to Fiskar Bay Hospital. A nurse directed her down a long hallway, brightly lit even now, close to 11:00 pm. The walls were painted peach pink and a pale turquoise blue. The hospital had survived attempts to downgrade it to a regional health centre, but there were doubts it would remain as a working hospital much longer. Roxanne turned a corner and saw Matt sitting outside a room further down the next hallway. She took the seat beside him.

"How come you're here?" she said.

"Sam and I are spelling each other off. I'm on until one."

"How is Bradley doing?"

"He has a broken collarbone. A bruise to the left side of the chin, marks consistent with thumbprints on his throat. Maybe concussion from having his head banged on the frozen ground. No head fracture."

"So they're keeping him overnight?" She got up and looked through the small window in the door. Bradley was sitting up in bed watching TV, his arm in a sling.

"Yep. The doc's been great. Says they can hold him here as long as we need. Do you want to talk to him?"

"No, let's wait until we find out how Axelsson's doing. Go home and get some sleep after this. Tomorrow might be a busy day." She turned and walked away, her phone to her ear, her boot heels clicking on the shiny, polished floor.

She drove straight to the RCMP detachment. The front door banged behind her as she entered. Sergeant Gilchrist was at the counter.

"Hey there. Thought you might show up soon."

"How come you're manning the front desk, Sarge?"

"Sent the rest of the guys home to get their beauty sleep. Waiting for you, right?" He grinned.

"Okay." She leaned on the other side of the counter. "Who do you think did it?"

"Well, it's obvious, isn't it? It had to be Brad. Look at the way that Axelsson fell. He was hit hard. Couldn't have been the old man. He doesn't have the strength. It's just what Brad would do. His dad's covering up for him."

"But you've still got John Andreychuk here?"

"Sure. He's not arguing about it. He thinks he's here for the night. I've got him all tucked in downstairs. Sound asleep last time I looked. We can leave him where he is until we know for sure."

So she should probably wait to interview him in the morning. "Does Bradley know that his father confessed as well?"

"None of us told him. Look, leave this one to me, Corporal. This is local. It's a clear-cut case of aggravated assault. Erik Axelsson got drunk and picked a fight with the Andreychuks and got beat up."

So that was what the sergeant really wanted to talk about. Roxanne wasn't buying it. "How did Erik find out that Brad told us he was having an affair with Stella Magnusson?"

"That's a no-brainer," Gilchrist said. "He'd been cruising the pubs all afternoon. If he didn't figure it out for himself the guys he drank with would have helped him."

"So they all want Brad put away?"

"Sure they do. He's always causing the bars grief on a Saturday night."

So Sergeant Bill wanted to be the hero that finally nailed Brad Andreychuk. She felt quite sorry to disappoint him.

"Look, Sarge, of course this fight is linked to the murders. Think about it. Erik and Stella were having an affair. Stella Magnusson was hit on the back of the head. Knocked unconscious. And now Erik probably needs brain surgery for damage also caused by a blow to the head. It's the same method, right? Isn't that too much of a coincidence? Then both Brad and his father confess to the assault? What do you know about Jeremy Andreychuk?"

"The kid brother? He's never been any trouble. Smart kid, took a bunch of prizes at school. He's not tough like Bradley. And he's in Winnipeg. What's the word on Erik Axelsson?"

"Not good. I just phoned Brian Donohue. Erik needs emergency surgery. They're bringing in a neurosurgeon. Is it true that Roberta Axelsson's gone to live in Winnipeg? She'll need to know. He's seriously injured, Sarge. He might die. In which case, we'll have another murder. That'll make three."

13

THE TEMPERATURE DIPPED to minus thirty-four overnight. It was too cold to run. Roxanne drove straight to the Andreychuk farm the next morning and parked out on the roadway behind an older green Ford Focus. Jeremy Andreychuk's, she hoped. The sky was banded with orange and yellow light towards the east, but clouds were massing on the western horizon. The weather was about to change again. She walked past Erik's truck. A yellow extension cord ran from the radiator grille to an electrical outlet at the side of the house. Izzy must have plugged it in for the night. Good. They didn't need a frozen truck to deal with on top of everything else.

There was no answer when she rapped on the door. No one was to be seen in the yard or around the workshop. She made her way to the far end of the yard, past the Andreychuk vehicles, and then down the path that led to the barn. There she found Izzy and a young man wearing a hoodie and jeans feeding rows of cows that munched contentedly in their stalls.

"Morning, Corporal! We'll be done soon."

Jeremy Andreychuk came over and introduced himself. He was smaller than his father and brother but he maybe resembled his mother, if you could imagine Maggie without the layers of fat.

"I got here an hour or so ago. Had a paper to finish, due in today, so I pulled an all-nighter and came out as soon as I'd sent it off to my prof. How can I help you, Corporal Calloway?"

He was a polite young man, unlike his brother.

"I can finish off here," said Izzy. "You head over to the house. I'll see you there."

Roxanne and Jeremy walked back, their breath turning to ice fog in the freezing air. Roxanne found herself looking forward to the warmth of the kitchen. This cold was bitter.

"My mother doesn't get up early but I'll get the coffee on." They entered the house through the back door. "Leave those boots on, Corporal."

Jeremy stuffed his feet into a pair of slippers. There were three steps up to reach the kitchen door, which stood open. Jeremy removed his parka and hung it on a hook. He reached behind the door, brought out a coat hanger and took her coat, all consideration and good manners.

"Have a seat." He filled a carafe with water, then turned on an electric coffee maker. They heard a toilet flush. "My mother must be up." He brought out mugs and a bowl of sugar. "My brother's under arrest?"

"He is. He confessed and we have his statement. How do you know?"

Jeremy smiled pleasantly as he filled a jug with cream. "I called the Fiskar Bay RCMP last night. You're still holding my father?"

"We have some questions that need answering," she replied.

"I've spoken to my father's lawyer. He'll be arriving in Fiskar Bay this morning. Any further questions will have to wait until he gets there."

So he hadn't just been working on a university paper.

Maggie Andreychuk appeared at the door opposite. She wore a large crimson caftan that billowed around her as she moved to the table.

"Is the coffee ready?" she demanded as she lowered herself onto a chair across from Roxanne. The carafe was half full. Her son filled a mug with the thick brew. Roxanne declined an invitation to have some of the same.

"I'll wait until it's done, thanks," she said.

"Why do you need to be here, Corporal, if you're holding my brother?" Jeremy asked.

"I want to talk to you, Jeremy," said Roxanne. "May I call you Jeremy?" She smiled. He nodded.

"How is Erik?" he asked.

"His surgery went as well as could be expected. He's in intensive care. The doctors don't know the extent of the damage to his brain, but he's still alive. So it's still a case of aggravated assault. For now."

"He picked the fight," Maggie growled. "It was self-defence."

"Shush, Ma." Jeremy sat down and placed a hand over his mother's. He turned to face Roxanne. Grey eyes, she noticed, cold like his mother's when he wasn't smiling. "So what else did you want to talk about, Corporal?"

"Stella Magnusson," she replied.

"Stella?" He didn't look or sound surprised. "Of course. I knew Stella. I worked for Stella. I liked her. I'm very sorry she's dead." He drank his coffee, perfectly at ease.

"What exactly did you do at StarFest?"

"Ticket sales. Box office. Festival passes. I did it for two years. First year I was on a student grant but last summer I was box office manager. I'd hoped to go back this year. It was a good summer job."

"Did you do bank deposits?"

"No." The question seemed to puzzle him. "I balanced out each day and handed the cash and charge statements over to Stella."

"So you didn't have access to any actual accounts? You never saw any financial statements, anything like that?"

"We had sales targets. We kept track of how sales were going. Compared them to the year before. That was all."

The back door opened and Izzy came in from the cold. She took off her parka and came into the kitchen in her socks, went to the kitchen sink and scrubbed her hands. She stood there, watching and listening.

"When did you last see Stella?" Roxanne continued.

"Just after New Year," Jeremy replied. "I went over for a visit. Had a drink with her. We talked about next summer and what she had planned for her trip."

"Were you in the habit of visiting Stella?"

"Sure," he said. "Used to take the skidoo over. There's a track over to her place, through the wood, behind the barn." His even tone matched Roxanne's. No worries. He smiled again.

"We noticed," she said. "Where were you on January 19, Jeremy?"

"The day you think Stella was murdered? I've already been asked that but let me check to be sure." He got up and walked over to where a backpack lay on a countertop. He had to know the answer. Why was he stalling? "How's your coffee, Ma?"

Maggie Andreychuk did not make a sound. Jeremy found an iPad, brought it back to the table and checked the calendar. They could hear a clock ticking out in the hallway.

Roxanne surveyed the kitchen. It was painted cream, with green trim. The floor was covered with beige linoleum. Colourful china plates were displayed on a dresser. Small appliances, a toaster, a mixer, were ranged on a counter. Geranium cuttings grew in pots on the windowsill. It was scrubbed clean, a typical prairie farm kitchen. What was it Jeremy and his mother didn't want her to know?

Izzy had remained standing, leaning with her back to the sink. Mrs. Andreychuk finished her coffee. Izzy fetched the carafe and topped up her mug. Maggie still said nothing.

"Here it is," Jeremy announced. "My parents came to Winnipeg on the nineteenth. I met them for a quick burger at the Burger King near the university, around twelve. I was in class all afternoon. It was a lab, so there'll be an attendance record. Then I worked a shift at the restaurant from six until after midnight. The next day was Saturday and I was home. My girlfriend can vouch for that. Just like I said already." He sat back, satisfied.

"Thank you," said Roxanne. "But something puzzles me. We've asked your father about the skidoo tracks that go from your barn to the Magnusson house and we didn't get an answer. And yet you tell me it was just you going to visit Stella, to talk about work. If that was all it was, why couldn't he just tell us? Why did he feel the need to cover it up? Mrs. Andreychuk, do you know? What was the problem?"

Any congeniality in the room vanished.

"What are you trying to get at? My Jeremy had nothing to do with Stella Magnusson getting herself killed!"

"Someone in this house thought it was important to cover up those visits, Mrs. Andreychuk. I have to ask why. Was someone afraid we'd find something out? Were you and Stella more than just friends, Jeremy?"

"We were not!" His answer came fast and sharp.

Roxanne retaliated as quickly: "You know what, we keep coming up against cover-ups." She turned back towards the mother. "Your son and your husband both tried to tell us that they were the one to hit Erik Axelsson on the head with that wrench, Mrs. Andreychuk, and they both can't have done it, so which of them is lying?"

"You know that. You arrested Bradley. It was self-defence."

Roxanne sat straight up, her hands in her lap. "But I'm not at all convinced that we do know the truth. I'm beginning to wonder if they're both lying. Your husband covered up for Jeremy about the skidoo tracks. Maybe he's covering up for him again. Maybe they both are. Were you here yesterday, Jeremy?"

"I was home working on that paper. My girlfriend…"

Roxanne barely acknowledged his excuse. "You see, Jeremy, I don't think either your dad or your brother picked up that wrench and hit Erik Axelsson across the back of the head with it. It's just not their style. They're both fighting men. They'd use their fists, and they'd want to finish it off face to face. But you, you're not like that, are you? You're smaller. Not so aggressive. Erik's a lot bigger than you are. You wouldn't have stood a chance against him in the mood he was in."

She put both hands on the table and leaned toward him. "You'd use the first weapon that came to hand and you'd take whatever chance you could to end the fight without getting hurt yourself. I think you came out that back door from the kitchen and saw your brother down and your dad being attacked and there was the wrench, just lying there. So you hit Erik Axelsson from behind and you put a stop to that fight before he did any real damage to your dad."

"I did not!" Jeremy exclaimed, his face inches from hers. "I wasn't here!"

Roxanne swung her head round and looked straight at Maggie Andreychuk. Two little eyes met hers.

"But you were here. It was you, Mrs. Andreychuk. You did it."

"Don't say anything, Ma!" Jeremy grabbed for his phone.

"He was like a madman, that Erik Axelsson. Going for my John. He's got a weak heart. He has a pacemaker."

"Shut up, Ma!"

"That Erik was going to kill him."

Roxanne rose to her feet. "Place Mrs. Andreychuk under arrest, Constable McBain, and then take her through to her room to get changed. We're taking her in."

"I'm calling the lawyer, Ma. Don't say a word!"

Roxanne glanced out the kitchen window. The clouds had thickened on the horizon to a threatening band of iron grey. A row of spruce trees stood like dark sentinels, guarding the way to Stella Magnusson's house. She reached for her own phone.

"I need to talk to Sergeant Gilchrist," she said.

IT WAS ALMOST lunchtime. Lentil soup was simmering in a Crock-Pot in Margo's kitchen. Sasha sat on a window seat overlooking the lake. Small, black-headed chickadees swooped from the telephone wire to a feeder filled with black sunflower seeds, chirruping despite the cold. The dogs were outside in the fenced backyard, hunting unsuccessfully for squirrels.

"The temperature's going up. We're going to get some snow again, and wind. Said so on WeatherNet. I hope Roberta isn't going to try to drive back in a snowstorm."

Roberta had emailed her friends. Erik hadn't regained consciousness. The doctors did not know how well he would recover from the damage to his brain. So she had decided to come home and take care of their animals.

"She doesn't say she's going to get back together with him again though, does she?" Margo was taking soup bowls out of a cupboard. Given her own experience, she had little time for husbands who played around.

"She visited him. In the hospital."

"Well, I suppose she would, wouldn't she? It sounds like he almost died. Must have been quite the fight."

"Erik's always had a temper on him." Sasha turned away from the window.

"Do you think she's telling the truth when she says he never gets violent?" Margo added more salt to the soup. "I hope she doesn't go back to him."

"I think Erik's useless. Just full of bullshit, most of the time. But she's crazy about the guy. And who'll look after him if he needs care after this?"

They were interrupted by a knock at the door. Annie and Panda walked in. Panda had a large tin between her mittened hands.

"Zucchini cake. Have you heard the news? They've arrested Maggie Andreychuk!" she announced, kicking off her boots.

"You're kidding!" Sasha got up from her seat by the window. "She's huge! She can barely walk. I saw her in the grocery store, weeks ago, shuffling along, hanging on to a shopping cart for dear life. Her husband was fetching all the stuff she needed from the shelves. I thought they would have charged that son of his, you know, Bradley. The one that's always in trouble."

"Nope. I called Matt. Bradley got a broken collarbone in the fight. They did arrest him but then that red-haired corporal from the Major Crimes Unit figured out it was Maggie." She brought the tin over to the kitchen counter.

Annie had unlaced thick-soled boots and pulled on felted slippers. She padded over to join them.

"So what was she doing? Trying to stop the fight?" she asked.

"It sounds like Erik Axelsson went crazy." Panda said.

"Drunk," said Sasha.

"He's not supposed to touch the stuff." Annie sat down, quiet and small, at the table. "That's why he goes to AA. He's been sober for years. He's fine as long as he stays away from alcohol. Being accused of the murder, Roberta leaving him, must have pushed him over the edge."

Margo knew that Annie attended AA meetings regularly in Fiskar Bay. She had never told them how or why she had started and the group did not ask. Some things about Annie were private. Panda would talk about most things but not if they related to Annie. Margo let the dogs in. They wagged their way around the table. Panda was good for a scratched ear. Annie ignored them. They went to the dog bed in the corner and snuggled in together.

"So see, maybe Roberta's right, about him never getting violent around her." Sasha said, joining Annie at the table. "If this doesn't knock him completely off the wagon they might be all right."

"He still had that affair with Stella," said Margo pointedly. "Don't forget, that's why she left him. Do you all want soup?" She reached for a ladle.

"How's she going to manage all those animals by herself?" Panda asked.

"She loves her goats." Sasha reached for a bread bun. "Don't know about the sheep and the chickens. They're a lot of work. If she got some help she might be okay, but I don't think she has enough money to pay anyone."

"She really is coming back up here today?" asked Annie.

Margo passed her a bowl. "I asked her if she'd like to come for lunch but she wanted to check in at the hospital first to see how Erik was, then head up the road in the afternoon."

"It's going to snow." Panda looked out the window and frowned. "Is there a snowblower out at Axelssons'? Didn't Erik use a tractor to clear that long driveway? We could go out there after it stops and help, Annie."

"You just want to drive that tractor," said Annie. "Sit down and eat your soup."

"Where's Phyllis?" asked Panda.

"Well." Margo took a deep breath and joined them at the table. "That's what we need to talk to you about."

"Phyllis? What's up with her? Is she sick again?"

"That's just it. She keeps getting ill. She feels nauseous and she doesn't know why. Sometimes she throws up. But did you know that she also gets an irregular heartbeat? Sasha and I stopped by yesterday and she started telling us about it, but George came in and acted like it's nothing unusual."

"He treats her with herbal medicines," Sasha whispered loudly, like it was some great secret. "Makes them himself from plants he grows in his garden in the summer."

"So? She believes in all that stuff," said Panda. "She was telling me all about it one day. Homeopathy. Alternative medicines. She was into it before she met George. Isn't that how they got together? Pass me a bun, will you?"

"No, no." Sasha was almost pounding the table, eager to get the next word in. "She met him online."

"She did?"

"Sure. She'd been checking out online dating sites. Said she'd gone on a couple of dates with other guys but they hadn't worked out. And then she met George and they just clicked."

"How long ago?" Panda appeared to be more interested in eating, as usual.

"Three years? I don't think it took long for them to decide to get married. How long is it since they moved out here? Two summers ago? She had a big house in the city. Crescentwood. Sold it and they bought the place out here."

"So she has money of her own?" Margo stopped chewing.

"Her husband was a lawyer, wasn't he? Successful. A QC. Don't know if George has any of his own."

"So are you saying that you think George is making her sick?" Panda put down her spoon. Her bowl was empty already.

"Well, maybe."

"But not deliberately!" Panda protested. Annie hadn't said a thing. She listened and ate methodically, spoonful by spoonful, but it was obvious she wasn't missing a word.

"We went online." Margo tried to explain. "We can't find out a thing about him. There are other George Smedleys on Facebook and Twitter, but none of them match this George. If he really is a naturopathic doctor, like he says he is, wouldn't you think he'd show up somewhere? There's not a sign of him. It's like he just doesn't exist."

"So are you saying you think George is a fraud?" Panda still sounded skeptical. "That he's poisoning Phyllis to get her money?"

Annie sighed. "I think Stella's murder has made us all too suspicious. We're all edgy. It's not like there's any connection between Stella and Phyllis."

"But maybe there is!" Sasha insisted. "He was the treasurer for the StarFest board. He was really keen to do that job, I remember. So he would have been able to have a good look at the books. What if something was wrong with Stella's accounts? What if George figured it out? He could have tried to blackmail Stella!"

"Or else George started fiddling the books and Stella found out," added Margo. It had all sounded so plausible when they had pieced it together yesterday. Now that they were telling it to Panda and Annie, she wasn't so sure.

"It's all *what if*. You don't really know anything," Annie said.

She was right. We just got carried away with the idea, Margo thought. But Panda was looking around the table at each of them in turn, an unusually serious expression on her face.

"Okay," she said. "I think you might be onto something. The RCMP are looking at Stella's money. I probably shouldn't be saying, but Matt asked me if I knew anything about Stella's finances. And I don't. I've never done the StarFest books, but I did sneak a look at some financial pages once when we were at George and Phyllis's. He'd left them lying at the front door. I just flipped through them, fast, but I think Stella had more money than shows up in the statements."

"So Stella was killed because of money?" Margo was encouraged again. Maybe they had got it right after all.

"And there we were all supposing it was about sex." Sasha hooted loudly. "So it just might be possible that George really is after other people's money? He tried to get at Stella's and ended up killing her, and now he's trying to bump off Phyllis, so that he'll inherit all her cash?"

"I don't believe a word of it," said Annie. "It's a great story but there's not a shred of proof."

"But maybe we should tell the police? Just in case there's something to it?" Margo had stood up to clear the plates.

"Tell them what?" Annie responded. "If they're looking into Stella's finances they'll find out what's wrong themselves. You can't accuse George of poisoning Phyllis. You're just making all that up."

"But we're not, Annie." Margo sat down again. "We looked online. Aconite. It's sometimes called wolfsbane. It causes vomiting. Irregular heartbeat. Phyllis's symptoms exactly. And it has a blue flower. There were all these blue flowers in George and Phyllis's garden this summer. It all fits!"

"I don't know." Panda fetched the cake from the counter and started slicing it. "What if you do accuse George and it turns out you're wrong? What's that going to do to Phyllis? She'll never speak to you again, and who could blame her? Maybe she really is just a bit sick. And if they want to treat it with natural medicine, that's their business. Lots of people have blue flowers growing in their gardens. You don't know that it's wolfsbane. You're just guessing. And you shouldn't believe what you read on the net."

"I suppose you're right." Margo collected the soup bowls together and went to put them on the counter. "These murders have shaken us all up."

"They've released Angus Smith's body," Sasha said, digging a fork into a piece of cake. "Funeral's tomorrow. Cullen United Church, but they're maybe going to move it to the legion. There's going to be a crowd."

"Wonder if they'll still do it if this storm dumps a lot of snow on us?"

"Dunno," said Sasha. She glanced towards the window. "I wish Roberta was here. Look, it's start to come down, and it's blowing. Going to be ugly out there on the highway. I hope she's okay."

14

THE SNOW HAD settled in by the afternoon. It came down thickly, in small white pellets that accumulated in cracks and folds and crannies, then slowly spread to fill the ground in a dense white cover. It was blown by a wind that had risen in the northwest, up on the tundra, and swept, unimpeded, over the flat prairie landscape. The sky was steely, the light filtered to a dim greyness. It was a miserable afternoon that matched the mood of the RCMP investigative team. Roxanne looked around the room. Coffee cups littered the table, along with notebooks, pens and laptops.

They were four in number. Brian Donohue had arrived from the city, with the snow at his back. Now he stood looking glumly out the window at the falling snowflakes. Izzy joined him. Roxanne overheard them talk about booking him into the hotel for the night.

"Guess so," she heard him say. He turned back to the table and looked in her direction. "We might have company. The Andreychuks' lawyer will probably be stuck here too."

Brad and his father had been released and allowed to go home. Maggie lurked, baleful, in a cell, while her lawyer tried to negotiate her release. Right now he was closeted with Sergeant Gilchrist. Roxanne knew how that would go. He'd get her out on a promise to appear in court. Maggie wasn't a danger to the public. Gilchrist had made it clear he didn't want her in a cell all weekend. He didn't have a bed wide enough for her. She said she suffered from sleep apnea. Izzy had had to lug her machine in with her, the one that kept her breathing at night. She hadn't stopped complaining since she arrived. She couldn't get comfortable. The food wasn't fit to eat. Gilchrist was going to be glad to see the back of her.

Outside, the thick snow muffled noise and had brought quiet to the town. People were going home. Downstairs, one constable manned the front desk. The rest were out on the highway, keeping watch as cars crept their way home through snow that was developing into a whiteout. Schools had closed early, yellow buses were ferrying children home and parents were trying to get back in time to meet them.

Izzy wandered back to the table. "Erik Axelsson's going to be okay?" she asked.

Donohue nodded. A lock of dark hair fell over his forehead. "It looks like he'll live. He doesn't remember a thing, what with the amount of booze he'd drunk and the whack on the head. And the surgery. They don't know how well he'll recover. He's still in the ICU."

Nothing like amnesia, Roxanne thought, to stop a line of questioning in its tracks.

"The Andreychuks are still suspects, though, aren't they?" Matt looked up from his computer.

"Sure they are. We've got two people that were hit on the back of the head. Same method, right?" said Roxanne. "We know that Maggie hit Erik hard enough to do him a real injury."

"It could have been a lucky swing," Matt reasoned, "but does it mean she could have done the same to Stella? Would Maggie have smothered Stella after?"

"Maybe it was Jeremy that did it." Izzy sat opposite Brian. "Maybe he was out here after all and they're all lying about that. Maybe he went over to Stella's place to visit her. What if he really liked Stella? Had a big crush on her?" She warmed to her theme. "I'll bet she led him on. It sounds like she tried it on with all the guys she met. Maybe he made a move on her and she laughed at him and he got so mad that he hit her. Maybe Jeremy's more like his mom than we think. He could have smothered her. And then his dad and Bradley chopped her up." She waited for a response. There was none. "We should have got some doughnuts," she muttered and went to root around in a cupboard. "There should be a bag of Oreos in here."

"Cut her up so they could incinerate her?" Matt called after her. "In the outdoor furnace behind the barn?"

"And then they changed their minds?" Brian shook his head. That lick of hair swung above his blue eyes. "The bone particles that were found on the saws from Angus Smith's place were Stella's. Why would they go to the trouble of taking her over to Angus Smith's to cut her up? They've got a workshop of their own. And plenty of saws."

Outside the window the snow was still coming down, thick and steady.

"But it could have been Jeremy that dumped the car at the airport. Isn't he small enough to be the guy on the airport surveillance video?" Roxanne asked.

"Think so. It's hard to see, it's so fuzzy because of the snow. Maybe."

This was getting them nowhere. Izzy had found the packet of cookies. She dumped it on the table.

"The Andreychuk lead is weak," said Roxanne. "We need to look at what else we've got."

They moved on to talk about Angus Smith. They knew by now that he had been stabbed in his own kitchen, in the early evening of Monday, January 29. It would have been dark when he was taken out to the lake, in his own truck, to his own ice shack, but there had been a moon that night. There would have been enough light to drive by with the truck lights out. It looked like his clothes had been removed in the house, to make it easier to push him through the ice hole. Someone knew that they'd need to do that. Knew what those ice holes were like. And knew where to find Angus's shack.

"There was a lot of blood," Brian said. "They might have wanted to get his clothes off so they could wrap him up, so they didn't get blood all over themselves, or the truck, or the rest of the house."

"They?" Roxanne asked. She had wondered about that herself.

"Or a strong person," Brian replied. "Angus wasn't big but he must have weighed over 145 pounds."

"It's got to be someone local." Matt was listening, twirling a pen between his fingers.

"Why's that?"

"Well, they didn't just know about Angus's ice shack. We're assuming that Angus was killed because he figured out that someone had used his workshop to cut up Stella's body, right?" It certainly was likely. "So they also knew how to find the key to the workshop. Knew there was a band saw in there and they also knew that Angus was staying with his daughter in Winnipeg. His wife was in the hospital. They must have known that too."

"That could be just about all of Cullen Village," said Izzy.

"Or someone from the city who comes out regularly."

The door opened. Bill Gilchrist stuck his head around the door. "Maggie Andreychuk's been sprung. The lawyer guy is taking her home before we all get socked in. The highway's dodgy. No visibility. It's coming down out there. I'm pushing off home. You don't want to stay too long or you might be spending the night right here." He whistled his way back downstairs.

"Let's get this done soon," said Brian. He sounded exasperated at being stuck out in Fiskar Bay, unable to make any real progress because of a snow day. Izzy was dunking an Oreo in a mug of lukewarm coffee. "What's happening with Stella's body?" she asked.

No one had claimed her. The police had been in touch with the parents, in Victoria, B.C. They were retired. The father had dementia and it sounded like the mother had enough on her plate with that. They hadn't been in touch with Stella for almost thirty years.

"Wonder what they fell out about?" Matt pondered. "There's no one else?'

"There was a brother but he died years ago. It sounds like the two old uncles who left her the house were the only family left." Brian was leaning back in his chair, arms folded. He had muscular arms and hands.

"So the parents are living all alone in B.C.? There's no other family left? And the mother doesn't even want to bury her? That is pathetic." Izzy nibbled on the soggy Oreo.

"We still don't know enough about her," said Roxanne. It was true. It was as if they had snapshots, ones that only showed what Stella wanted them to see. What had she been hiding? "Leo Isbister says she slept around with lots of guys. She was only married once as far as he knows, to Freddie Santana, but that was years ago."

"And there's still no sign of a will," said Brian. "At least, not so far. No executor, nothing."

"Guess it's hard to write a will when there's no one to leave anything to." Izzy reached into the bag for another cookie. She appeared healthy and fit. There wasn't a scrap of fat on her. Roxanne wondered how she did it.

"So who would want to kill her for her money?" asked Matt.

"What money?" Brian raised an eyebrow at him. "She was only earning $30,000 a year from the festival. She racked up about $10,000 in expenses as well. She did a major trip early each year, officially scouting for the festival, and a lot of visiting and sight-seeing while she was at it, but the business covered that."

"So how did she pay for renovating the house?" Roxanne interjected. "Even with the money for expenses, it doesn't match her lifestyle. She had the best of everything. She dressed well. Apple computers, the SUV's almost new. Even her luggage is top quality."

"Maybe the old uncles had a stash hidden under the bed," said Izzy. "Or she got a pile when she split up with that Freddie guy."

"My aunt Panda thinks she was putting money away somewhere." All eyes turned toward Matt.

"Really? How does she know?" Roxanne asked.

"Panda's an accountant. She's audited the books for some arts groups so she knows how they work. She figured out that the money and Stella's lifestyle didn't match, but she hasn't ever worked for Stella so she wasn't really sure."

"Was she ever on the StarFest board? Got a look at the books?"

"Not really. She got a quick peek at them once, that's all."

"Wonder who audits Stella's books," Brian said. "We should check."

"So it's possible she's been siphoning off money, and if so, how and to where? Could she have another bank account?" Roxanne felt more optimistic. This was as good a lead as they had right now. It fit with Stella's laptop and cellphone being missing. Someone didn't want them to know something and if it was financial, that might be why. "Who do we think would want to kill her because of the money? If she was embezzling funds, who might find out?"

"Smedley. The creepy little guy that's the treasurer." Izzy sounded cheerful again. Brian got up and looked at the whiteboard.

"All right. You need to talk to the board members, soon as this snow clears. George Smedley, Sasha Rosenberg, the Halliday woman. They're all down at Cullen Village, right? The rest?" There were two more.

"Gone south for the winter," said Izzy. One was in Arizona, the other in Mexico. Brian turned back to face the room. "Let's wrap it up and see how bad the roads are out there. We might not be able to get very far tomorrow until everything gets dug out."

"Your room's booked at the hotel, Sarge. I sent the confirmation number to your phone." Izzy was already on her feet, reaching for her boots. "You coming, Matt?"

Brian turned to Roxanne. "Want to leave your car plugged in here? We could go over to the hotel in my SUV." It made total sense. There was no good reason she should say no, except that she didn't want to get too close to this very attractive guy. Another cop. Not a good idea.

"Okay," she said.

They all stomped outside into the storm, with scarves wrapped around their faces to ward off stinging snow pellets. They tried to keep the wind at their backs as they swept snow off their cars and scraped ice off windshields. Izzy waved goodbye out of the window of Matt's car as they left. Soon Brian and Roxanne were chugging slowly along the single open track that led to the hotel. The wipers swept back and forth, struggling to keep a semicircle of glass clear. Snow was blowing straight down in the light from the headlamps and in the cones of orange light cast by the streetlamps. There was no one else about.

They pulled into the hotel parking lot. Brian found a spot close to the door. Wind gusts blew the snow across the beam from his headlights. A deep drift lay along the side of the building. He stopped the car but kept it running. The inside of the car was warm.

"You're Jake Calloway's widow," he said. The question caught her off guard.

"How did you know about Jake?" Her voice came out flat and unemotional.

"I was there, at the funeral," he said. "I walked behind his coffin."

The RCMP had arrived from all over Canada that day. They always did when one of their own died on the job. Jake had stopped a speeding truck on the Trans-Canada Highway, a routine call. But the driver had had drugs, and a gun. Jake had been shot point-blank. Died instantly, they said. It could happen to any one of them, just as it had happened to Jake. So the Force had marched, rank on rank of red serge, their polished boots drumming out a requiem on the tarmac. It had been more than two years ago.

"I remember seeing you," he said. "You held up well that day."

"Thanks." Her mouth was dry.

"Look," he turned off the engine. "We're stuck here for the night. We might as well keep each other company over dinner, right?"

"Sure," she said. Of course they could. They stumbled through the snow into the bright warm lights of the hotel.

15

THE SNOW STOPPED overnight. In the morning the sun shone. Roxanne walked between piles of snow two feet high to the RCMP building. Work crews were out clearing roads and parking lots. Blowers spouted snow off driveways. She spotted Brian Donohue's SUV outside the doughnut shop. He had offered to drive her to work in the morning but she had said she'd get there herself. She couldn't run in this snowy mess but she could walk. And it gave her some time to think about the night before. Brian had turned out to be good company. Over dinner, she'd told him about Finn, about how having her sister to care for him had brought her to Manitoba. He had two kids of his own. He shared custody with his ex. He was hoping to get promoted to inspector. In the RCMP that meant an administrative job. If he stayed with the Major Crimes Unit, it would keep him closer to home. He had a live-in girlfriend. Her name was Sally. Of course he had. That caused her a rueful smile. So when she finally admitted to herself that she really liked a guy it turned out he was taken? She saw Matt and a couple of other constables in the RCMP parking lot, shovelling. Her own car was sheathed in snow, looking like an igloo. When she went upstairs she found Izzy McBain already at her laptop, StarFest brochures scattered around her, making lists.

"Sponsors. Just wondered what they'd say if we asked them how much money they gave Stella for StarFest."

"Leo Isbister said he donated $3,000 a year." Roxanne hung up her parka. "Why don't you make a list of the artists who played there, too? And phone some of them. Find out what she was really paying them."

"They live all over the place," said Izzy. "B.C. The Maritimes. The States."

"That's okay. Do what you have to do. Within reason."

The door opened. Brian arrived, a tray of coffees in his hand. His smile was friendly as he handed one to her.

"Black for you, Roxanne. Cream and sugar for Izzy."

Matt came in, rubbing his hands from the cold. He wrapped them around a warm cup and took a seat.

Izzy glanced up from her screen. "StarFest didn't have a board for the first couple of years. Sasha Rosenberg's been a member from back then. And Roberta Axelsson, Erik's wife, was on it for a while."

"We should talk to her." Roxanne was glad of the coffee. It was strong and hot. She and Brian had finished a bottle of wine last night. She had drunk most of it.

"I met her in Winnipeg, at the hospital," said Brian. "Isn't she staying there with family?"

"Do you think she could have done it? Killed off Stella because she found out about her and Erik?" Matt said. Roxanne found the idea surprising. She hadn't considered that. Yet.

"No!" For Izzy it was unthinkable. "She didn't know about him and Stella. That's why she left him." She frowned at Matt and went back to studying her laptop.

"Still." Brian hadn't taken off his jacket. He was heading back to the city. "Matt has a point. If she's still in Winnipeg, I can talk to her."

Roxanne needed to get going too. "Matt," she said. "Why don't you come along with me to Cullen Village. See if we can catch those StarFest board members. We can take my car. I'll meet you outside."

She went to the window and clicked the remote starter. The car lights flickered, barely visible under the snow. She went downstairs and stopped in at the women's washroom. Kathy Isfeld was rinsing her hands at the sink. Her pale image looked at Roxanne from the mirror.

"Kathy," said Roxanne. "Do you know anything about why Stella Magnusson quarrelled with her family? Way back, when she first lived here?'

Kathy turned to the paper towel dispenser and pulled out a couple of sheets. She wiped her hands dry. "Don't really know," the reflection in the mirror said. "Stella was a few years behind me. But everyone knew she was a wild one. Story was she got herself into trouble. They sent her away and she never came back." She dropped the towels into the wastebasket.

"Stella got pregnant?"

"That's what people said." Kathy shrugged and walked towards the door.

"So she had a baby?"

Kathy turned and looked directly at Roxanne. "Or she got rid of it. Who knows?" And she disappeared out the door.

When Roxanne got to her car, it had been swept clean of snow. "Thanks, Matt." They drove through high snowbanks that narrowed streets and blocked sightlines at intersections. She told Matt what Kathy had said. Maybe the family had felt disgraced by Stella's behaviour. It happened in small towns back then. If Stella had been sent off to have a baby, by herself, still in her teens, it could explain the rift in the family. Had she aborted the baby? Or did she have the child and put it up for adoption? Matt got on his phone to Izzy. Maybe she'd have time to check that out.

"Izzy says Roberta Axelsson's back home at her farm," he said.

"Right," said Roxanne. "We'll go there after." She pulled into the Smedleys' driveway.

THE PHONES WERE buzzing in the village. Sasha called Margo.

"Roberta's home! She made it through all that snow yesterday. Panda phoned me. She called her and offered to go help her dig out but Roberta says she's okay. She got the snowblower going and blew a path to the barn, then she called a guy that lives past her place and he's going over with a tractor to clear her driveway."

"She's okay out there by herself?"

"Panda says she sounds fine. Alice has left lots of goat milk in the fridge so she's going to make soap. I'm going to call her after this."

"You do that. Maybe we should go by and visit? Just to make sure she's okay?"

"I'll ask." Margo had barely hung up when the phone rang again. Panda.

"Oh good," Panda said. "You're home. Sasha's phone is busy. I just drove past George and Phyllis's. My nephew Matt and that woman RCMP officer were ringing their doorbell."

"Really? I wonder if the police are getting suspicious about George?"

"We could call Phyllis in a while and find out."

"You do that." Margo didn't want to appear too snoopy after their visit to Smedleys. She'd leave that call to Panda. "I think we should go and check up on Roberta."

"Good idea. We could take lunch. I've got a chunk of pork in the slow cooker at home."

Shortly after, Sasha called back. "The police are at the Smedleys!"

"I heard. Wonder what that's about?"

"I'll see if Phyllis wants to come with us to Roberta's for lunch, then we'll find out."

"That's happening? You talked to her?"

"Well, yeah. She wasn't keen at first. Did the whole 'I want to be by myself' thing. She's trying to figure out what she's going to do. Says she likes being out there on her own. Likes having the place to herself."

"So she's not scared?" Margo knew that you could enjoy being alone, up to a point. Her children worried about her being lonely, but she liked being able to do what she wanted when she chose. After years of taking care of a family, it was a luxury. Sometimes she would get up on a sleepless night, make a cup of tea and go back to bed and read until she was tired again, Bob sprawled at her side. A single life had its advantages. "Too bad she doesn't have a dog for company. Or a cat."

"Erik doesn't like them. Won't have animals in the house. She's not going to be able to live there by herself, you know. She'll never be able to cope with all that work on her own. And the farm's probably not hers to have."

"Isn't she entitled to half of it?"

"What use is half a farm? That place is all or nothing. Anyway, I told her that the police had been banging on the Smedleys' door and that got her interested. She wants some time to finish making soap so I said we'd be there by one. Can you bring something?" The conversation was interrupted by the sound of Lenny baying loudly. "Hang on. Someone's at the door. Probably just the Jehovahs."

Margo waited and listened. Sasha's doorbell was ringing.

"It's the RCMP!" Sasha came back on the line. "What do they want with me? I'll call you back." She hung up. Margo thought for a moment, then opened her laptop and found a photo of aconite. She was sure she'd seen something like it in the Smedleys' garden. She'd print it and take it along. Show it to Panda and Annie if she had a chance and see what they thought.

IT WAS ALMOST noon when Roxanne and Matt reached the Axelsson farm. Roberta did not appear pleased to see them. She wore old, shabby, comfortable clothes. Her hair was tied back in a bandana but some stray yellow ringlets had escaped.

"It's really not convenient. I'm making soap. You'd better come through while I finish this batch," she said. "Keep your boots on." She turned on her heel and led them through the house to a warm, sweet-smelling room. A hot plate, strainers, moulds, various jars and bottles lay on shelves. There was a makeshift countertop.

Some shelves held empty, clean containers and others were filled with white and pink lotions, neatly labelled. One was devoted to rows of soap squares, in different pale hues flecked with herbs, tied with straw ribbon or coloured strands of wool.

Roberta stirred a pot on a hot plate. She added some aromatic oil to it and mixed in a handful of dried herbs, like an ancient alchemist. Or a witch. A Leonard Cohen song was playing in the background. She turned it off. She pulled a flat metal tray onto the counter beside the hot plate, then went back to stirring.

"Is there any more word on how Mr. Axelsson's doing?" Roxanne asked.

"No. We're just going to have to wait and see about that. You'll probably know before me."

"We need to ask you some questions about Stella Magnusson's music festival."

"Me? What on earth for?" She stopped stirring and regarded them with surprise. "I haven't been a part of that for years."

"But you used to be. You were on the board of directors, weren't you?"

"Sure. Back in the beginning. But I gave it up. I left StarFest ages ago. I don't know what goes on with it now." She turned her attention back to her soap making.

"What made you leave?" Matt Stavros asked. "Wasn't it a good place to sell stuff like this?"

"The Constellation Crafts Corner?" Her voice had a bitter edge. "Sure, it was okay. But it only happened for one weekend in the year. I do the farmers market in Fiskar Bay now, every Saturday, all summer long. That works better for me."

"So that was why you left StarFest?"

She lifted the pan off the hot plate, was about to pour the contents onto the metal tray, then stopped. She sighed and pushed back a stray strand of hair. Her face was pink from the heat.

"Hey, why don't you go through to the kitchen and take your jackets off? The kettle's on the stove. Get it going and we'll have some tea. I'll finish this off and be right with you. You can hang your jackets behind the door."

Before long she had joined them, made peppermint tea for herself and coffee for them, put a plate of sliced ginger cake on the table and sat down.

"This is great coffee," Roxanne said. That got a grudging smile.

"Glad you like it. Have some cake."

Roxanne took a slice to humour her. "You were around when StarFest started?"

"Sure I was," Roberta said. "We'd been living here about three years when Stella showed up." She took a breath, remembering. "We were all happy to see her. Well, Erik and Mike Little were. They both knew her from before, right? And Stella was something new. She was full of ideas. She had the money to make it happen, too. She fixed up that old house. Hired carpenters. Got it done right."

"You saw her often?" Matt asked.

"Once a week at least. We'd eat dinner. Talk. Play some music— well, the guys did. Sometimes we all sang. She had great stories to tell about people she'd met. She'd lived in L.A., you know. And she'd been to Nashville. That impressed the guys no end. I hadn't a clue Erik was still carrying a torch for her." She gazed out the window, blinking, as if she were going to tear up.

"Anyway, Stella started talking about StarFest quite early on. And it did sound like a great idea. Showcase some of our own guys, like Erik and Mike. Get them an audience. She'd managed to find some gigs for them already. That's why they're still out there, working most weekends. They're working her old contacts. They'd never have done it without Stella." She went quiet again and sipped her tea.

"So you helped get StarFest going?" Roxanne prompted again. The cake was really good. She resisted taking another slice.

"Yup. It was fun. It really was, for a couple of years. Hard work, though. The land had to be got into shape. The guys worked their butts off. For free. For Stella, I suppose, but I didn't know that then. She sold us on the idea that it was for us, for local artists, that it would be a cultural hub, that's what she called it. And we all bought it. Should have known when she named it. We all thought it would be the Cullen Village Music Festival. Or Interlake, maybe. But no. Stargazer. 'People can camp out under the stars and listen to the music,' she said. 'It's romantic.' It was that, all right." Roberta looked weepy again.

"But it was Stella's own business?" Roxanne brought the conversation back to practicalities. Roberta fished a tissue out from a pocket and blew her nose.

"Sure. Stella was always in charge. We were her unpaid labour. But we didn't think of it like that, because the guys got to do their thing. They were writing their own songs. And the craft corner was like a little village of its own, we all hung out together, all weekend. We'd put up display tents. Musicians who weren't on-stage would come by and busk. And Stella got the word out. She was good at that. People came. It didn't take long for the concerts to sell out."

"So why did she create a board of directors??"

"She wanted to go after government grants. So she had to have a board. It didn't change anything. It was just the same old gang, really. We got together three or four times a year. Stella told us what she had planned, we said, 'Fine, let's party,' and we did."

"But you got a look at how the money was managed?" Roberta had become quite animated. She appeared to be enjoying telling them all about it. She spoke freely, without any guile. Roxanne couldn't imagine that she was masking a murder. That she'd carried out the deed herself.

"I never paid much attention to that. Didn't care as long as it all happened. I was selling enough stuff to make it worth my while. Stella had started paying the guys for performing. It was all great."

"So why did you quit?" Roxanne probed further. Roberta's brows knitted. She gulped down some tea.

"It was a couple of years later. StarFest was beginning to get a name for itself. Then one night there was a meeting at Stella's. She told us what she wanted to do for the next year and it had all changed. Our guys were gone. All the locals were, except the crafters. She was bringing in people from Toronto, Newfoundland. A lot of Winnipeggers. She said it was time for StarFest to move on, to grow up. Grow up? Like we were all children? I got so mad at her. 'No,' I said. 'It's all about you, Stella. That's what this is all about. You don't give a damn about us. You only care about yourself. You've used us,' I said, 'and I'm out of here.' And I left. Never went back.

"She did use us. The guys just sucked it up. I thought Mike was going to cry when he heard. But Erik, he just shrugged. 'Guess that's it,' he said. What a joke.

"So there. We got suckered by Stella Magnusson. I sure did. I didn't kill her, though. I just wish she'd been exposed for what she really was. People thought that she was so great. Still do. But she was bad, through and through, out for herself and no one else. And I thought that long before I found out she was fucking my husband. Do you want any more coffee?"

Matt flicked a glance at Roxanne. Had they heard enough?

She had one more question. "Sasha Rosenberg stayed on with StarFest?"

"Sasha likes the craft corner. She's taken care of it since I left. It works for her. Sasha makes some big ceramics. And sculptures. It's a lot of work to cart all that heavy stuff to a site and set it up for a sale. She only has to do it once a year. And StarFest is big now. She does well off of it, all in one go. But it sounds like that was going to stop too."

"What do you mean?"

"No one's told you Stella was going to close that down too next year? She wanted the craft space for a second stage. Someone told me at the farmers market. I'll bet Sasha knows."

The doorbell rang. The door opened. Panda Stavros walked in.

"Look who's here! Matt! My favourite nephew!" Roxanne watched as a large, dark-haired woman breezed into the room and flung her arms around Matt. He wormed his way out of her grip and reached for his jacket. A much smaller woman followed her. Annie Chan.

The big woman looked towards Roxanne. "The famous Corporal Calloway? Are you staying for lunch?"

"No, we're not," said Matt, heading for the door. "We're just leaving." The last thing he wanted was to be stuck at a table with Corporal Calloway while his aunt interrogated them about the case. You never knew what Panda might say.

"Heard you two have been out all day quizzing half the neighbourhood." Panda turned towards Roberta. "Phyllis can't come. She needs to stay home and take care of George. These guys paid him a visit today and he's all freaked out about it. See!" She turned back to Roxanne and Matt. "You never know what you might find out if you stay and listen."

"No, thanks. We have to get back to the detachment." Matt handed Roxanne her parka.

"Well, come for dinner again, Matt. Soon." Annie Chan leaned against a counter, looking mildly amused.

"Yeah, bring that cute blonde cop chick with you this time," added his aunt.

"I'll call you. I'll be out at the car." Matt escaped, leaving Roxanne to thank Roberta for her help. She turned to Annie Chan and reached out her hand.

"You are Annie Chan, right? So glad to meet you. We have your drawing of Stella Magnusson on our bulletin board. Thanks for that," she said.

"You're welcome," was all Annie said, coolly dismissive. Still, Roxanne had finally met her.

She could hardly suppress a smile when she reached the car. "That's your aunt? She's as big as you are! She almost lifted you out of the chair!"

"Not quite. She's five eleven. Sometimes I wish Panda would keep her mouth shut."

"Oh, I don't know. She told us we've shaken up George Smedley," said Roxanne. "That's good to know." A small blue Honda waited for them to pass at the end of the driveway. Sasha Rosenberg peered at them through the window as they drove by.

IZZY HAD BEEN busy while they were gone. They hardly had enough time to get their parkas off before she spoke.

"I phoned Freddie Santana!"

"The guy Stella married? In L.A.?" Roxanne asked, surprised.

"Well, you said I could do U.S. calls, right? So I got his secretary and left a message. I didn't think he'd call back but he did. Do you know that nobody had thought to tell him Stella was dead? He was kind of annoyed. Says he wants to know when the funeral is. He might come up for it."

"Could be long enough before that happens." Matt sat down beside her.

"He says Stella was always on the make. Thinks she stashed a pile of cash while she was married to him. Couldn't prove a thing, he says. She was too smart. Said he wasn't surprised somebody had done her in. She was bad news and she had it coming to her. His words."

"So he doesn't know what she did with the money?"

"Not really. But she did have at least one bank account in her married name, as Stella Santana. He thinks she maybe had one in Grand Cayman. They used to holiday there sometimes. I called the guys in Winnipeg. They're going to check it out." She sat back, a grin on her face, pleased with herself. "Want to hear more? I've been working while you've been out schmoozing. Leo Isbister says he gave Stella $3,000 as a sponsorship, right?"

Roxanne nodded.

"Well, that's not what it says here." She waved a financial page. "Two thousand. I got hold of another couple of sponsors to find out what they said they gave and matched it against how much it says here and bingo! She reported less, for all of them. She had at least twenty sponsors. The official take was about $25,000 annually so she probably skimmed seven or eight thousand every year. And then there's the artists."

"You phoned them too?"

"Not many, but I got hold of an agent in Toronto who said he told his clients not to work for Stella. She was paying them less than scale. Says she'd call them directly and given them some sob story about how it was such a little, low-budget festival and how it needed a boost from someone of their calibre and how she'd make sure they had a good time when they got here to make up for it.

"This agent said she'd get these guys on Skype and bat her eyes at them and they'd agree to do StarFest for a lower fee. Couldn't tell me how much, though. He threatened to cut them out of his books if they did it again, he said. So I checked, and again, that's not what the financials say. According to the records she was paying a decent rate. I checked back with him to make sure. So there! She's been pocketing the difference. Stella was fiddling the books."

"Guess we should leave you stuck in the office more often," said Matt.

"Not likely," Izzy retorted. "You need me at Angus's funeral tomorrow." The funeral had been delayed because of the storm. "I'm the one who knows everybody that'll be there. And I'm going anyway. Angus Smith was a good guy."

Roxanne rocked back in her chair. "We should all go. Did you manage to find out anything about Stella and a baby?"

"Not today. It's Saturday. Government offices are all closed."

They were done for the day, early. The highways were open again. There was no snow forecast. It took only an hour and twenty minutes to drive into Winnipeg. Roxanne would get an evening with her kid and commute back tomorrow for the funeral.

16

CARS WERE PARKED nose to tail around Cullen Legion Hall. Roxanne found a spot two streets away. The building was plain, rectangular and large enough to hold more than three-to-four hundred people. It was packed with Angus Smith's friends and neighbours. Coat racks stood by the front door, filled with winter parkas and the occasional fur coat, still the best, some locals insisted, for keeping out the bitter Manitoba cold. Archie Huminski from Cullen Dump sat near the back, wearing his best suit and a tie. A plump, grey-haired woman sat at his side. Mrs. Huminski, maker of cookies? He spotted Roxanne and got to his feet, indicating that she could have his seat. She shook her head and went to join Izzy, past row upon row of occupied chairs. They found a place to stand along the wall near the front. From there, they could see most of the crowd. Judging by the nudges and whispers, their presence had also been noted.

Matt was sitting beside his aunt Panda and Annie Chan. Bill Gilchrist had arrived, with Constable Mendes at his side, both of them in uniform. They took up a position opposite her. We are too obvious, Roxanne thought. We should have stayed at the back.

She could see Sasha Rosenberg sitting beside Margo Wishart, the woman who had found Angus Smith's body. George Smedley and his wife were seated a couple of rows behind them. The ever-helpful Jack Sawatsky was moving around, finding seats for elderly people with canes and a very pregnant woman. He wore the green uniform jacket of the Royal Canadian Legion and appeared to be one of the organizers. He caught her eye and nodded his head in acknowledgement.

The legion's colour flags stood in a rack beside a polished table. On it was a funeral urn, a lidded earthenware pot glazed in green and blue. Roxanne recognized Sasha Rosenberg's work. There was a framed photograph of Angus, wearing the uniform of a captain in the Princess Patricia's Canadian Light Infantry. Two large vases of flowers stood either side of a small model boat carved to look like one of those used to fish the lake in the summer months.

John Andreychuk sat with his two sons. There was no sign of Maggie. Roxanne made a mental note to text Brian Donohue when the ceremony was over, to let him know that Jeremy was here, not in Winnipeg. Brian had planned to talk to him some more about the StarFest money while he was in town.

The Smith family trooped in and took up their seats in the front row. Angus's wife, Millie, was still recovering from hip surgery and needed a walker. The daughter's eyes were puffy. There were two male adults and another woman, three children, two of them in their teens.

The local United Church minister, a woman with short grey hair, conducted the service. Roxanne had not been raised in any religious faith. She was startled to hear the power of the Almighty being invoked to come to her and her colleagues' assistance, so that they might "come to a swift and just conclusion, and help restore harmony and goodwill to this beloved community." Amen to that, she thought. It was too bad that bowed heads did not allow her to see if there were any twitching eyelids or licked lips that might indicate a flicker of concern or guilt.

An old soldier talked of Captain Smith's career in the Canadian military. He had served in Bosnia and in Kosovo. "He was a true Canadian peacemaker," the old man told them. "Spent the rest of his years determined to do good in this world." A trumpet played the last post. Uniformed legion members took up the flags and dipped them towards the ground in Angus's honour. Roxanne swallowed. Since Jake's death, would ceremonies like this always get to her?

One of the family men was Angus's brother. He said what was expected, spoke of a good father, the faithful husband, told stories of Angus the fisherman, of the things he and his carpentry group had built. He took the model boat into his hands.

"When the spring comes," he said, "we'll put my brother's ashes into this boat and set it on the lake, out on the water, and we'll light it on fire. We'll let you know when we do it and we'll have a barbecue afterwards. You're all invited."

The crowd smiled and nodded. No one mentioned that Angus Smith hadn't deserved to die the way he did, at the hands of a murderer, but at the end of the service, Roxanne found her hand being shaken by people who wished her well and every success.

"So you know it wasn't Brad Andreychuk that did it?" Archie stood at her elbow.

"Can't talk about that with you, Archie," she said. She looked over to where the Andreychuks stood, two men the same age as Brad at their sides. Were those his buddies, Mitch and Billy? Otherwise, they were isolated and ignored.

"That business with Erik Axelsson should never have happened," said Archie. "Bradley had no need to try to pin the murder on Erik. I don't blame Maggie for trying to defend her man, we all know John Andreychuk's got a pacemaker, but what Brad did was wrong. People around here remember things like that." As Roxanne wondered how she could change the subject, Archie continued, "Hear you've been talking to George Smedley."

"Can't talk about that either," she said.

"Gotcha, milady," he replied. "You should come see me one of these days. You know where to find me. Kettle's always on."

Right, she thought, so that I can feed the gossip mill.

"Look." Izzy returned to her side with a plateful of food in her hand. "They've made real funeral sandwiches." Hatches had been opened at the other side of the hall. Tables were set up, trays of food laid out. Coffee and tea urns hissed on the counter.

"You hardly ever get these anymore," Izzy was gleeful. "See, they've even got the round, cherry ones." The sandwiches were crustless, layered, from different breads and with fillings. Some were rolled and cut like pinwheels. The ones Izzy had mentioned were brown bread, filled with a mixture of cream cheese and chopped maraschino cherry. "They're the best." Izzy devoured one in two mouthfuls. "Here's my mom." A round-faced woman came up and was introduced. The talk was all about Izzy being in the Force, the food, the funeral service. Not a word was spoken about murder.

"You're not eating?" Izzy's mom looked at Roxanne.

"Corporal Calloway doesn't eat this kind of stuff," said Izzy.

"I'm supposed to be training for the marathon," Roxanne explained. "Although I'm getting out of shape. There's nowhere to run inside and it's either too cold or snowy out."

"Really?" said Izzy's mother. "There's a walking track in the community hall at Sprucewood." The village she mentioned was a few miles west of Fiskar Bay, near the McBain farm. "They'd let you run there, if I asked them. Izzy, why didn't you say?"

"I never thought." Izzy swallowed another mouthful. "I still think you should come and skate with me and my hockey team, Corporal. That's the best way to burn off steam. Then you could eat properly."

"Don't be cheeky, Isabel," said her mother.

John Andreychuk and his sons were making their way to the door. The crowd parted in front of them to let them through, but otherwise they were treated as though they were invisible. This is how a small town works, Roxanne thought. It has its unspoken rules. You help those who follow them, exclude those who don't.

Matt joined them, with his aunt at his side. She really was almost as tall as he. Annie Chan looked tiny beside her.

"Good funeral," said Panda. "I like it when it's organized so everybody knows when to stand up and sit down and nobody gets to go on too long." She was interrupted by a disturbance behind them. George Smedley was supporting his wife, who was buckling at the knees. Izzy seized a chair and the rest moved to help, but it was Annie Chan who took control of the situation.

"Get your head down, Phyllis," she instructed. Phyllis's face was a sickly shade of green and she was shaking. "Breathe in now, in and out."

"She said she felt sick," George blurted.

"We need to clear some space here," Roxanne said to Matt. Bill Gilchrist came up with a man at his side.

"Harry here's a paramedic," he said. "He'll take care of her. Another guy's gone to get equipment."

"I used to be a nurse," said Annie. She continued to reassure Phyllis, to calm her down, to get her to breathe slowly and steadily.

"My heart, it's racing." Phyllis gasped for air. Annie put a hand on each of her shoulders. "It's okay, you're going to be fine." As soon as they could, the medics ushered Phyllis to a side room. George went to fetch the car.

"She's going to be all right," said one of the medics. "Probably just the crowd and the excitement." Annie rejoined them.

"You were a nurse?" Roxanne asked her.

"I was," said Annie. "A long time ago, but you don't forget. I think Phyllis was having a panic attack."

George reappeared. He looked shaken.

"Are you all right to drive, Mr. Smedley?" asked Roxanne.

"Oh yes!" he said. "She was perfectly fine, you know. She hasn't had one of these turns for a while."

"They're a regular occurrence?'

"No, no, not regular. My wife is very sensitive," he continued. "She gets upset easily. Today has obviously been a little too stressful for her. I'll get her home, to bed. She'll be all right, she always is. Can you show me where they've taken her?"

Matt showed him to the room where Phyllis was sequestered. Annie and Panda were talking to Izzy. They said goodbye. Izzy turned back to Roxanne, all smiles.

"Dinner is on. Tomorrow night. Annie Chan's going to cook Chinese."

Gilchrist had taken his leave of Angus's family. He came to join Roxanne. "You got that George Smedley in your sights?" he asked her.

"We're checking him out, Sarge. There are financial issues with Stella's business. And something's a bit off about him."

"Guy's a little creep, if you ask me."

"Do you know much about him?" she asked.

"Nah. Nothing much. He's one of those not-quite-retired folks who show up here now and again, all touchy-feely, smile too much. They move here, stay for a year or two, then they move on. He won't be here by this time next year, I'll bet. If you're going to pin this on him you'd better get moving," he added with a laugh. "Hear you've been talking to Leo Isbister too. Word is he's on the agenda for the next council meeting at Fiskar Bay. Did he tell you that?"

"No," she said. "Didn't tell me very much."

"Figures," he said. "Sharp fella. Never know what he's really up to. Problem is our council doesn't know either. See you back at the office."

She watched him move to the door, shaking hands as he went. It looked like he knew almost everyone in the hall, like Izzy, who was moving around from group to group.

There was a lineup to say goodbye to the family. The mother's face looked drawn, but composed. She sat, enthroned, in a large chair. Angus's son did most of the talking.

"Mom's going to be moving to the city," he said to Roxanne. "She'll be staying with my sister's family while we find a place for her. The house is going to go on the market soon."

"You need to check with us about that," she responded crisply. The house was still a crime scene. "We may need you to hold off on that for a while."

"We have to get going on this," the son insisted. "Mom's money's tied up in the house."

"We won't delay any longer than we need to." His mother looked helpless. It was so soon after Angus's death. Didn't she need more time before they made these changes? The daughter joined them.

"Not that we're going to get a decent price for it, after what's happened there," she complained.

"What's going on with Dad's saws, the ones you confiscated?" demanded the son.

"All in good time," Roxanne said. "We may need to hold onto them as evidence."

"Christ," he said. "Are you saying you'll need to keep them until there's a trial? You haven't even arrested anyone yet."

"The investigation is proceeding as it should," she replied, feeling no need to sound anything but professional. "You know who to contact if you need to, don't you?"

He frowned at her, put off by her manner. She took advantage of the pause in the conversation to say goodbye to the mother and wish her well. How did a good and generous man like Angus Smith end up with such pushy offspring? The paramedics who had tended to Phyllis Smedley were standing by the door.

"What do you think was wrong with her?" she asked.

"Annie Chan was probably right," said one of them. "Looks like it was a panic attack, but she should get checked out. We wanted to take her to the hospital but her old man insisted that she'd be better off home, and she went along with it."

She thanked them and found Matt. "Annie Chan was a nurse?" she asked.

"She was," he said. "A long time ago, right after she left school. She hated it. It was her dad's idea. Good Chinese father, you know, making sure she'd always have a decent job. It was Panda helped her to go to art school. First she rescued Annie, then she rescued me." He looked across the room toward Annie and Panda.

"You needed rescuing?"

"Sure. I was a bad kid. Almost ended up on the wrong side of the law. It was Panda talked sense into me. She took me in, you know. I lived with her and Annie all through university."

Maybe Matt was the wrong choice for this case. He was too close to Izzy, too close to his aunt. But he was thoughtful. He asked good questions. She enjoyed having him on her team.

"I hear you and Izzy are going to their house for dinner tomorrow."

"We are. I need to talk to Izzy. Warn her not to say too much or it'll be all over Cullen Village by morning." When he smiled it lit up his whole face.

"Corporal!"

Roxanne turned to see Margo Wishart approaching. She was smiling too. Brown eyes crinkled at the corners and each cheek creased into a dimple. She wore a soft brown hooded coat that reached almost to her ankles and a paisley scarf in shades of brown and purple hung around her shoulders. Her hat and gloves were in her hand. "Can I have a word with you?" The Scottish accent was quite distinct.

"Sure. Now? Or I could drop by your house tomorrow."

"Oh no! If they see your car, the whole village will know you've been to see me."

"How true," said Roxanne. They both laughed. "Come by the office in the morning? Around ten?"

"All right." Margo pulled on her hat. Dark brown fur framed her face.

"Can you give me some idea what this is about?" Roxanne asked.

The dimples disappeared. "It's regarding George Smedley," Margo said.

17

IZZY WAS ALREADY working at her laptop when Roxanne arrived back at their office the following morning

"My mom says, can you call her when you have a minute? She needs to meet you at Sprucewood Hall so she can get you signed up and give you a key, then you can go in and jog when nobody else is there."

"I don't jog, Izzy. I run."

"Right," said Izzy. "Whatever."

"I get a key?"

"Gonna cost you ten bucks, I'm to tell you."

"That's all?"

"Yep."

Margo Wishart came through the front door promptly at 10:00 am. Today she wore a red puffed jacket with a hood, which Roxanne hung up for her. Under the jacket was a cream sweater in an unusual, asymmetric cut, topped with a scarf streaked with warm browns. Her clothes blended with the colour of her hair. She wore earrings, sculptured bronze. A large leather bag was slung over her shoulder.

Izzy came downstairs wearing her parka. "Coffee?"

"Oh yes. That would be lovely." Her eyes crinkled, the dimples appeared on each cheek. This was a woman who smiled a lot. Roxanne led her to an empty room.

"Did you want to make a formal report?"

"Oh no, no, nothing like that. I just want to talk to you." Margo looked curiously around her. "I've never been in a place like this before," she laughed, a little nervously. "It's a bit like being in the movies."

"How would you like to begin?" Roxanne sat.

Margo took the seat opposite. She hesitated. "This is a bit embarrassing, Corporal. I don't really know if I should be here at all. Everything I am going to tell you is purely speculative. There's no real evidence at all. But my friend and I are worried about Phyllis Smedley. We wouldn't want to see her come to any harm."

"Your friend being who?"

"Sasha Rosenberg."

"Ms. Rosenberg is not here with you?"

"No. I didn't tell her I was coming. We've talked about it, whether we should tell you what we suspect. There's a group of us. We get together quite often. A book group. Sasha and I discussed it with them and they thought that we might have it all wrong. As I said, we have no facts to back up what we've been thinking." She smiled ruefully.

"These friends, do they include Panda Stavros and Annie Chan?"

"Yes! How did you know that? And Roberta Axelsson, I expect you know her too."

"Yes, we do."

Izzy appeared at the door with a cardboard tray containing two paper cups of coffee and a plate of pastries.

"Did you go out for these? You should have said. Let me pay you for mine." Margo reached for the bag at her feet.

"It's okay. They're on the house." Izzy left. Roxanne peeled back the lid on her coffee.

"Phyllis Smedley is another one of your friends?"

Margo emptied a container of cream into her coffee and stirred it. "She is. But she doesn't get together with us very much. She spends a lot of time with her husband, George. We were going to leave you to get on with your inquiries and say nothing. But then Phyllis had that strange turn yesterday. She keeps getting sick, Corporal. It's not the first time. Sasha and I are worried that something is happening to her."

"Something like what?"

"Well," said Margo. "It's like this…" And she proceeded to tell Roxanne all she knew about Phyllis's illness and how it connected to aconite poisoning. She spoke about George's naturopathic business and how they could find no record of it online. "I teach at the university, Corporal. I know how to do research. And I cannot find a single trace of that man."

She talked about how George and Phyllis had met through an internet dating site. How recent the marriage was. How Phyllis would probably have been left quite comfortably off when she had been widowed.

"And I know that sounds like bad gossip, Corporal, but her first husband was a successful lawyer. She owned a big house in Crescentwood before she and George moved out to Cullen Village. It's a cliché, isn't it? The well-off, lonely widow being taken advantage of, but it happens, doesn't it? And Phyllis does seem to be very dependent on George. She goes along with everything he says. He doesn't think she needs to see a regular doctor, but she has recurring episodes of irregular heartbeat. He treats her for it himself. Shouldn't she be getting that checked out by a regular doctor?" She looked at Roxanne over the rim of her coffee cup, her eyes bright with concern. "We've been told that you are investigating the StarFest finances…"

Roxanne was startled. She tried not to show it. "Did Ms. Rosenberg or Mrs. Axelsson tell you that?"

"Panda Stavros, actually."

Roxanne should have guessed. She noticed a hint of laughter in Margo Wishart's brown eyes. The dimples appeared again. "Look, Corporal. These murders are the talk of the whole village. Cullen Village is a small place. Stella Magnusson and then Angus Smith both being killed has shaken it up. Made everyone suspicious.

Made us question whom we can trust. So of course we want to know as much as we can about what is going on. It's an awful thing to happen in a place like ours. It's like a virus that's eating away at what holds us together.

"I thought that if you suspected George of something already, you should know about this. That's all." Margo drained the last of her coffee and rose to her feet. "Please be discreet if you decide to follow up on what I've said. I don't want to make a bad situation worse. I just thought you should know." She rearranged the scarf around her shoulders.

Roxanne and Izzy watched out the window as she walked to her car, her hood pulled up to ward off the cold. They turned back into the room.

"Nobody ate these?" Izzy helped herself to a lemon Danish and listened as Roxanne related the story. "She thinks George Smedley is after his wife's money and he's poisoning her?"

"Says he might be growing aconite in his herb garden. She showed me a photograph of what it looks like. It'll be under two feet of snow right now and frozen solid if it's out there."

"And it connects to Stella Magnusson because they think George Smedley was after her money too?"

"She admits it's all guesswork. There's nothing to prove it."

"Well," said Izzy, "She's right about one thing. George Smedley doesn't show up anywhere online. I looked. I can't find a thing either."

"He's not on Facebook? Twitter? LinkedIn? "

"Nothing. He's not listed as a naturopathic doctor anywhere. There's a list of all of them, the ones that are registered in Canada, by province. He doesn't show up. There are two colleges, one in Toronto, one in Vancouver. I tried calling but I just get machines. I've left messages."

Roxanne sighed. "I don't think he can be poisoning her. We don't see much of that any more. It's too easy to track poison with modern medicine. Aconite poisoning would show up and lead us straight back to George Smedley. He's not stupid enough to risk that. But if his wife's having panic attacks, we have to wonder why. Maybe something is going on that makes her anxious enough to trigger them."

"Like knowing that George murdered Stella? And Angus Smith?" Izzy had demolished the pastry. She dusted sugar off her hands. "Just supposing! If he did it, someone had to help him move those bodies, and who else is there but her? My aunt had heart palpitations for a while. Turned out to be an overactive thyroid," she said, then picked up a second cake and bit into it.

"But that wouldn't explain the nausea or the breathlessness. You saw her. She turned green. Izzy, how do you eat all that sugar and not put on weight?"

"I'm an active girl," Izzy said, pulling the pastry apart, "with a healthy appetite. We could run down to Cullen and pay the Smedleys a visit. Just drop by to see how she's doing?"

"No, we don't want to set off any more alarm bells. Not yet. You've got dinner tonight at Annie Chan's, right? Maybe you'll find out something there."

"Oh!" Izzy remembered something. "Matt talked to his aunt. You're invited, too, if you want to come."

Should she go? "It's supposed to be a family dinner, isn't it?"

"Oh, come. You can take the heat off me, and it'll be fun. You want to see where the famous Annie Chan lives, don't you?"

She did.

"Well then!"

MARGO GOT HOME to find a message from Sasha on her answering machine. She called back.

"I'm home," she said. "Do you want to go for a walk?"

"You've got to be kidding. I took Lenny around the block. That's as far as I'm going today. Phyllis called. She wants to know if we want to go over there and play Scrabble tonight. Do we?"

"With her and George?"

"No. He's gone down to the States to pick up some supplies for his business. He's staying overnight."

"He's what? He's gone away after she was so sick yesterday?"

"That's what she said."

Margo sat down at her table, by the window that faced the frozen lake. Bob the dog, who had heard the word "walk," sank to the ground at her feet. His head drooped down onto his paws.

"Sasha," she said. "I did it. I went to the RCMP and talked to that woman officer. I told her what we've been thinking about George."

"You didn't! I thought we agreed not to."

"Not unless she got sick again. And she did. You saw what she looked like. I've never seen anyone actually turn green before. I can't believe those paramedics didn't take her straight to the hospital. Anyway, I was leaving the funeral afterwards and I saw the corporal so I talked to her and made an appointment to go and see her. This morning. I've just got back."

"And you didn't call me? I'd have come too."

"I didn't want to get you involved." Margo had thought about it but she knew from experience how Sasha's flair for the dramatic could embellish a story. Margo didn't want them to look like two gossipy old friends with overactive imaginations but she wasn't going to tell Sasha that.

"It's done," she said. "If there's any fallout from it, it's going to be my problem." Then she thought again. "Do you think I should phone and let the police know that George has gone south of the border?"

"Don't think there's anything to worry about." Sasha dismissed the idea. "He's done it before. He has a post box at Pembina."

Manitobans who bought goods from companies in the States sometimes had them mailed to a postal warehouse in North Dakota, just over the US border. They would drive down and bring the materials through customs in person, rather than trusting them to the expense of Canadian postage rates and an unattended postal customs check. It was a three-hour drive from Cullen Village to the border.

"It's still funny that he'd go off by himself and leave her at home, after yesterday."

"We would find out all about it if we went to play Scrabble," said Sasha hopefully.

"I don't know." Margo hesitated. Was it right to go when she'd just cast suspicion on the Smedleys?

"Oh, Margo. You didn't say anything bad about Phyllis, did you? It was George that you told on." That was true. "Shall we take some wine along? I've got a big bag of Cheezies."

"That might be pushing it." Margo laughed in spite of herself. "I could make popcorn." She was never sure how seriously Phyllis took the health food regime.

They hung up. Margo pulled her hooded jacket back on and went to find a leash.

"Come on, Bob, we both need a walk."

The dog bounded to the door, wagging his long tail. She'd go and try to walk away the dull feeling of dread that had lingered since she had made the decision to speak to the police.

IT WAS DARK by late afternoon. Coloured lights, strung along the eaves of houses and wrapped around evergreen trees, made the village appear cheerful and bright as the day turned to night. Margo and Sasha sat on either side of a Scrabble board, nibbling on pieces of homemade crispbread, loaded with seeds. It didn't taste bad, and they had each brought a bottle of wine along. Margo was driving, but Sasha was enjoying a third glass. Phyllis took her time to play and was happy to talk instead. She hadn't gone to Pembina with George because he thought she should have a couple of quiet days to herself to recover, but really, she told them quite smugly, she thought he wanted to shop for a present. Her birthday was coming up soon.

"So he'll be back home tomorrow?" said Margo, staring at a rack of consonants, no vowels.

"Absolutely. He has clients to see in the city on the way back. One of them needs a special food supplement. He'll be able to give it to him."

It all sounded just fine, thought Margo. What was I worrying about?

A FEW KILOMETRES west, Roxanne was sitting at Panda and Annie's dining table, eating Szechuan noodles. Other dishes of food were laid out, crispy beef, a spicy chicken dish, tofu and vegetables, meat on skewers.

"Annie made her favourites," said Panda.

"It's all so hot!" The Chinese food Izzy was used to was of the milder, sweeter, Cantonese-Canadian variety. Out in the country cafes where it was served, you were still automatically given a fork to eat with.

"I cooked it mild." Annie looked up at her. "Don't you like it?"

"It's great! I'm just not used to this heat." Izzy picked up her bowl and chopsticks and tried to imitate Panda. For her, it was fiery.

Roxanne was enjoying the food. She was reminded how different life was out here in a rural community. In the city you got used to being able to eat food from all over the world.

"You should try eating in Chengdu," said Panda, reaching for a skewer. "There, it's really hot. Burns the roof off your mouth."

"Does not," said Annie. "Have some more tea, Izzy. Roxanne?"

It was a night off. She'd asked them to drop the job title while they were off duty. She liked that too. She'd be Corporal Calloway again tomorrow. Times were changing in the RCMP but some of the old formalities that propped up the hierarchies still needed to be observed.

"How come we don't get this kind of Chinese food here?" asked Izzy. She drained her teacup. Annie filled the little cup again.

"You can," she replied. "My mom, she was born in Szechuan, she gets what she needs sent over, or buys it in Winnipeg, in Chinatown. So I ate a lot of this food when I was growing up. She makes a great fish dish with chili broth. Here, she uses whitefish. I sometimes take her one, fresh out of the lake, when I go to visit."

"Where do they live?"

"Virden." That was a small town to the west, near the Saskatchewan border.

"Did they run the local restaurant?" Roxanne asked.

"Oh yes. I waited table when I was a teenager," said Annie, laying down her chopsticks. Everything she did, even the way she spoke, was clean and neat. "But I was an only child and I was a girl. The restaurant wasn't going to go to me. I have a couple of male cousins. One of them got it. Not that I wanted it. I couldn't wait to get out of that town. And I didn't want to end up like my mother, cooking chickens and chopping vegetables all my life. Try some of this beef. It's very chewy." Annie picked up some pieces of dry fried beef and dropped them into Izzy's bowl, then passed the dish to Roxanne.

"So that's when you became a nurse?"

"That was my dad's idea. I wasn't given a choice. He really wanted what was best for me, but I didn't like nursing. Then I met Panda and I was able to quit."

The lower floor of the house was built on an open plan. The kitchen area was behind a counter, the table set in front of it, opposite a large wood stove that warmed the whole house. Tall windows faced into the blackness of a dark wood. The nearest neighbours were a couple of kilometres away. Annie's paintings hung on either side of the room, brightening the room with their rich colour.

"Annie's studio is upstairs," said Matt as the meal drew to a close. "Can you take Izzy and Roxanne up to have a look?"

"No." Annie stopped clearing dishes from the table. "Not right now. I'm working on something."

"What is it you're doing?" Matt sounded surprised. Was Annie usually so reluctant to show people her work? "Is it something to do with the case? Like the drawing you did of Stella?"

"Never you mind." The corners of Annie's mouth flickered. She picked up the used bowls and moved towards the kitchen. "You're not going to see it right now." Then she turned and smiled at them all. "It's going to be a surprise. Maybe when you find the murderer I'll let you have a look."

"It'll be finished long before then at the rate they're going," said Panda. "Let's move over to the sofa. Have you ever eaten Chinese candy?"

Izzy and Matt sat down. Roxanne stopped to study a painting on the wall. It was darker than the rest, browns and black with vivid splashes of yellow and purple. Panda passed around a bowl of little wrapped candies. "Did you know," she began, "that George Smedley's taken off down to the States for the night and left poor Phyllis home, all on her own?"

"He's what?" Izzy and Matt said, simultaneously. Roxanne stared at Panda. "He's gone where?"

"Oh, just down to Pembina to pick up some stuff for work." Panda was delighted by the reaction. "Maybe he'll go as far as Grand Forks. He's supposed to be back tomorrow."

"What else do you know, Panda?" Roxanne asked.

"Nothing. Phyllis is at home right now, playing Scrabble with Sasha Rosenberg and Margo Wishart. She's fine. Wow. You really think George Smedley did it?"

18

THERE WERE FINGERPRINTS all over the StarFest binder that George Smedley had left at the detachment earlier for Izzy McBain. None of them belonged to a person of that name. Most of them matched someone named George Devine. He had a record, going way back. He'd done time, twice, in Nova Scotia for fraud. Most recently, he'd been taking on different identities, cheating people, mainly women with money. His last victim had been divorced. He'd robbed her of most of her life savings before he got caught. His mug shot showed a little man with thinning hair several shades lighter than George Smedley's. He had a trimmed beard but otherwise looked exactly like him. Margo and Sasha had been right to be suspicious after all.

Emails buzzed back and forth between the Fiskar Bay RCMP detachment and Brian Donohue in Winnipeg. Soon, a picture emerged of a man who had taken the identity of someone who was dead by getting a copy of the death certificate and building a life from there. The original George Smedley had been a market gardener, near Ottawa, with a reputation as a herbalist, dead ten years. Devine had taken his name and his interests and built a new persona. He had done some online courses in alternative medicine while he was in jail, and became Dr. George Smedley, naturopath.

His car was found sitting in the parking lot behind a holistic health centre in a fashionable area just south of Winnipeg's downtown. That was where George had rented an office. He met clients there twice weekly. The car had been left there sometime on

Sunday, when the place was closed. He definitely had not driven south to Pembina, North Dakota.

"We've got airport security and the border guys all watching out for him, but I doubt we'll catch him. He'll have changed his appearance," Brian told Roxanne over the phone.

"Shaved off the moustache?"

"Maybe added a beard again. More hair. Dyed it. He probably had another identity ready to use in an emergency. He's thought this all through beforehand. The car's been parked where there are no surveillance cameras. He's had an escape route all figured out."

"How would he have left the office? By cab?"

"We're checking. There's a hotel within walking distance. He could have picked one up there. Or taken a bus. Sunday service is slow but he'd have been close to a major bus route. It's been hours. He's long gone. It's not going to be easy to track him. Do you think he's the killer?"

"No, I don't." Roxanne had already given that some consideration. "There's nothing in his record that points to violence. He's a liar. A fraud. A thief. But he always talks his way out of trouble. Even in jail, he avoided fights. He doesn't get physical."

"He could have got into something that pushed him too far this time," said Brian.

"And if he did, he would have needed help to dispose of those bodies. Devine has always worked alone in the past. He's a loner. This would be way out of character. I need to get to Cullen Village and talk to his wife."

"I'll keep checking in," said Brian. "If you need me, holler."

PHYLLIS HAD SLEPT in. She was still in her pyjamas and a fluffy pink housecoat when she answered the door.

"Goodness, Corporal, it's you again. And Constable Stavros! Did you need to speak to George? He isn't here." She paused, a worried look on her face. "Nothing's happened, has it? He's all right?"

Roxanne and Matt assured her that to their knowledge George was alive and well. They soon found themselves in the Smedleys' pastel living room, seated in overstuffed armchairs.

The news that George Smedley was an alias, that the man she had married was a fraud, appeared to come as a surprise, but Phyllis recovered remarkably quickly. She opened up her iPad straight away to check her bank account. Their joint savings account had been cleaned out. Almost $10,000 was gone.

"George insisted that we should always have ready cash available in case of an emergency," she said. She did have investments of her own, she told them. She was quite sure he would not have had any way to access that money.

"My son, Ross, is an investment banker. He takes good care of my portfolio. George would never have been able to get at it."

She had paid for his car. It had cost more than $40,000. It was news to her that the car was, in fact, leased. George must have pocketed the cash. She had also given him money to set up his business, to pay for furnishings and supplies. She had no idea that the space he had rented came already furnished, so another $25,000 was gone.

"He told me that he had gone into business with his previous wife, that they had run a health clinic. She managed it poorly and that was one of the reasons they split up. He said that the divorce settlement had left him with very little money," she explained. "I wonder if there ever was another wife, apart from the women he's cheated?"

Roxanne told her about his criminal record and the time he had spent in jail.

"Oh, Corporal, I do feel foolish. My son is going to be so annoyed about this. Ross never wanted me to marry George. He said that he was a fraud right from the start. That he was after my money. He didn't come to the wedding. Now it looks like he was right. I wonder if I'm legally married, if George Smedley doesn't exist?"

Roxanne wasn't sure. "Is he named as a beneficiary in your will?"

"I'll need to change it! I was going to leave this house to him, and a living allowance. Ross advised me not to leave him a chunk of money. I'm going to have to talk to my lawyer."

"Did George know what you were going to leave him?"

"Not really." Phyllis gave her a sly look. "I just told him I'd leave him a little something."

"When did you last hear from him?"

"He emailed last night. Look." Phyllis opened up her email and turned the iPad screen so that Roxanne could see it.

"Night night, sleep tight. See you tomorrow. XXX George," Roxanne read. It had been sent from his iPhone.

"Can you forward that to me?" Matt asked Phyllis, taking out his own phone. He gave her his contact information.

"Your house will have to be searched by a team from the Forensic Identification Unit," Roxanne said. "They're on their way here from the city."

"I hope they aren't going to make a mess. He took his laptop with him, but his office is through there. His lab, he called it." Phyllis waved towards the end of the hallway. Roxanne wondered why Phyllis was not more upset. There were no tears, no outrage. Phyllis seemed more concerned with the practicalities of what should have been devastating news.

"Your husband used medicinal herbs?" Roxanne asked. "He grew some of them in your back garden?"

"Oh, yes. Rosemary. Lovage. Echinacea. Mint. All kinds of things."

"Wolfsbane?"

"I don't know that one," she said.

"Blue," said Roxanne. "About three, four feet high. Bell-like flowers."

"Like delphiniums?" Phyllis's face lit up. "We have those, out at the back. I love delphiniums."

"You've been sick recently, Mrs. Smedley. Your husband always treated your illness himself?"

Phyllis smiled a confidential smile. "Well, Corporal, he liked to think he did. I just went along with it to keep him happy. But I still went to my old doctor in the city for check-ups. She's a lovely woman. I didn't want to lose her as my doctor. I didn't tell George, didn't want to sound like I didn't believe that he could cure everything that ailed me using naturopathy. Not that his treatments weren't helpful, often they were. But I did think I should see a regular doctor as well, so I did. On the quiet. I'd tell George that I was going to visit an old friend. Well, I was, wasn't I?"

"Did you tell your doctor about these fainting spells you have? Like yesterday?"

"Oh yes. I have panic attacks. I've had them before. I'm not good at handling stress. She gave me a prescription. I keep the pills in an old purse in my closet. George never knew I had them. Do you want to see them?"

"In a moment. Has something been stressing you out lately, Mrs. Smedley?"

"Corporal, how can you ask that? Since poor Stella was murdered I've just been a bag of nerves."

"And the medications your husband gave you. Did you take them?"

"Yes, I did. I don't think they made much difference. I often don't take my other pills though—the ones my real doctor prescribed. They make me feel woozy. I should have taken one before I went to that funeral, then I wouldn't have had that embarrassing turn. I've been taking them since then. George thought he'd cured me."

That also explained her present calm demeanour. Phyllis was sedated.

"Mrs. Smedley," Roxanne asked, "do you know where your husband was on the evening of January 19th and also on the 29th?"

Phyllis looked perplexed. "Why are you asking that? Aren't those the dates of the murders? Stella's and Angus Smith's? What are you suggesting, Corporal?"

"We need to ask." Roxanne gave her what she hoped was a reassuring smile.

"You think he's a murderer? That's just ridiculous, if you don't mind my saying so. George may be a bit dishonest but he's not capable of killing anyone."

"You're sure of that?"

"Look, Corporal. I always knew there was something wrong with George's story. I thought he might not be telling me the exact truth. But you know what, I liked him. I enjoyed his company. He took good care of me, and I like being married. I hated being a widow. I am surprised that he was breaking the law as badly as you say he was, and it does look like he has stolen quite a lot of money from me. But George is a wuss, Corporal. He's a total wimp. I lived with him for almost three years. I know that. He'd never be able to kill anyone. He's just doesn't have it in him to do that."

"January 19th and 29th?" Roxanne reminded her. Phyllis reached for her iPad and opened the calendar.

"There we are! We didn't go anywhere on the 19th, so we must have been here, at home. Together. I would remember if he'd gone out anywhere without me. It hardly ever happened. And on January 29th, we went into Winnipeg for a matinee concert and then had dinner. We didn't get home until after nine. We're usually in bed by ten. Are we about done here, Corporal? I'd like to get dressed before your forensic colleagues arrive, and I do need to call my son and also my lawyer." She rose to her feet.

Roxanne stood too. Black and white framed photographs on the walls, mostly shots of the lake, caught her attention. Pelicans swooped in to land. Narrow wooden swimming piers stretched out over the water. She spotted a photograph on the far wall, in a prime spot.

"Isn't that Stella Magnusson?" There was no mistaking the high cheekbones, the shining blonde hair reflecting stage lights.

"I took that at StarFest a couple of years ago," Phyllis said proudly. "It was in last year's brochure. Stella was so appreciative."

"Constable Stavros will wait until the Ident team arrives. Would you like to call a friend? Maybe you would prefer to get out of the house while they search?"

Phyllis's spine stiffened. "I'm not going anywhere, Corporal. I'm staying here to keep an eye on things. I'll expect a full inventory and a receipt for anything you decide to remove. Will your people take long? I might want some company this evening. I think I might cook dinner and invite some friends over. Tell them the news myself."

Matt's eyes widened in alarm. Panda Stavros would probably know more than they did before the night was over.

"You know what? I think I am hungry. Constable, would you like some lunch? A sandwich? Corporal, you can stay and have one too, if you like."

"No, thank you." Roxanne made her way to the door. "You'll be sure to let us know if you think of anything? Or if you hear from him again?"

"Oh, I doubt I will. I think he's gone." It was the first time, in the whole interview, that she had looked sad. She still hadn't shed a single tear.

BY THE TIME Roxanne got back to the office, there was more information for her. The payments on the car lease were two months in arrears, as was the rent for George's office space. There were traces of hair in a sink in his office, so the moustache was probably gone. Would his wife have a photograph of him as he was now, without facial hair? Probably not, she thought. They'd check his old files. Perhaps get a forensic artist onto it. The clothes he had been wearing as George Smedley were hanging in a closet in his office. No one else had been near the place that Sunday to see him come and go. There was no sign of a laptop. His work files remained, but it did not appear as though he had had many clients. All his bookings had been made through a shared front desk. There were boxes of manufactured food supplements in a cupboard and bottles of pills and liquids with Latin names. Those had been taken to the lab.

What else might he have done to cover his tracks? Moved money around online? There was no report of anyone like him being seen boarding a plane, a train, a bus, or renting a car. George Smedley had quietly and efficiently vanished.

19

"SHE JUST REFUSED to leave."

It was the following morning and Matt was telling Roxanne and Izzy about his afternoon at Phyllis Smedley's.

"The Ident guys really wanted her out of there. She wasn't having any. 'I was married to a lawyer,' she said. 'He was partners with Alexander Lazar, the well-known criminal lawyer. I expect you've heard of him. I am going to call him, he'll be happy to advise me. Do I need to ask him to have a word with you?'"

It was no empty threat. Lazar was well-known in the courts as a tough negotiator.

"You should have seen her," Matt continued. "'It's not as if there's been a murder here, is it? It's not an actual crime scene. You only need to remove items that are in his office, don't you?' They took out box after box. It was like a little chemistry lab in there. He was grinding up dried herbs and putting them into capsules. No computer, though. He must have used the laptop and that's disappeared with him. They couldn't find any records. Nothing like that."

"They searched the rest of the house too?"

"Yup. The bathroom. And the bedroom. She sat in the corner directing traffic. 'That's George's night table. That's George's closet.' Then she found out they were going to dig up her delphiniums. They had to clear away the snow and hack at the roots with an axe. They were frozen solid. 'What on earth do they think they're doing, Constable?' she asked. I just acted dumb. I wasn't going to be the one to tell her that we thought her husband might be trying to poison her."

Roxanne had driven out first thing to Sprucewood Hall to meet Izzy's mother. The walking track would be fine for running and the price was certainly right. She'd arrived too late to run though. There had already been walkers striding around the circuit. She'd picked up a schedule and the promised key. She could get there early most days and put in a few laps before the regulars arrived.

She had checked in with Brian Donohue. George's email to Phyllis on Monday night had been sent from Pearson International Airport, Toronto, he told her. It was now Wednesday. George could have gone anywhere in the world from there, assuming he had a passport for whatever identity he had assumed. The materials taken from the Smedley house would take some time to analyse. They could find no banking information in the name of George Smedley apart from his joint account with Phyllis, or anything recent in the name of George Devine. It was frustrating how easily he had disappeared.

The two constables from the Ident team who had been sent out to search the Smedley home had been less than happy. One had given Brian an earful. His complaints echoed what Matt was telling them.

"She sat there with a notepad watching every move we made over the top of her glasses. Took photos on her iPad. It was like we were the criminals. Kept threatening us with Alex Lazar. You know what that jerk's like. We got out of there as fast as we could."

Roxanne faced Izzy and Matt. "Sergeant Donohue is going to stay in the city and see if he can get hold of Jeremy Andreychuk. Find out if he knew anything more about the StarFest money," she said.

"So we're back to that?" Matt asked.

"It looks like we've got another dead end." Roxanne sounded exasperated. Izzy looked out the window.

"Why is your aunt Panda pulling into the parking lot, Matt?"

"She is?" He took a quick look. "Phyllis Smedley was having them over for dinner last night. She might have something to tell us."

Matt headed downstairs to the front office. Roxanne followed. Izzy lingered on the stairs, curious.

Panda came in the front door, stomping snow off her boots onto the doormat. She waved away Ken Roach, who was manning the front counter with a big, mittened hand.

"It's not you I want to talk to, Constable, it's him." She pointed towards Matt. "That's my nephew."

Sergeant Gilchrist poked his head around his office door. "Personal visit, is it?"

"Personal be damned," said Panda. "I'm here to help them with their inquiries. I've got something to show Roxanne."

Roach and Gilchrist exchanged a glance as Roxanne joined Matt at the other side of the counter. How come they were on first-name terms?

"See this?" Panda dropped a brown envelope on the countertop. "It's from Annie. She's at the dentist. I said I'd bring it in." She pulled off her mittens and opened it up. It contained a white paper napkin. She laid it out flat. "See," she said. "Phyllis said you didn't have a good photograph of George without his moustache, so Annie drew him for you."

They looked at it. On the white napkin, folded square, was a line drawing in fine black marker.

"Geez," said Bill Gilchrist, "that's pretty good. Bet that's what he really looks like."

Panda glanced upstairs to where Izzy was watching. "Hi, Izzy! You got a crime wall like on TV up there? Are you gonna stick it up there?"

"Tell Annie thanks," said Matt. "Was that all you had to tell us?"

Roxanne stood beside Gilchrist and studied the drawing. "She really has got him," she said.

"You know,"—Gilchrist rubbed his chin and looked up from the drawing to Panda—"your pal, she could apply to be a real forensic artist if she wanted. They make good money. Maybe she could do another one, with a beard."

"Annie Chan is famous, Sarge!" Izzy came down the staircase. "That's probably worth loads of money."

"You can keep it after this is all done," Panda said to Roxanne. "Souvenir. Annie said to tell you. But right now someone needs to talk to me. I've got stuff to tell you. There's what's left of an hour until I have to go and pick up Annie. Can we go upstairs? See where you do the real work?"

"Sorry, Panda. That room is off limits. There's an interview room available. We could go in there."

"Nope. I've got a better idea. How about I take my favourite nephew out for a coffee and tell him what happened when Phyllis Smedley took us out for pizza last night." Panda played her ace and grinned. She pulled her mitts back on.

"Can I join you?" Roxanne wasn't going to miss this. She put the drawing back in the envelope. "Is it okay if we copy the drawing? Send it out internally? We won't tell anyone that it's an Annie Chan."

"Sure," said Panda. "Are you buying?" Roach watched as Izzy passed jackets over the banister and the women walked out the door.

"What the hell, it's just a doodle on a napkin," he muttered as Gilchrist passed him on the way back to his office.

The local Tim Hortons was like all the others across Canada, decorated in varying shades of brown and beige, with plastic tabletops and glass countertop displays of doughnuts and muffins. There was bright signage advertising soup-and-sandwich combos and serving staff with professional smiles, even in a smaller town like Fiskar Bay. At mid-morning there was a smattering of older customers, retired people, three men at one table, heads together as they talked, a couple of single people reading the newspaper while their coffee cooled, a couple staring over each other's shoulders with nothing much to say to each other. It was warm inside and smelled of coffee, cinnamon and newly baked buns.

Panda inspected a rack of muffins. "I'll have that cranberry one." She pointed to the biggest. They found a corner table, away from prying ears.

"Phyllis is calling herself by her name from her first marriage. Johnson." Panda announced, pulling the paper casing off her muffin. "Kinda funny, isn't it, being married to someone who doesn't exist anymore?" They sipped their coffee. In house, it came in a real mug, instead of the usual paper, take-out kind Roxanne and Matt had become used to.

"So she took you out for pizza? She said she was going to invite you over for dinner but the guys were there all afternoon."

"She's dead annoyed about that. Said they took so long she didn't have time to cook anything. So it was pizza, here in Fiskar Bay, instead. Her treat. She got Margo to drive her so she could drink some wine."

"Was she celebrating or drowning her sorrows?" Matt continued. Roxanne let him do the talking, an easy chat between him and his aunt.

"A bit of both, maybe. Turns out things weren't so great between her and George anymore. She says she was getting fed up with him fussing all over her. Thinks she maybe got married too soon after her first husband died. 'I was lonely,' she said to us, 'I didn't know what to do with myself. I couldn't believe my luck that I found a partner again, and George, he was so, well, attentive.' You know how she speaks." Panda was doing a decent job of mimicking Phyllis. She was catching the polite, mannered cadence of her voice perfectly, and having fun doing it. And enjoying an audience.

"She ordered a Hawaiian pizza. I hate it." Hawaiian pizza has a pineapple and ham topping and was said to be a Canadian invention. "She ate most of it herself. I think she's making up for all that health food she's been eating. The rest of us ate the pepperoni.

And she'd ordered two bottles of wine, but Margo was driving and Annie doesn't drink, and I wanted to keep my head clear, so she and Sasha drank most of it. She got really chatty." She got back to telling them what Phyllis had said.

"She says it was lovely at first. They had a new life together, they moved out here, a new house, it was all quite exciting, but after a while it all got to be a bit much. George wanted her to be with him all the time. She said she used to be glad when he went into the office in Winnipeg. It gave her a day to herself. But then he wanted her to drive into town with him, to keep him company on the road, he'd say. She'd go and shop while he was at work or meet an old friend for lunch. But she was never getting any time on her own, in her house, and she missed that. When she was married before, she didn't see her husband for days on end. He worked long hours, even on weekends. She had lots of time to do what she wanted to do. 'I would have liked to be able to go for walks by myself with my camera, but I couldn't,' she said. 'I used to watch all of you getting together and I could make it to the book group, but that was about it. I wasn't able to have my own friends out here. It was like George had gobbled up my whole life. He was beginning to get on my nerves.'

"We told her we had thought they were devoted to each other and she laughed. 'That's what George wanted you to think,' she said. 'And I suppose I did play along. The good wife. It's how I was brought up, to have good manners and be considerate, you know, but sometimes inside I was seething. I think that's what was making me sick. I knew I'd made a mistake and I didn't know how to get out of it.'

"We couldn't believe our ears. 'Why didn't you just leave him?' we asked her. And she said, 'What? Leave the house? I paid for it. I wasn't going to be the one to leave. I'm quite comfortably off, you know, and George, well, he said he didn't have any money. He told me his last wife cleaned him out—isn't that a joke? So if I'd asked for a divorce, he could have come after me for support and he probably would have got it. I wasn't going to let him have my money.'

"And we said to her, 'but he did, didn't he? He got away with a whole lot of your cash.' 'About a hundred grand,' she said. 'And now he's gone. I think I got off lightly.' Then she poured herself another glass of wine and downed half of it. Can you believe it?" Panda tore off a piece of muffin. "Wonder how much she's really worth," she said as she popped it into her mouth.

"Who was there besides you and Annie?" Matt asked. She washed the muffin down with a mouthful of coffee. "Margo. Sasha. Roberta didn't come. Hey, that's something else you should know. She went to Winnipeg and fetched Erik home."

"So he's been forgiven?" Roxanne couldn't keep quiet any longer.

"Not yet, she says, but she didn't think she could leave him in the hospital with nowhere to go when he got out. And they were dying to get him out of there. You know what those city hospitals are like. She'll get over the affair with Stella, of course she will. She's mad about him. It's those old Viking good looks. He's had to have the hair cut, she says. They shaved half his head for the surgery. Maybe he doesn't look like one anymore."

Matt had finished his coffee. "That's it? We done here, Panda?"

"No!" She leaned across the table and lowered her voice. "Did you really think that George Smedley was trying to poison Phyllis?"

"Who said that?" Matt asked, though he realized the question might be futile. What the grapevine didn't know it made up and sometimes it got it right.

"You did! That's why you dug up her delphiniums. You thought they were aconite! That's hilarious." Panda's voice had risen.

"Shh, Panda." Matt looked cautiously around. No one appeared to have heard her.

"Sasha told her. Gets loose lips when she drinks too much, and she must have drunk a bottle of wine herself. She told her that Margo had been to see you guys. Margo sat there looking like she wished the ground would swallow her up. Phyllis got really mad at her. How could Margo not have had a quiet word with her, stuff like that. Margo said that she'd been worried about her. We said we all were, but then Phyllis knew we'd been talking about her and that got her even madder.

"'The police got suspicious because you interfered,' she said. She was sitting right across the table from Margo, just about spitting at her. 'That's what really drove George away, it's all your fault.' So she probably isn't telling the truth about being glad he's gone. Maybe she's kidding herself. Who knows? Anyway, Margo got the blame. Phyllis isn't speaking to her anymore. She asked Annie and me for a ride home. She's talking about going to visit her son and the grandkids in Boston. Don't know how Margo and Sasha did, driving home by themselves. I think Margo's pretty mad at Sasha for telling. So they've all fallen out with each other." She clambered to her feet. "I'd better go get Annie. She hates the dentist, she won't want to be kept waiting. Hey, gimme a hug."

Soon after, Roxanne and Matt stepped around a snowbank and slid back across a road still covered with a skin of slippery, packed snow. Panda got into her truck. Roxanne and Matt made their way around the side of the RCMP building.

"So Phyllis Smedley's planning a quick trip to the States?" Matt said. "Is it all a scam?"

"You think she and George planned the disappearing trick? That she's planning to rejoin him south of the border?"

They walked in the front door of the office. A young woman stood in front of the counter, Sergeant Gilchrist and Izzy behind. The woman turned to look at them. Her hair was almost all white, spiked and tinted in shades of green and purple. Rings and studs fringed her nose and ears. She wore a pale layer of makeup and her lips were painted a deep purple. Dark smudges and black liner framed eyes that were a startling ice blue. She was dressed entirely in black, from her leather jacket, to her leggings, to her thick-soled boots.

"Here's Corporal Calloway and Constable Stavros now," said Gilchrist. "This here is Maureen Penner." The woman held out a hand laden with silver rings.

"Hi there," she said. "You can call me Mo. Stella Magnusson was my mom."

20

MO PENNER HAD arrived in Fiskar Bay in a beaten-up old Ford Fiesta driven by her boyfriend, Keenan. They had followed Roxanne's car to Stella Magnusson's place. Now they wandered from room to room, fingering the furniture, checking out the appliances, the rows of glasses and dishes on shelves. The big piano impressed them. So did the Apple TV. And the well-stocked wine rack.

"How big is it?" Mo looked out the window.

"Eighty-six acres, I've been told," Roxanne replied.

"So how far does it go?"

"I'm not sure. Those trees are at the property line on the west side." Roxanne pointed in the direction of the Andreychuk farm. "It goes way back from there."

"Cool house," said Keenan. He was as pierced and studded as Mo. His dark head was shaved. He sported a stubbly beard and a tattoo could be seen creeping up from the back of his neck onto the base of his skull. He dressed similarly to Mo, except his coat was of ancient, worn tweed. They had not removed their outerwear. The heat in Stella's house was turned down as low as possible to prevent the pipes from freezing. It was cold enough that you could see your breath when you spoke.

Back at the office, Mo had pulled a birth certificate out of a pocket and waved it under Roxanne's nose.

"It's a copy. I've got mine at home. You can have this one. Look what she called me. Ariel Star Magnusson. And they changed my name to Maureen Penner. How boring is that? I thought I'd start calling myself Star Magnusson but Keenan says he likes Mo, says it suits me. Maybe I'll change it to Mo Magnusson. I kinda like the sound of that."

She'd been born in Brandon, Manitoba, twenty-nine years ago. Her mother was named on the certificate as Stella Louise Magnusson. Her father was not named. Stella must have been eighteen. How had she ended up in Brandon?

"You were adopted?" Roxanne asked.

"Yeah. Two weeks old, my mom says. I grew up in Winkler, a good Mennonite girl."

Winkler lay in a part of Manitoba known as the Bible Belt, largely settled by people of the Mennonite faith. They practised pacifism, which caused them to migrate every time armed conflict arose in the country where they lived. They spoke a form of Low German, were religious conservatives, but were also shrewd and successful prairie farmers. The towns where many of them now lived had flourished. Mo Penner did not look at all Mennonite but the hair without the dye, the face minus the decorative metal, were all Stella's.

"Did you get in touch with her?"

"Tried. I phoned at first. Left a message. She didn't reply. So then I wrote her a letter. She wrote back. Said she'd never wanted kids, still didn't. Wanted me to leave her alone. So I did. No big deal."

"Do you have a copy of the letter?"

"Not on me. I can get it. It's in Winnipeg." If Mo had a birth certificate and a letter from Stella acknowledging that she was her child, she probably really was who she said she was. So when she had said she wanted to see Stella's house, Roxanne had agreed to take her. She was also curious to see how Mo would react.

"Can I take photographs?"

"No."

"Why not?"

"Because it's still related to a crime and it isn't yours," said Roxanne. It wasn't yet, but who else was there to inherit? "You know Stella's parents are still alive? They live in Victoria. He's got dementia."

"Oh. Well, won't matter that he's forgotten me then, will it."

"I can give you their address."

"Sure." Maybe Mo's grandmother would like to know about her granddaughter after all these years, even if she hadn't wanted to stay in touch with Stella. Mo was still busy scanning each room and its contents with those blue eyes, making an inventory in her head.

"Where's her computer?"

"She had a laptop and an iPad. They're missing. So is her cellphone. Her work computers are with us, in Winnipeg. They'll be returned."

"So who lived here before?"

"Two old uncles. Bachelors. There was no one else to leave it to."

"And now there's just me."

"Maybe." They were in the hallway lined with photographs. Keenan was picking out a tune on the piano. He wasn't bad.

"Hey, babe!" he called. "Can we keep this thing?"

"There's no will, right?" Mo was checking out the photographs. Roxanne stared at her. "How did you know?"

Mo laughed. Her tongue was studded. "Figured it out! See this one?" She was focused on an old black and white photo in a black frame. "That's my mom, right? Must be younger than me in it. Think I look like her?"

The photograph was the one Roxanne had seen before, from the years when Stella was still in her teens, in the Winnipeg band. She and Mo certainly looked alike. Keenan came up behind them and looked over Mo's shoulder.

"Sure do," he said. "She was great looking, your mom, eh? Just like you." He peered closer at the photograph. "Hey, isn't that the Isbister guy there, playing the bass?"

Mo elbowed him. Too late.

"Leo Isbister?" The guy in the picture had long hair and was a lot leaner, but the smile was unmistakably Leo's. "You know him?"

Mo stared back at Roxanne. The blue eyes had gone a shade darker.

"I'm taking you back to the office, Maureen. We need to talk some more."

MARGO OPENED HER door. Sasha stood on the doorstep, a flat plastic container held in both hands. She was wearing a long raccoon coat that she'd picked up at a thrift store and a brown, fur-lined hat with ear flaps that made her look remarkably like her hound, Lenny. Large round sunglasses covered her eyes.

"Oatmeal cookies. Peace offering."

Margo regarded her from the doorway, then opened the door wider. "Oh, come on in. I'll make a pot of tea."

"Coffee would be better."

"Hung-over? Serves you right."

Sasha stepped out of her boots, reached into her pocket, pulled out well-worn sheepskin slippers and hung her coat up in a closet. She patted Bob the dog. "At least Bob's glad to see me."

"He knows you've brought cookies. Are you keeping those sunglasses on?" Margo poured coffee beans into a grinder.

"If we're sitting at the window, like usual, yes."

"You don't sound very apologetic."

"And listen to you, all judgmental, as usual." Margo had been raised Presbyterian, Sasha had gone to synagogue. Neither now attended, but it was something they enjoyed sparring about. "Wasn't so hung-over I couldn't bake. I took a batch of these over to Phyllis."

"And how's she doing?" Margo brewed the coffee.

"She's worse than me. Didn't drink much when she was married to the health nut so she's out of practice." Margo smiled in spite of herself. She put mugs on the table.

"The coffee's going to be strong."

"Oh, good." Sasha seated herself at the table, her back to the window and the light. She opened the cookie container, took out a cookie and gave the dog a piece. "I talked to Roberta as well, on the phone, for ages. She's put Erik in the spare room for now. He won't be there for long. She's figuring out how to forgive him, I can hear it, the way she's talking. But for now she says he's home because she wants to stay on the farm."

"Well, that's true, isn't it?" Margo brought over mugs and a jug of milk.

"Yeah, but it's only half of it. She's nuts about him, I tell you. He'll be back in her bed in no time."

Sasha affected to be finished with men. She had been married twice and had had several other relationships. Now she proclaimed that she was an independent woman and being single suited her just fine. Margo didn't believe a word of it. She brought the coffee to the table and helped herself to a cookie.

"These are okay."

"Okay? They're fantastic, aren't they, Bob? You haven't asked me if Phyllis is still mad at you."

"Is she?"

"Yep. All of us, not just you. Says we're always sticking our noses into everyone else's business, that's what she hates about small towns. No privacy. Well, I said, that's the price you pay for us taking an interest, Phyllis. We look out for each other. We've got each other's backs. That shut her up."

"No word about George yet?"

"Nothing. She's not getting to go to Boston. The RCMP called her and told her she can't leave the country, needs to let them know if she's going anywhere. Wonder who told them that she was thinking about going? Bet it was Panda."

"Has Phyllis figured that out for herself yet?"

"Probably. She's talking about selling the house and getting a condo in the city but she's not allowed to do that either. Or get rid of George's clothes. She's got them all boxed up ready to go to the Goodwill."

"So she's going to have to stay out here for now?"

"Sounds like it. She's got plans for George's home drug lab. 'One good thing, the RCMP cleared that all out for me,' she said. 'I might make it into a photography studio for myself.' We talked colours. She's going to pick up some paint chips tomorrow and I'm going to help her decide." Margo looked out the window, over the white expanse of the lake, streaked with blue shadows.

"It cracked last night," she said. "Sounded like a pistol shot."

"The lake?"

"Way out there." The lake water shifted and moved under the surface of the ice. Sometimes it caused a crack, a fissure that formed a ledge when it refroze. "It was a really loud bang. Look at it, all white and blue and perfect, but it's not, is it? It's full of cracks, where the ice has split and it's frozen together again. It's not perfect at all."

"Hey, it's February. Another month and it'll start to melt. Don't you like when it breaks up and you can hear all the little bits of ice banging up against each other around the edges? When it makes that tinkly sound, like little bells? I love that. And then it'll be summer and we can swim and eat ice cream."

Margo wasn't convinced. "I have a feeling this is all going to get worse before it gets better." Sasha passed her the cookies again.

"But it will. Right? It has to get better."

MO PENNER LEANED back in her chair in the interview room looking bored. She seemed quite familiar with police protocol. Her sparky chat was gone. Now she was sullen.

"You don't need to keep Keenan."

"We'll talk to him after we talk to you, if we have to. How long have you known Leo Isbister?"

"Dunno."

"Yes, you do. Where did you meet him?"

Silence.

"Did you get in touch with him or was it the other way round?"

Mo slammed her booted feet onto the ground and glared at Roxanne. "None of your fuckin' business."

"Oh, yes it is. Think about it, Mo. You're probably Stella Magnusson's heir. No one stands to benefit from her death more than you. So did you and your boyfriend come out here and kill her so you would get her house and her money?"

"There's money?" Her look challenged Roxanne across the table.

"Might be. Do we need to go and ask Leo Isbister what he was talking to you about?"

"I didn't have anything to do with her murder. Didn't even know she was dead until yesterday."

"How come? It's been all over the news, TV."

"Don't pay much attention to that stuff."

"So Leo told you?"

Mo's eyelids flickered. She sat up and hauled a booted foot up onto her chair. She was wearing a sleeveless tunic over a long-sleeved sweater and leggings under her coat.

"Can I take off my boots?"

"Not here." Roxanne tried to ignore the distraction. Mo was acting more like a teenager than a woman of twenty-nine. Was this arrested development? A reaction to stress? "Tell me about Leo. Sooner we're done, sooner you can go."

Mo put the foot down and stretched both legs out in front of her.

"I thought he might be my dad," she said.

"Leo?"

"Yeah, sure. Why not? Once I knew that Stella was my mom I tried to find out everything about her. Do you know she was once married to Freddie Santana? The filmmaker? Long time after she had me. He's not my dad. Anyway, I found out she was in this band, there's some old tapes of them on YouTube, and I figured out she must have known them round about the time she had me, and her and Leo, they looked like they had something going on, so I found out who he was and I showed up on his doorstep one night. Have you seen where he lives? On the riverbank? In Winnipeg? It's huge!"

"You went to his house?"

"Sure. Keenan drove me there and waited in the car. His wife didn't look very pleased to see me, but Leo was cool about it. Told me to come to his office the next morning. I really hoped he would be my dad but he isn't. How come you know he told me that she was dead?"

"Because he didn't know about it either until a couple of days ago. He was away in Costa Rica."

"He's got another house there. I've seen photos. I'd like to go there someday. And a cottage out here. Anyway, he phoned me yesterday, to tell me he was sorry about my mom. And Keenan and me, we talked about it and we figured we should come out here and tell you who I am, because you should know. So see, we did the right thing and what do we get for it? Shut up here in jail, being grilled by you, accused of murder."

Roxanne sat back. She might as well let Mo go for now. She had no grounds to hold her.

"Where are you going to be staying tonight, Mo? Do you have an address?"

"No. Ask Keenan. He's got friends out here. Want my phone number?"

"And your email. And your address in the city. Do you have a job?"

"I work in a pet store. I'll give you that address too. I've got a shift tomorrow night, it's late closing. Can I go now?"

"If we need to know more I'll be in touch." Roxanne stood up. Mo was already halfway to the door. She stopped and turned.

"Hey, you don't know a guy called Erik Axelsson, do you?"

"Yes," said Roxanne. "I do. He lives near here. Why do you ask?"

"Well," said Mo, "Leo told me yesterday that that's my dad's name. Erik Axelsson."

It didn't take long for Mo and Keenan to escape the office. They sauntered out to their old, once-red car, hand in hand.

"You gave her directions to Axelsson's farm?" Roxanne said to Sergeant Gilchrist as they watched them go.

"Sure, I did. Everybody around here knows where Erik lives. Someone else would have told them."

There was a burst of music, loud and metal, from upstairs. Izzy had found Stella and Leo's band on YouTube. Roxanne turned back from the window.

"So," said Gilchrist, "Erik was messing about with Stella Magnusson back when she was still in high school and Leo Isbister knew all about it?"

"That's the story. We'd better let Brian know. He's in the city. He can go talk to Isbister."

Kathy Isfeld glanced up from tabulating figures on a calculator. "Don't need to," she said, in her quiet, whispery voice. "You can catch him here tomorrow. He's got a meeting with the town planning committee tomorrow afternoon. Want me to get you an agenda? You could pick him up right after."

21

ROBERTA AXELSSON WAS furious. "Can you believe it? He and Stella had a baby? When she was still a kid? He must have been ten years older and he just walked away and left her to get on with it? That makes me sick."

They were in Roberta's kitchen. Margo went to fill the kettle. Sasha had called her as soon as she heard from Roberta. They had driven to the farm right away. An eviscerated chicken lay on the counter. Beside it was a bowl of chicken guts.

"How about I put this in the fridge?"

"I was going to stuff it and roast it. Sage and onion. His favourite. Can you believe it?" Roberta pulled a big pot out of a cupboard and filled it with water. "There was me thinking we might still get back together. He was getting well again, so quickly. He'd gone out to the barn, to clean it out." Manitoba sheep had to be wintered inside. "I thought I'd have him back to his old self in no time. That bringing him home had been the right thing to do. Fresh air, good homegrown food, you know? I killed that chicken myself." She dumped the carcass into the pot and lit the stove. "Now it's going to be soup."

"You'd forgiven him? For the affair with Stella?" Margo made herself busy looking for mugs and milk. Roberta was storming around her kitchen fetching onions, carrots, a knife in her hand. Sasha had parked herself safely behind the table.

"No," Roberta barked. She put down the knife, pulled a bandana off her head and rubbed it, blonde curls falling over her forehead. She had thought they might be able to get together again. Erik had paid dearly for his mistake, she said. He could have died. Maybe he'd learned his lesson. He'd never wandered before. Maybe they could work it out. Not now.

It was only an hour since everything had fallen apart. A small reddish car had chugged up the driveway. Roberta had had no idea who might be coming to call. Probably someone lost, she thought. Looking for directions. She'd been working on the chicken, had blood and grease all over her fingers. They needed scrubbing. The car had stopped by the time she had dried them. The couple that stepped out wore dark clothes, with big boots. They'd walked up the driveway, holding hands. The girl's hair was all spiky, white, purple and green. He had a scruffy beard and a black cap pulled down over his skull. They didn't look threatening but they did look strange. Goths, you know the type. Roberta had opened the inside door but kept the outside storm door locked to be on the safe side. Margo was relieved to see Roberta stop pacing. Now, she stood by the stove, the water in the pot gurgling behind her.

"She reminded me of someone right away but I couldn't figure out who. I asked if they were looking for someone. And she said, yeah, did someone called Erik Axelsson live here. She has these eyes, you know, just like Stella's, but there was all this black liner. And studs, along her eyebrows. I didn't get it right away. 'Oh yes,' I said. 'He's in the barn. How come you know Erik?' all innocent like."

The pot came to a boil. The lid rattled and steam spurted out of it.

"'You know Stella Magnusson?' she said to me. 'That woman that got killed? I'm her daughter. My name's Mo Penner but I think I'm gonna start calling myself Mo Magnusson.'

"And I knew. Instantly. That explained the likeness. Her hair's blonde at the roots, she's got the cheekbones and of course the eyes."

The pot boiled over. Water sizzled and spat on the hot plate. Margo gently moved Roberta aside. "Go sit down," she said, reaching for a cloth. "I'll deal with this."

"I just felt cold," Roberta said. She sank into a chair. "I told them to come into the house. I couldn't leave the two of them out there on the doorstep to freeze. I left them here and I went to the barn to find Erik. But first I asked her, this Mo woman, how old she was. She said she was twenty-nine. Doesn't look like it. She looks way younger. But Erik was living in Fiskar Bay thirty years ago. So was Stella. I knew exactly why she was here."

Margo put a mug of tea in front of her. She put a spoonful of honey in it and stirred. "Drink it," she said.

When she opened the barn door, Roberta continued, Erik had been pushing a wheelbarrow full of manure towards her. He'd smiled when he saw her, put down the barrow and stood tall to stretch his back, but his expression changed as he noticed that she was not smiling back. He was wearing a soft cap. The side of his head where they had operated was still covered with a bandage and the rest of his hair was cropped short. She'd trimmed it for him herself, the previous night.

"You have visitors," she had said, watching his face.

"I have?"

"A young woman called Mo and her boyfriend Keenan." He hadn't reacted to Mo's name.

"What do they want?" He'd pulled a rag from his pocket and was wiping his hands clean.

"I didn't ask. Didn't have to. She's twenty-nine years old and she looks like Stella Magnusson." His eyes had widened. There was a slackening of the jaw. "She says that Stella was her mother. Guess we both know why she wants to see you, Erik."

He had stepped towards her. She had stepped backwards.

"Don't come near me, Erik." Her teeth had clenched. The words came out like a hiss. She'd taken a breath before she spoke again. "They're waiting at the house. I'm going to go back there. I'll give her your truck keys. And you can go somewhere else to talk."

"But Roberta—"

"Don't 'but' me, Erik. You know what this is all about. You and Stella Magnusson, you go way back. Way, way back. You had a daughter with her? And you told me that you and Stella were just 'having a bit of a fling' like it was nothing serious? What kind of a fool do you take me for? For God's sake, Erik, I need you to get out of my life and never come back. We are over."

Then she had turned and walked out of the barn. She hadn't looked back. When she got inside, she'd reached into a bowl near the door and lifted out his keys. She'd pulled the house key off the ring.

"I was so calm," she told Margo and Sasha. "I knew exactly what to do."

She had found Mo and Keenan in the kitchen looking suspiciously at the chicken carcass and the bowl of bloody guts that lay beside it. She'd held out the truck keys.

"Here," she'd said. "Your dad's coming to meet you. Give him his keys, would you?" Mo didn't argue. She'd taken the keys and gone to the door.

"She said 'Sorry,' as she opened it. I told her it wasn't her fault."

Erik had already reached the path to the house. Roberta had watched from the kitchen window. He'd stopped in his tracks when he saw Mo. They stood looking at each other.

"He smiled all over his face when he saw her," said Roberta, sipping her tea, quiet now. "Like he recognized her. He could see Stella in her, probably. Mo handed Erik his keys and she and her boyfriend went to their car. Erik came back towards the house, but I beat him to the door. I told him he wasn't welcome. To go away and not come back. And I closed the outside door. Locked it."

He'd stared at her through a glass window frosted with ice, then turned and walked away. She'd watched until he got into his truck, backed it up and drove off after the little red car.

"I talked to Lizzie, my daughter," Roberta said. "She's taking the day off tomorrow." Today was Thursday. "She can stay all weekend and bring the kids. I'm going to be fine."

BRIAN DONOHUE HAD arrived from Winnipeg, eager to hear the latest developments and to interview Leo Isbister later that afternoon.

"He'll be done by three. I'll go sit in on the meeting and pick him up when he's finished."

"Kathy Isfeld says the room will be full," said Izzy. "You'd better get there early if you want a seat."

Roxanne was happy to pass on the meeting. She had been around small prairie towns long enough to know that these could go on longer than expected, and this one was going to be contentious. Many local tradespeople would welcome a new development and the jobs it would bring. New buildings meant more revenue for the town. But the project involved draining some of the wetlands and the environmental lobby would be out in full force to defend the health of the lake, which relied on the wetlands to filter the water that fed it.

On the other hand, Roxanne had made the first contact with Leo Isbister. She'd been keen to continue that line of investigation herself. Now that it was happening on her turf, she wanted back in on that interview.

"I've got questions I'd like to ask him," she said, looking up from her laptop.

Brian glanced up at her. "Email them to me," he said, "and I'll ask him."

So he didn't want her sitting in on the interview? What was that about? Did he want to take the credit for the Isbister lead for himself and cut her out of that part of the investigation? So much for teamwork and collaboration. He really was ambitious. Getting something on Isbister would probably score him points with their bosses. It could help him get that promotion he wanted. Izzy cut across her line of thinking.

"Hey," she said from the window. "Mo Penner and the Keenan guy just drove up beside the Timmie's. And Erik Axelsson's right behind them in his truck."

"Really?" Roxanne crossed over to look. Matt was close behind. "When did he get out of the hospital? Shouldn't he still be recovering?" They watched Erik swing out of the truck and follow Mo and Keenan into the shop.

"It looks like there's nothing wrong with him," said Matt.

Izzy had pulled out her phone. "Bet he's back at Roberta's. I'll call my mom. She'll know."

"Would he have known he had a daughter before this?" asked Brian.

"He must have," said Roxanne. "He'd have known there was a baby, anyway, even if Stella didn't acknowledge him as the father."

Izzy ended her call. "Roberta brought him home yesterday. He's living back at the farm. Roberta must be so pissed off if she knows about Mo."

"Could Roberta have known about her before this and killed Stella?" asked Brian. "Does she have an alibi for the time of the murder?"

Izzy looked dismayed. She really didn't want Roberta to be guilty, but this time she didn't protest.

"I'll go and ask her," said Roxanne. Brian Donohue still sat at the table working on his own computer. She was glad to have a reason to get out of the office. "And, Matt, go down there and keep an eye on the coffee shop. Bring Erik in here when he's done talking. Hold him until I get back."

"I can interview him," said Brian.

"It's okay. You don't want to be late for that meeting." Roxanne smiled sweetly, then followed Matt to the stairs. "You take care of Isbister and I'll deal with this."

ROBERTA AXELSSON LOOKED frustrated when she saw Roxanne on her doorstep. Her face was red and her hair was dishevelled but she appeared more annoyed than upset.

"What are you here for?" She stood in the half-open doorway.

"Can I come in?"

"Erik's not here," said Roberta. "It's him you want to talk to, right?"

"No. It's you."

"Oh, great. Come on in then." She opened the door wide and walked down the hallway. "Hang up your coat and help yourself to a pair of slippers," she called behind her. "I suppose I'd better make more tea."

Roxanne looked at the basket of hand-knitted slippers. They were not her style, but she thought she'd better comply. She chose the least bright pair and padded into the kitchen. A pot bubbled on the stove. It smelled like chicken soup.

"If you're here to tell me about Erik's misbegotten daughter, you're too late. She's been here already." Roberta reached for the teapot. "What do you take in your tea?"

"Black's good. You didn't know about her?"

"Me? No. Last to know. Isn't that always the case? Have a seat. Do you like goat cheese?"

She reached into the fridge, brought out a bowl and indicated a chair at the table.

"You didn't know that he was involved with Stella Magnusson years ago? When they first knew each other?"

"No, how would I?" She bustled around the kitchen, put bread on the table and sliced it up. Roxanne watched how expertly she wielded the bread knife. "Some people go off their food when bad stuff happens. Not me. I just get hungry. Eat up, Corporal."

She slathered butter on a slice of bread, put it on a plate and added a large spoonful of creamy white cheese. "I just made that yesterday." It wasn't what Roxanne ought to be eating, but she reached for the plate. A friendly chat at the kitchen table might yield results.

"She must have just been a kid," Roberta continued. "What was he thinking of? And he gets her pregnant and then what? He doesn't marry her, does he? She has to go away and have the baby by herself and get it adopted. Poor Stella. I never thought I'd ever say that." She bit into a mouthful of bread and cheese.

"She put the baby up for adoption. Then she was able to get on with the rest of her life."

"No thanks to Erik." Roberta's mouth was still full of food. "You know what, Corporal? He's just plain useless. I've kicked him out. Again. This time it's for good. I don't want to have anything more to do with him. I'm getting a divorce."

"When did you find out about Mo?"

"She came here, looking for him. Her and the boyfriend. God, she looks like Stella."

"Where will Erik go? Does he have any other family? In Winnipeg?"

"Sure. He has a couple of kids, both grown. But they won't have anything to do with him. He treated their mother badly. Real bad. Drank too much back then. You know what, I'll bet he married her on the rebound from Stella."

"He was drinking when he met you?"

"He went to AA. He's been going ever since and he's been okay. Stayed off it all these years."

"And you two always got along?"

"I thought so. Stupid me. He must have been mad about Stella the whole time. His other wife and me, we were just second best." Her face drooped but then she held her head back up. "So we're done, me and Erik Axelsson. Too handsome for his own good, that's Erik, Corporal. He gets away with murder, that's his problem." She put her hand over her mouth. "Never said that, did I?"

Roxanne had no doubt that Roberta Axelsson was telling what she believed to be the truth. Mo's existence had been a surprise to her.

"What will you do now?" she asked. "We're going to need to know where you are for the time being."

"We'll have to sell this place, but meantime I'm staying put. I'm not letting him move back in."

"You're going to be here alone?" Roxanne wondered how safe that was, if Erik got drunk again.

"No. My daughter Lizzie's coming out, soon as she's finished work. She's staying all weekend. Bringing the grandkids." So she'd have company for now. "Mike Little is Erik's best friend. If you're looking for him, he'll probably know where he is."

Roxanne took her leave. "The bread and cheese was delicious," she said. It was. It had reminded her of being at her grandmother's farm when she was little. She took out a card and gave it to Roberta. "My cellphone number is on this," she said. "You need me, you call, right away." It wouldn't hurt to be on the safe side. Roberta had come to the door with her and was pulling on a jacket.

"I'm going to go talk to my goats," she said as she stomped off towards the barn. Roxanne checked her phone before she drove away. There was a text from Brian.

LEO ISBISTER AT TIM HORTONS. WILL CHECK.

She drove back to Fiskar Bay, fast.

22

ROXANNE ARRIVED IN time to see Mo Magnusson and her boyfriend, Keenan, leaving the coffee shop. Their rusty Fiesta was parked at the roadside. Roxanne pulled up right in front of it.

"Hey, you looking for my dad too? You missed him." Mo flashed a silver-studded grin as she opened the passenger door. "Can you move your car out of the way? I've got to get to get to Winnipeg in time for work."

Roxanne looked past her. She could see Brian Donohue and Matt Stavros crossing the parking lot. So they'd lost track of Erik Axelsson? Both of them avoided looking at her as they walked briskly towards the RCMP building. She got back into her car and pulled it forward so Mo and Keenan could drive out. Mo gave her a cheery wave as she passed. Roxanne caught up to Brian and Matt upstairs in their office. Matt appeared sheepish but Brian was unapologetic.

"Hey, it happens," he said. "He went out the back door, to go to the bank. We came in the other way."

The bank was across the street. Roxanne noticed Izzy reach for her phone. Calling Roberta? How much money could Erik Axelsson access?

"Isbister had shown up and Erik took off right away," Matt added, trying to placate her. "At least that's what Mo says. Didn't want to spend time with him."

Roxanne was not going to be appeased. "So why did both of you have to go into the coffee shop?"

"Isbister and Axelsson were both there. My decision," Brian said, dismissively authoritarian. He sounded annoyed. That was fine by her. She was thoroughly pissed off. And she had thought he was attractive?

"Except Axelsson wasn't yours. He was mine. Why didn't one of you keep an eye on the truck? Matt, I told you to watch out for him."

"Bad timing," Brian answered instead. "Axelsson must have got to his truck while we went into the shop for coffee. We were looking the other way."

"So he's gone. And now he's out there with cash in his pocket."

Izzy got up and reached for her parka. "He could have gone to Mike Little's. I know where he lives. Hey, Matt. Let's go find him. We'll check the bars if he's not there."

They disappeared off down the stairs, leaving Roxanne and Brian alone. The phone rang. It was Roberta, calling back. Erik had emptied most of their joint account. He'd walked off with almost a couple of thousand bucks.

"Did you not think, Roberta? Couldn't you have transferred some into your own account?"

"Don't have one."

"You shouldn't be out there alone."

"Lizzie took the afternoon off. She'll be here soon. Not to worry, I know how to handle Erik."

"Lock your doors, Roberta."

"Okay, okay. I'll be fine." She hung up.

Brian was leaning against a wall, arms folded. "So he's out there drowning his sorrows with a buddy. Nothing illegal about that."

"He's recovering from a head injury and he gets violent when he's drunk."

"So, tell Gilchrist. He can handle it. It's not our problem, is it? We've got a murder to solve. Why are you wasting time on a small-town drunk that we know has an alibi? Did the wife have anything to do with it?"

"No. I don't think so."

"Well then. And there's Angus Smith. Did they even know him? They don't live near Cullen Village. Erik Axelsson has nothing to do with the murders. This line of investigation is dead. Give it up. I'm going to go and get some lunch before this planning committee meeting."

That was her told. He was team commander, after all. That was an oxymoron. All command and no questions asked. So much for teamwork. He turned on his heel to leave. She spoke to his back.

"I want in on that interview," she said. "Sir." If he wanted protocol, he could have it. "If I'm the investigator on this case, I need to know what Isbister has to say."

"No problem." Suddenly the hostility evaporated. He relaxed, actually smiled, back to his good-looking self. "Come along to the meeting if you like. I'll buy you lunch first."

"That's okay," she said, refusing to be charmed. She needed to skip lunch anyway, after what she'd eaten at Roberta's. "I'll be here when you bring Isbister back for questioning."

Once he was gone, she looked at the whiteboard on the wall. Brian was right that this was a dead end, but so many leads in this case were. The Andreychuks, George Smedley, they all led nowhere. Isbister was interesting. He might know something about Stella Magnusson's money, but he'd been out of the country at the time of the murder. It was another watertight alibi. She sat and stared at the board, running different scenarios in her head. Something was missing, some vital bit of the puzzle. She couldn't figure out what it might be.

KATHY ISFELD EXCUSED herself from her desk at 1:45 precisely. She returned an hour later. The meeting that was predicted to take all afternoon had lasted exactly twenty-two minutes. The lake support group had been out in full force, with placards and photographs that described how the new development would damage the lake's ecosystem. They'd packed the seats in the chamber. She'd seen Sergeant Donohue there, sitting in the back row. She'd found a space just in front of him. She didn't think he'd recognized her out of the office.

Leo Isbister had been introduced. Everyone waited to hear his pitch. He didn't deliver. He agreed with the ecologists, he said. They should protect the wetlands. He wanted them to know that he was a progressive developer, one who listened to the community's concerns, who took the needs of all stakeholders into account. And in this case, he had decided that Isbister Homes should withdraw its application for development and respect the natural habitat. He hoped they would be able to do business at some point in the future, but as of now he had no plans for development in the area. He thanked them for their attention.

"All the lake supporters cheered," said Kathy in her tiny voice. "It was quite exciting. A lot of the guys who have businesses around town aren't too pleased. You could tell by the looks on their faces."

"Guess they'll be over here real soon then," said Sergeant Gilchrist. "Him and Sergeant Donohue."

"Here?" Kathy had taken up her usual position at her computer. "They're not coming here. They've gone to the hotel."

"What?" Roxanne couldn't believe it. She reached for her phone. There was nothing from Brian. A text from Izzy said that Erik Axelsson had been at Mike Little's house earlier but Alice, Mike's wife, had insisted he leave. She and Matt were checking the bars. No luck so far.

"Leo Isbister's lawyer spoke to Sergeant Donohue after the meeting," Kathy whispered. "I was standing right there. He asked him to meet them in the lounge at the hotel at three."

It took Roxanne ten minutes to get out of the building, into her car and down to the hotel. She found Leo Isbister comfortably ensconced in an armchair beside a blazing log fire, a bowl of nuts on the table in front of him. He'd ordered whisky. The hotel's selection of malts was limited. Glenlivet would have to do. Brian sat on one side of him and on the other was a man wearing an impeccable tan-coloured suit, a pale yellow shirt with a lilac tie. His soft leather briefcase sat on the table in front of him. Any surprise they had at seeing her was quickly suppressed, especially by Brian.

"Well, well, the gang's all here," said Leo. He introduced the third man as Ivan Gregory, his lawyer. Of course he was. Sleek and foxy. "Have anything you like, Corporal. Ivan's sticking to a soda. He's driving. And your buddy here's having a Coke, since he's on duty. I guess you are too."

Leo sniffed the malt and sipped it, looking smug. A server hovered. Roxanne ordered a mineral water. Gregory searched his briefcase for some papers and looked at them over the top of gold-rimmed reading glasses.

"I act on behalf of Mr. Isbister and his company, but Ms. Stella Magnusson was also a client." Gregory laid an envelope on the table. "She invested in a real estate company. Central Holdings. They own rental properties around the city. These papers will provide you with the details."

Brian opened the envelope, glanced at the contents and passed them to Roxanne. A bottom-line figure of just over $1,685,000 jumped out at her.

"Central Holdings is a subsidiary of Isbister Homes?" Brian asked.

"No, Sergeant. Definitely not. It's a separate enterprise. Mr. Isbister's finances in no way connect to those of Ms. Magnusson."

Roxanne's drink appeared at her elbow. "So she was using this company to launder money?" Was that why the bosses in Winnipeg were so interested in Isbister? Was Brian involved in a related investigation?

"All our dealings with Ms. Magnusson were legitimate," said the lawyer.

"See," Leo drawled from the depths of his armchair, "Stella had money when she came back from the States, from when she was married to Freddie Santana. Divorce settlement and some other stuff. She used some to fix up the house. And she asked me where she could put the rest. I sent her to Ivan here."

"Her investment paid off," the lawyer added. "She did well from it. It's built up over the years."

"And she added to it?"

"She did. When she could." Leo swirled the amber liquid around in his glass. "Stella had a head for business. Smart girl."

"So why is there no will?" Roxanne asked.

"Ah, but there is." Ivan Gregory produced another envelope, Houdini-like. He slid it across the table. "Your copy. She left the bulk of her estate to her daughter, Ariel Star Magnusson, a.k.a. Maureen Penner. There's a small bequest to Mr. Isbister here, for all his help. That's all. It's very clear. I am her executor."

Again, the document was passed from one to the other. It was dated over nine years earlier. The witnesses were a legal assistant and another lawyer from Ivan Gregory's firm.

"Stella got a letter from Mo about ten years back," Leo explained. "Didn't want to get involved with her, but she did take an interest. She asked me to keep an eye open for the kid. So I did." He looked pleased with himself.

That didn't mesh with Mo's story, Roxanne thought. Which of them was lying? "You know we've been looking for this?" she said.

Both men smiled at her, one showing his teeth, the other tight-lipped.

"We thought we'd wait until you found the murderer," said Leo. "Didn't want to get mixed up in that. Taking your time, aren't you?"

"And we didn't want suspicion falling on Maureen. She doesn't need that," Ivan Gregory said smoothly.

"Very thoughtful of you." Brian pocketed the copy of the will. "You'll know where Stella Magnusson did her personal banking, then?"

"I don't," said Leo. "But Ivan does."

Stella had used a credit union. Ivan gave them the address. The original documents were in a safety deposit box. Had they found the key? They hadn't.

"Well, you'll just have to search a little harder, won't you," said Leo. Then he leaned forward, put down his empty glass and smiled like he was having fun. "Relax. Ivan has access. We're here to help."

Ivan Gregory closed his briefcase with a snap. "My card." The lawyer passed them each one.

"The lady's got mine already," said Leo breezily, and they were gone.

"So that answers some questions," said Brian. "Took their time telling us. I need to get straight back to Winnipeg."

Roxanne's phone had vibrated ten minutes earlier. Izzy had sent a text. EA BOUGHT VODKA. PAID CASH. Not good news. Roxanne called her. Erik had dropped into the liquor mart two hours earlier. He could be anywhere, drowning his sorrows.

Roxanne stepped into her car and watched Brian drive off in his. Her running gear was in the trunk. It was late afternoon, and the knitters and quilters at Sprucewood Hall would have gone home. People ate early in this part of the world. Supper was often at five. Soon she was there, running circuits. She had the track to herself. She'd get some laps in, clear her head, and try to figure out what was eluding her. Even with this new information, something was still missing.

ROXANNE WAS DRIVING back from Sprucewood when her phone rang. Roberta Axelsson sounded scared.

"He's coming up the driveway. It's got to be him. He's driving fast."

"Don't let him in. We're on our way."

Roxanne put out an all-car alert as she drove, lights flashing, to the farm. She didn't have far to go. She pulled into the driveway to see Axelsson's truck skewed in the middle of the parking space in front of the house, the driver's door hanging open. The door to the house was also open.

She pulled up alongside the truck. From the car door, she saw Erik Axelsson back out of the house. He turned his head and saw her.

"She's got a gun! She's crazy!"

He stepped backwards onto the step, holding his hands up. Then he backed down another step. A younger version of Roberta Axelsson appeared in the doorway. She was holding a shotgun.

Roxanne reached for her own weapon. She could hear a siren in the distance. And another.

"Put down the gun, ma'am!" she called. She stayed by the car.

"Tell him to back up," the woman called to her. She was pointing the gun straight at Axelsson. "You, back up!" She took a step towards him. He took two more steps back and reached the ground.

"You need to drop that gun, right now!" Roxanne shouted. She'd moved closer, into the cover of Axelsson's truck.

"That's my house!" Axelsson was flailing his arms in the air, shifting drunkenly from one foot to the other. The cap on his head had fallen to one side. It didn't quite cover the bandage on one side of his head. "It's mine! She can't lock me out!"

"Get back!" The woman in the doorway stayed where she was.

"Walk backwards, Erik! Walk back towards me!" Roxanne shouted. The sirens were coming closer. Erik turned to face Roxanne.

"She's mad, just like her mother!" He lurched in Roxanne's direction, away from the house. The woman on the step lowered the gun.

"Let's talk about this, Erik." Roxanne stepped out from the shelter of the truck. "Ma'am, put that gun down!" she called again. Roberta's daughter, Lizzie, propped the gun against the doorjamb. Roxanne put away her weapon.

"He kicked the door in," Lizzie called to Roxanne. "He hit my mom."

Erik turned, ran for the door, jumped up the steps and grabbed for the shotgun. Roxanne raced towards him. When she tackled him, he had raised the butt of the gun above his head, ready to hit Lizzie.

He fell sideways off the step into the snow. Roxanne landed on top of him and twisted his arms behind his back. The cap had come off. His face appeared gaunt without the hair.

"Don't move," she said. The yard was illuminated by red flashing lights. Matt ran to her side. "Cuff him."

Izzy had picked up the shotgun. She cracked it open. It wasn't loaded. Matt and Sam Mendes got Axelsson to a police car. The door to the house was hanging off its hinges.

Roxanne walked into the kitchen. Roberta was sitting on the floor, leaning against a counter, a child in her arms. Her left eye was red and swelling. Her daughter was soothing a crying baby.

"I've never seen him like that, Corporal. He was like a madman. He was yelling that he was going to kill me."

Roxanne turned to the daughter. "You heard him say that?" Lizzie nodded her head in agreement. Matt walked into the room.

"We've got him in the back of the car," he said. "We'll charge him with assault. Lock him up for the night. You'll have to wait until he's sober to interview him."

"Get him for unlawful entry as well. Driving under the influence. Uttering threats. We need to get this woman to the hospital to get that eye checked."

23

"HEY, CORPORAL!" SERGEANT Gilchrist beamed approval when Roxanne arrived at work next morning. "Hear you took Axelsson out at the knees. Rugby, eh? You never told us."

"How come you know about that, Sarge?"

"Roberta Axelsson's daughter's been on Facebook. And Twitter. Posted a photo of you and your team. Izzy showed us."

Roxanne hadn't played since she left the University of Regina more than twelve years ago. How had Lizzie tracked that one down?

Kathy Isfeld looked up at her over the top of her glasses. "Breakfast TV wants to know if you can be in Winnipeg at seven tomorrow for an interview," she said. "And some woman from CBC News is trying to get hold of you." She appeared quite excited, for Kathy. She was almost pink.

Izzy trotted downstairs, her laptop open on her arm. "Have you seen this?"

Roxanne looked at a rugby team lineup, years ago. She'd weighed more then. She barely recognized herself. The comment read: "A shout out to Corporal Roxanne Calloway of the RCMP who single-handedly stopped my maniac of a stepfather from killing me and my mother last night. He's a major suspect for the murder of Stella Magnusson. Hope they lock him up for good."

The phone rang. Kathy Isfeld picked it up. "Who? The *Free Press*? Give me your number. I'll tell her you called."

"Oh," said Roxanne. She had no idea how to handle this.

"Hey, you're famous!" Izzy closed the laptop. "Maybe I should take up kickboxing."

Gilchrist grinned at her. "Think you're tough enough already, young lady."

Izzy made to punch him. He dodged it. This is still what it takes, Roxanne thought. Beat up on a guy and you'll win their respect.

"How's Axelsson?"

"Hung-over but he'll be okay for questioning."

They had all worked into the evening the previous night. Roxanne had waited at the hospital to get a statement. Roberta had double vision in her eye, but they thought it would clear. She had applied for a restraining order. A carpenter had shown up later in the evening to fix the front door of her house. Then there had been a report to write. Roxanne wanted to make sure that her version of the story was in to HQ before any other. Brian had instructed her to drop the Axelsson lead. It could look like she'd ignored that order. But she hadn't. She'd responded to a call for help. By the time she'd sent the report off, it was too late to call her son and wish him goodnight. She felt bad about that. She'd gone straight to bed.

Matt Stavros shouted from upstairs. "Lizzie Maxwell's on CBC radio." He leaned over the banister, holding out his phone so they could hear.

"He's a crazy drunk," they heard Lizzie say. "Came flying at me. He was going to hit me over the head with the butt of a gun but the corporal, she ran real fast and jumped him, just in time. Knocked him right off the step, gun and all. He said he would kill my mother. I think he would have killed me too."

"So Corporal Calloway saved your life?"

"For sure. Well, I might not have died but I'd have been injured, real bad. She was great. And she took my mom to the hospital after. She deserves a medal."

"A dramatic rescue by an RCMP officer at Fiskar Bay last night. We'll continue to track this story." The news reporter signed off. Roxanne looked around at the smiling faces. She felt embarrassed.

"How about we talk to Erik Axelsson together, Sarge?" she said to Gilchrist. "And if anyone else calls from the media, I'm not available."

ERIK WAS SLUMPED in his chair, grey-faced, his head sunk between his shoulders. The bandage covered a large patch of his skull above his ear. The rest of his hair was cropped short. It was mostly grey. He looked almost ordinary. Gilchrist turned on the recorder. Axelsson raised bloodshot eyes.

"It's not break-and-enter when it's your own house!"

"Assault, Erik." Gilchrist took the seat opposite him. "You hit your wife hard enough to give her double vision. She's getting a restraining order. It's her house, too, and right now she's living there. You won't be going back there for a while. Get used to the idea."

Roxanne took the seat beside Gilchrist. The look she got from Erik was baleful.

"I'd had a drink. I don't remember," he muttered. Then he went silent and clenched his hands.

"You were going to hit your stepdaughter with the butt of a gun. You'd have got her head. You would have knocked her out cold."

"I didn't hit her."

"Because the corporal here stopped you. You can't deny it, Erik. We've got three witnesses."

Axelsson sat up straight, trying to focus his bleary eyes.

"So that's it then? What are you asking me all this stuff for if you know already?"

"You threatened to kill your wife," Roxanne said.

"Did not."

"Is that what happened with Stella?" She fired the question back, in no mood to play games.

"What do you mean? I didn't kill Stella!"

"Really? She was hit across the head with a blunt instrument. You punched your wife in the head last night. You swung at your stepdaughter's head with a gun butt. It's a bit of a coincidence, isn't it? Do you always aim for women's heads when you get mad at them? Is that how you killed her?" Roxanne watched him glance from one corner of the room to the other, as if he was trapped.

"It isn't! I didn't!"

"Did you drink some wine together? You and Stella?"

Erik's gaze shifted towards her, his brows lowered.

"Did you get into an argument?"

His lips compressed. He wasn't saying anything.

"Did you get angry and then hit her? What did you use? The poker?"

"I've got an alibi!" he shouted and sprung to his feet. "You know that!"

Gilchrist rose and faced him. "Easy, Erik!"

Axelsson sank back down into his chair.

"I'm not sure you do have an alibi," Roxanne said. She leaned back in her chair and spoke quietly. "Sure, you fixed a car the day Stella died. And you picked up some parts from the garage. But that was at lunchtime, right? You could have been finished earlier than five. You could have had a couple of hours to go and visit Stella. Did you ask the guy whose car you fixed to say you worked until five that day? Do we need to go and talk to him about what happens to people who commit perjury?"

"I didn't kill Stella! I couldn't hurt Stella!" He slumped again. His head sagged. "Stella was different."

"How was she different?"

"She just was." He folded his long frame back into the chair.

"Her body was cut up after she died. Who helped you do that?"

He exploded up onto his feet, leaned across the table and yelled at Roxanne. "Me? Cut her up? That's crazy. You're crazy."

Roxanne didn't move. "You've said that before. You say we're all crazy, Erik. Your wife. Your stepdaughter. Now me? I'll tell you what's crazy, Erik. It's taking Stella Magnusson's frozen body to Angus Smith's workshop and cutting it into pieces, then putting it into garbage bags and leaving it out to be picked up and taken to the dump."

"Christ, no!" He sat down again, his back straight, glaring at Roxanne.

"After that you went back, didn't you? You killed old Angus Smith. Then you took his body out to his ice shack and sunk him in the lake."

"I did no such thing! I never knew this Angus Smith guy! He had an ice shack? How would I know that? I never met the guy. I know nothing about him."

"Don't give me that. Angus liked a drink. You and Mike Little, you play the bars. I think you knew Angus Smith. Angus liked to talk when he'd had a beer or two. About fishing. About his workshop."

"Look, lady." Erik's tone changed. Weariness replaced combativeness. "Stop trying to pin this on me. I never knew any Angus Smith. I didn't kill him and I didn't kill Stella. And I'm not saying anything else." He turned to Gilchrist. "I get a phone call, right? I want to call my daughter, Mo. She'll get someone to take care of this. I need a lawyer."

Gilchrist reached out to stop the recorder. He hesitated. He glanced at Roxanne and then back at Erik. "That girl's got the money to pay for a lawyer for you, Erik?"

"Leo Isbister's going to make sure she gets Stella's money," Erik replied.

"What do you know about Stella's money?" Roxanne interjected.

"Hell, I dunno. That's all Mo said when Leo came into the coffee shop yesterday. 'This is Leo, remember him, he used to know my mom too. He's going to make sure I get all my mom's money.'"

"Did she say anything about a will?" Roxanne asked.

"No. What will? Doesn't matter. She'll get the house and all Stella's stuff, right? There's nobody else that Stella could leave it to."

"How about you, Erik? Did you think Stella would leave something to you?"

"Nah. Not me. Wasn't like that with me and Stella." He drooped in his chair again.

For once, Roxanne felt almost sorry for him. Gilchrist walked around the table and helped him to his feet.

"Let's get you back to the cell, Erik, then we'll get that phone call set up for you." He stopped before they reached the door. "If I was Mo Penner's dad and I really wanted to help her—and you, Erik—I'd tell her to find herself a decent lawyer. Right away. One that works for her, not for Leo Isbister. Okay?"

Erik blinked. He looked puzzled. "Sure. Okay. I'll tell her."

Roxanne said nothing as she walked back to the upstairs office. She sat down at the table, deep in thought.

"I'm going for coffee," said Izzy.

Roxanne looked up, reached for her bag and pulled out a wallet. "I'll buy. Get us some muffins. A bran one for me."

"Got an appetite now you're famous, ma'am?" All Izzy got in reply was a raised eyebrow. She hurried for the door. "I'll be right back. You want to check your emails."

Roxanne had lots of mail. A staff sergeant in charge of communications wanted her to refer all media questions to him. That suited her just fine. There was one from her sister.

"That was you they're talking about on the news? I told Finn. He's so excited." He'd be at nursery school right now. She would have to catch him tonight on FaceTime.

Her supervising inspector sent congratulations. That was good. He'd got her report, then. There was nothing from Brian Donohue.

Bill Gilchrist had returned from the cell unit and clattered upstairs. "You sure went for Axelsson," he said. "You don't still think he's the murderer, do you?"

"No," she said. "But he's given me an idea."

Izzy appeared with muffins. Gilchrist parked himself at the table and reached for the bag. "What's all this about money and a will?" he asked. They didn't know about yesterday's interview with Leo Isbister. She filled them in.

"Stella had money. A lot of it. More than a million plus the house and everything in it."

"Wonder how long it'll take that Mo kid to get through that," said Gilchrist.

Roxanne thought for a moment, then said to Izzy: "Can you call her? Tell her we've got the keys to her mother's house and we'll get the car to her as soon as she wants. The sergeant here told Erik to let her know she should get herself a decent lawyer. Make sure she knows that."

Sometimes it didn't hurt to do someone a favour. If she hadn't given Roberta her phone number, last night's assault could have ended very differently. They wouldn't have got there in time and someone would have been hurt. Badly. Being nice to Mo Penner wouldn't hurt.

The sergeant lumbered off back downstairs. Now she could chase up a new lead on the Magnusson case.

"We've been coming at this from the wrong angle," she said to Matt and Izzy. "We've been focussed on looking for Stella's killer. And that gives us too many options." She sipped her coffee. "Stella's life was complicated. Some people loved her, like Erik Axelsson, or admired her, like the Smedleys. Other people couldn't stand her. There are plenty of them. We keep bouncing from one lead to another and so far they've all led us nowhere. But if we concentrate on Angus Smith's killer instead, it's all much simpler." She noticed that she had their attention. They were listening closely. "It came to me when we were interviewing Erik. He can't be Stella's killer because he didn't kill Angus. He knew nothing about Angus. Whoever killed Angus knew where he lived, knew the setup of the workshop."

Matt sat bolt upright. "Knew where to find the key. And that he was away around the time Stella was killed."

"Knew that he was an ice fisherman," added Roxanne.

"And knew which shack was his," said Matt.

"There's a lot of people at Cullen that knew all that." Izzy sounded dubious.

"Yes," Roxanne continued. "But how many of the guys who did woodwork with Angus and who fished also knew Stella?"

"That takes us back to Bradley Andreychuk," said Matt.

"Maybe he didn't know about the workshop." Izzy looked at him across the table.

"He might. He and Angus drank in the same bars."

"But he wouldn't know where to find the key."

"Unless someone told him. We can check it out." Roxanne ended the discussion. She was on the right track. She knew now where she needed to start looking.

24

THE TABLE AT Margo's house was set for lunch. Panda had made moussaka and Annie had stir-fried chicken and vegetables. Sasha had shredded carrots and beets into a red and orange slaw. Phyllis had baked a lemon mousse cake and Margo had bought a crusty French loaf.

"See," Sasha crowed, "It always works." They never planned who would bring what to a potluck lunch but they always ended up with an acceptable mix of food. "Did you hear on the radio? Erik Axelsson went after them with a gun."

"He was going to shoot Roberta?" Phyllis asked.

"Sounds like it. They interviewed Lizzie, Roberta's daughter. She said that the woman cop stopped him just in time. They'll have to lock him up now, won't they?"

"When's Roberta coming?" Margo had asked them to come early so they would all be there to welcome Roberta. It also gave them a chance to catch up on new developments before she arrived.

"One. Not long now. Lizzie is dropping her off."

"She can't drive herself?"

"Erik hit her in the eye."

"She can't take him back after this. He's dangerous." Sasha flopped into her favourite seat, with her back to the window.

"Who knows," said Panda. "We didn't think she'd bring him back home last time."

"Yes." Annie put a bowl on the table. "But he's never threatened her before. It's too bad. He's stayed off the drink for years. He needs to get sober again."

"Do you think so? He got Stella pregnant years ago and did nothing about it. Then he got together with her again while he was married to Roberta. And then he gets drunk and tries to kill her? If I was her I'd run for my life," said Sasha. Margo agreed with her.

"You're not Roberta," said Annie. A knock at the door interrupted them. Roberta herself was standing on the doorstep. Her daughter was driving away.

"Lizzie doesn't want to stay for lunch?" Margo asked, being polite, but they did want to have Roberta to themselves.

"She's gone grocery shopping. She'll pick me up later. And I need a break already." Roberta was pulling off a hat and coat as she spoke. A wad of gauze and a plastic eye shield covered her eye. "She is so bossy! I could have driven here myself. My other eye's just fine."

"That one's turning purple already," said Sasha. "He must have hit you real hard."

"Is it true he tried to shoot you?" asked Phyllis.

"No. Who said he did?" Roberta planted herself in a large chair at the end of the table. "Lizzie threatened him with the shotgun but she was just trying to scare him off. It wasn't loaded. Hey, the cops have got him locked up and I'm done with him. What's for lunch?"

They took the hint and found their places around the table.

"So," said Sasha. "You met the kid? What's she like?"

"Stella gone Goth." Roberta grinned at them. The patch made her look like a pirate, even if it was white, not black. "Studs, black gear, spiked hair. Calls herself Mo. I suppose she'll get Stella's place."

"Is she artsy? She could keep StarFest going. Just a different kind of music, right? Really loud. The Andreychuks next door would really love that." Panda laughed. "Pass me that coleslaw, would you?"

Phyllis looked up from buttering a slice of bread. "There's money too, though, isn't there? Don't the police think Stella was stealing money from StarFest? That's why they were after George. They thought he'd found out about it and was blackmailing her."

"You knew she was altering the accounts, too, didn't you, Panda?" said Margo.

Panda stared at her, a fork of food halfway to her mouth. "Not really," she replied. "And I wasn't blackmailing her, either."

Margo was surprised at the edge to her voice. For a second, no one spoke. That wasn't funny.

"Nobody here knew that Stella had a baby?" Annie's voice broke the silence. She was sitting beside Panda, as usual. Sometimes Panda polished off everything on her plate and then finished Annie's as well.

"No. It had to be years ago." Sasha reached across the table for another spoonful of stir-fry.

"Almost thirty," said Roberta. She was eating like she hadn't seen food in months.

"Mo was born in Brandon. Stella must have had her right after high school. She was still just a kid."

"Why Brandon?" Sasha continued. "This stuff is really great, Annie. Hey, you grew up in Virden, right? That's near Brandon. You must know the place?"

"No. Not much." Annie wore a blank expression. There was another moment's silence, broken this time by Panda.

"She had to stay home and make wontons. Right, Annie?"

Annie brightened up. "That's right. Me and my mom hardly ever got to go. My dad did the shopping trips by himself."

Panda looked around the table. "What are you going to do now, Roberta?" They were all dying to know.

"I'm staying put for now."

"Can you manage out there by yourself?" Margo stood and picked up the empty teapot.

"A guy who keeps sheep called me this morning. He's maybe going to buy the flock. I can manage the chickens and goats for a while and I make some egg money. That'll give me enough cash to get me by for now. Do you know what that jerk, Erik, did? He went to the bank and cleaned out our account. He didn't even leave me half. So I guess he really doesn't care one bit about what happens to me. Lizzie says I'll get half the value of the farm. It'll have to be sold."

"Will you move back to the city?"

"Dunno. Don't want to. Lizzie is dying to put me into a 55-plus high-rise near where she lives. She just wants an unpaid babysitter, if you ask me." She stared out the window, at the vast expanse of the lake. "I can't buy Erik out or keep the farm going by myself. But can you see me living in an apartment in Winnipeg? After living out here?"

Phyllis got up. "Time for cake!" she said cheerfully. She fetched it and began to cut it up.

ROXANNE PULLED IN beside Archie Huminski's shack at the dump. There was no sign of Archie, but smoke rose straight up from the shack's tall, metal chimney and a dirty old truck was coming down the hill towards her, belching ice fog from its exhaust. More smoke puffed above the area where wood and lumber were stored. Archie must be burning it off. Another vehicle was parked where old electronic equipment was stashed. The truck stopped, a window was rolled down, a short conversation ensued, then Archie cruised towards her. She got out of her car. Archie climbed out of the truck to meet her.

"Ah, milady. Get yourself in out of this cold." Inside the shack, the wood stove burned. Archie indicated a chair at the worn, wooden table. The kettle sat on top of the stove. He took two mugs from a shelf and a bowl of sugar.

"Got no milk but I've got cookies." He opened his usual tin and put teabags in the mugs, then topped them up with hot water. "So you came to visit after all."

"I did."

He put down a mug for her and one for himself. "Bad business about that Axelsson guy. Hear you got him real good, though."

"Something like that," she said.

He peered at her. "So what is it you want to talk about?"

"I've been wondering if you can tell me more about Angus Smith."

"Not the Magnusson woman? Just Angus?"

"For now."

"Well, it's funny you should ask that." He sat on the other side of the table cradling the warm mug in his hands. "We've been talking about him a lot, me and Jack Sawatsky."

"You have?"

"Yeah. I mean, nobody had it in for Angus. That Stella woman, she got up people's noses. But not Angus. People liked Angus. And Jack, he feels real bad. He was supposed to be looking after the place while Angus was in Winnipeg, when Stella's body got cut up in the workshop."

"Did Angus figure that out?"

"Oh, right away. Well, he knew somebody had been using the place. He was on the phone to Jack the day he got back home. Said it was too clean."

"Wasn't Angus pretty tidy?"

"He was, but there's tidy and then there's clean, know what I mean? Jack didn't know anything. He thought maybe one of the guys had stopped in to work on something, but why wouldn't they say? And who was fussy enough to clean the whole place up? George Smedley, maybe. He could be a bit of a clean freak. But he said no, it wasn't him." He pushed the cookie tin towards her. Ginger snaps.

"Jack asked George?"

"Sure. Talked to a few guys. That was the Monday, the day before they found the body. That shook them up. Angus and Jack, they went for a drink after. Angus was sure, right away, that someone must have cut up the body at his place. He had a good setup, a big table, saws, well, you've seen it, right?"

"Archie," Roxanne interrupted. "They were both interviewed here, the day they found the body. Why didn't they say anything?"

"They didn't really know, for sure. Angus had an idea who might have done it. But he couldn't say just then. He didn't want to blame somebody, then find out he was wrong. He wasn't ready to tell. He kept it to himself. He asked around again. Made sure it was none of the guys who had been in the workshop."

"Aren't there lots of them? Half of Cullen Village knows about Angus's place, right?"

"Yeah. But he'd changed where he hid the key in the summer. It was only the guys who came since then who knew where to find it. That meant there was only about ten of them. And then there's the ones who knew where Archie went fishing as well. Only about six more of them knew that."

"Did George Smedley?"

"No. George never went fishing. Wasn't his thing. Jack says so, and he would know. He can give you the list of all of the guys who knew, if you ask him."

"Couldn't you have told me this, Archie, after we found Angus's body?"

"Hey, lady, don't blame me. I told you to come talk to me. That very day. And again, the day of the funeral. It's not my fault that it's taken you this long to drop by."

She remembered him standing, waving to her, when she was leaving the frozen lake late that afternoon, and standing in the Legion hall wearing his suit. She realized why he couldn't come to her. That would be telling and men like Archie didn't do that. She had needed to ask, and he had invited her, twice. She hadn't taken his invitation seriously.

"Is there more that you know?" she asked

"Well. Yeah." He pursed his lips and breathed deeply. "Me and Jack, we sat here one day and Jack says, whoever did it had to know Stella Magnusson as well, right? Because whoever killed her killed Angus."

Roxanne nodded her head. "Did you think about the Andreychuks?"

"Bradley? He was never in Angus's workshop. Probably didn't know that he was away in Winnipeg either."

"How about his little brother, Jeremy?"

"No. He was pals with Stella. I don't think he and Angus knew each other, though. But there's something else, milady. Something you don't know about. And it fits much better."

"What's that, Archie?"

And so he told her. Roxanne sat back and listened, incredulous. Was he right or was what she was hearing just village gossip?

MARGO WISHART KNEW. She found it hard to believe, but she was sure. She didn't know how or why it had happened, but she knew who had killed Stella. She half listened as her friends chattered on. Margo found it hard to join in the conversation. She wished everyone would leave. She was relieved when Roberta finally announced that it was time to call her daughter and get picked up. Margo needed time to think.

Soon, Lizzie showed up with both children. Phyllis took charge of the baby.

"I can't think how Stella did it," she said as she bounced him on her knee. "Gave up her baby and walked away."

"She didn't have much choice." Sasha sat beside her. The baby was chortling. "If you'd been pregnant at seventeen, what would you have done?"

"Maybe she knew, back then, how Erik gets when he has a drink in him. Maybe that's why she wouldn't marry him," said Roberta, shrugging her arms into a parka. "And then she came back here all those years after and he was sober. So they got together again." She pulled up her zipper. "You know what? I'm tired of the whole thing. Don't want to think about it anymore." She took the baby from Phyllis and soon left with her brood.

Phyllis was giving Sasha a ride home. Panda reached into the closet for her coat and Annie's. All four of them walked down the driveway together. Margo waved goodbye and closed the door.

She noticed that Sasha had left a bag behind with an empty dish in it. It lay on the floor beside the closet door. She'd have liked to call her back so she could talk to her about what she was thinking. It might help to say it out loud, but only to Sasha, not with Phyllis hovering. She put the dog outside, into the fenced back yard. There would be no walk tonight for Bob. It was too cold anyway, crisp and clear. It was getting dark. The stars were coming out over the lake.

She loaded the dishwasher, let the dog back in and pulled a bottle of red wine from the rack. A Shiraz. That would do. She poured some into a glass and sat down at the window to watch the last light fade. She needed to remember exactly what had been said. And what had not been said. The doorbell rang. Sasha, she thought, back to get her dish, probably out walking Lenny in spite of the cold.

She went to the door, eager to invite Sasha back in, her dog barking beside her. She opened it. It wasn't Sasha. She stood rigid, appalled. The dog sensed her fear. The fur rose on the back of his neck and he began to growl.

25

BY THE TIME Roxanne left Archie's shack, the sun had gone down. It was dark over Cullen Village but, in the west, pink light glowed on the horizon. The stars were coming out. No moon. It was going to be crisp, dark and cold tonight. Roxanne drove slowly through the village, thinking about what Archie had told her. She was not ready to act on it, not yet. She couldn't be sure that he was right, but if he was, she wanted backup. She needed to talk it over, but with whom? Brian Donohue was the obvious choice, but he was in Winnipeg and she wasn't sure where she stood with him after he'd tried to cut her out of the Isbister interview. Izzy, if she could get her alone, but she was probably at Matt's right now, looking forward to a night off.

She passed Angus Smith's house. It was dark, apart from an orange yard light. Tape was still strung across the driveway. Along the lakeshore, the lake gleamed silvery cold. It was never entirely dark out here in wintertime. Even starlight was enough to reflect off snow or ice. Out on the lake was Angus's shack, where he'd been lowered into the water. Further along she passed the place where they had dug his body out, through all that ice. The pile of blue chunks had been removed and the hole had frozen over, although markers still showed the indentation that had been left, to warn off any passing snowmobiles.

She was at the north end of the village now. A car was parked beside the road. A woman was outside it, trying to catch a black dog, running loose. Roxanne pulled over and wound down her window.

"Do you need help?" she asked. The woman came towards her.

"Freya Halliday, village councillor." She extended a hand. "Aren't you the RCMP officer? The one in charge of the murder investigation?"

"Is that your dog?" asked Roxanne. The black dog was standing some distance off, near a street light, watching, staying out of reach.

"Not at all. It looks like Margo Wishart's. Can't imagine why he's running loose.

Roxanne got out the car. What was the dog's name? She couldn't remember. "Here, boy." Roxanne liked dogs. Finn hankered for one, but they couldn't have one, not with her job. "Come, boy."

She crouched down, held out a hand. The dog approached cautiously, his head down, the tail wagging tentatively. As soon as he sniffed at her fingers, she scratched his ear, then reached for his collar.

"You know where she lives?" she asked the woman. She didn't want to get sidetracked into taking care of a stray dog tonight. "I think I have a piece of rope in the trunk. You can use it as a leash."

Roxanne handed the dog to the woman and gave her the rope. Soon she was on her way again. There was time to go to Sprucewood and run. After, she would go back to the hotel and call Finn before he went to bed. Then she'd email Brian. It was the best course of action. He was in charge, after all. He'd probably come out tomorrow. She would like to be the one who solved this case, but she couldn't act alone on this new lead. And maybe it was just another dead end. Maybe Archie had it all wrong.

She had just let herself into Sprucewood Hall when her phone buzzed. "Hi, Matt," she said.

"I've just had a call from Phyllis Smedley. She's at Margo Wishart's house in Cullen Village. Sasha Rosenberg is with her. They say the Wishart woman has gone missing. Shall I go there and have a look?"

"How long has it been?"

It had been two, three hours. Not long, but the murders, and the fact that Margo Wishart had visited the detachment earlier and her dog was running loose, added up to something. But what?

"I'll see you there," Roxanne said. When she got to Margo's house she found Sasha and Phyllis seated at Margo's table. There was no sign of Margo. The dishwasher had finished a cycle. It was still warm. Margo's car was gone, her red puffer jacket was gone, her boots were gone. An open bottle of red wine sat on the kitchen counter, a used wine glass beside it. On the table was an almost empty bottle of brandy and a crystal tumbler. The same black dog she had seen earlier came to meet her and then went to lie down in a dog bed in the corner.

"She must have just gone out," Roxanne suggested. "She forgot about the dog."

"Never," Sasha asserted. "No way she'd leave that dog outside loose on a night like this. And what was he doing out on the street anyway? She has a fenced yard. Freya Halliday brought him over to my place, to see if he really was Margo's dog. The house was all locked up. The dog was hungry and thirsty. Margo would never leave him like that. Something's wrong here."

"How did you get in?"

"Spare key. I have hers and she has mine. Freya's gone home, had to feed her husband his dinner, but I called Phyllis and she knew how to get hold of Constable Stavros."

"It is very strange," said Phyllis. "We were here this afternoon. She didn't say a thing about going out this evening."

"Who else was here?"

"Roberta Axelsson. Panda and Annie, you know them?"

"Did anything unusual happen?"

The two women looked blank. Nothing. They'd talked, that's all. It had been after 4:00 pm when they left. They had all gone at the same time.

Matt came through a door that was connected to the garage. "Everything's locked up. I can't see anything unusual. Maybe something unexpected came up? She has a cellphone?"

"I tried," said Sasha. "Says it's out of the area."

Roxanne looked at the brandy and the wine bottles. "Does she drink much? When she's alone?"

"Not really," said Sasha, her brow furrowed with anxiety. "Hardly ever. A glass of wine, maybe. Not enough to get drunk."

"And she wouldn't drive when she's drunk," Phyllis added, her voice sharp and insistent. "We had dinner recently and she was driving. Didn't touch a drop. Look, there's been two murders already. And my George has gone missing. You might have caught him if you'd been quicker off the mark. Shouldn't you be organizing a search?"

It was still only three hours, but she had a point. Did they know Margo's licence number? No, but she drove a blue Honda Civic. Did she have relatives? There was a daughter in Toronto, a son in Vancouver. Was there a recent photograph of her anywhere?

Phyllis thumbed through images on her phone. She found Margo's Facebook page. "She didn't take selfies. But there's this." The photograph was of the book group. Margo sat in the middle, Sasha and Roberta on one side, Panda and Annie on the other. Phyllis had taken the photo herself.

Matt had gone to his car to fetch bags for the bottles and glasses. He'd have to find a way to recork the wine. She followed him outside. "Okay, let's do it. Find the number of the Honda and get a call out on it. I'm going to go and talk to your aunt and Annie Chan. What's the quickest way to get to their place from here?"

"I can take you." He had his phone out already. "Or I could call Panda. Will I get her to meet you at the detachment?"

"No," she said. "I need you to take care of things at this end. Send these two home and stay here. Margo Wishart might show up. Call me if she does. Now, which way do I go?"

MARGO WISHART STRUGGLED to regain consciousness. It was too dark to see anything. And cold. She was disoriented, her hands felt numb. She patted her body. She must be wearing her thick, puffy jacket, but no gloves. That was not good. Her head hurt. She touched her forehead. It was sore, tender, crusted with something. Blood?

The taste in her mouth was disgusting. Stale brandy. A memory swam into focus of eyes that were hard and hateful, a long, shiny blade, the threat of death, having to drink, glass after glass. Her mouth was dry. Had she vomited already? She should be more drunk than she was. Maybe danger had helped sober her.

She was lying at an awkward angle, her head lower than her feet. There was something solid underneath her, under her belly, rectangular and hard. She touched it, felt around with her palms. Her fingers were stiff and cold. She recognized the console of her car. That was where she was, sprawled over the front seats, in the dark, somewhere out in the cold.

She reached out and touched the steering wheel. Above and to the left there were rectangles of faint light. She squinted at them, forced her fingers to grab onto the wheel. It was frigid, but at least it wasn't metal, so her skin didn't freeze to it. She pulled herself upright. She needed to get her fingers warm so they didn't get frostbitten. She pushed each icy hand up the opposite sleeve. This jacket was not warm enough. She had a big down-filled parka for going outside at minus forty. She wished she was wearing it now. She would die out here in the cold if she didn't get help. But that was the plan, wasn't it? She remembered. This was supposed to look like an accident, like she had driven into the ditch, drunk. And then she had frozen to death, out here in the dead of winter.

Where was she? All she could see was grey light through the windshield. It was frosted over. So was the side window. Reluctantly, she pulled a hand out of the sleeve and felt around for a handle. She wound the window down, about three inches. It was even colder outside. Above, the sky was thick with stars. A satellite blipped its way across the dark expanse. Just you and me out here, she thought. The only things moving on this black, lonely night.

She wound the window up again, unlocked the door and pushed up against it. It was heavy at this angle. She got it six inches or so open and pushed her head outside. The air was so cold she could hardly breathe. She could see the edge of the road, up above her. The car was deep in a ditch, in a snowdrift. Should she try to climb out? You were always told to stay in the car. Don't leave it. Wait to be found. Would anyone be looking for her? Would they find her, out here? She remembered hearing of a man who lived in the village, whose car had stalled on a cold night and he'd tried to walk home. He hadn't made it. He had frozen to death. They had found him in a heap at the side of the road.

She was shivering. She flopped back into the driver's seat and the door slammed shut above her, like she was being shut in a tomb. She realized that she hadn't been belted into the seat. She stuck her cold fingers into her pockets. No wallet, but there was her cellphone. She pulled it out and clumsily poked at the screen. There was no service. Of course there wasn't. Just how remote was this spot? It had been chosen deliberately, so no one would come by and find her. A road not travelled, at least on cold winter nights, one where she wouldn't be found for a long time. She was entirely alone. The car, she knew, had been cleaned out of anything that might help her survive. The blanket she kept for the dog on the back seat, her winter survival kit, in the trunk, with its candles and matches. Flares. A small shovel. A tin that you could melt snow in. She was thirsty. Perhaps she could eat snow? The passenger side of the car was buried. She could open the window and grab a handful. But swallowing it might make her colder, and what would that do to her hands? The last thing she needed to do was get them wet and have that moisture freeze on her skin.

She had a thumping headache. It was difficult to think straight. She took her right hand out of her pocket and reached for the ignition. Her cold fingers remembered where it was. Muscle memory. The key was there. She turned it. The engine coughed then died, and she remembered something else. The tank had been drained, deliberately, while she had been sitting at her table, forcing down all that alcohol. There must have been enough gasoline left to get her here, wherever this was. The engine must have been left running while she lay here, unconscious. How long had that been? The whole plan was so thoroughly thought out, so ingenious. It was just like the other murders.

The cut on her forehead throbbed. How had that happened? She had no recollection. She reached for the glove box and felt around in it. There had been a flashlight. It was gone. So was the bag of candies she kept there, so she could suck one on a long drive home, when the greatest danger was that you might fall asleep at the wheel, mesmerized by the straight road ahead. Now she was in real danger. She wouldn't be found in time. She would freeze to death out here. She would die.

Her finger touched the dashboard. She remembered that there was a bar at the top, one with the red triangle on it. Hazard lights. Why hadn't she thought of that before? She didn't have gasoline but her car battery was good. She pressed. Red lights blinked on, wreathing her car like a beacon, on and off, on and off. Would they be reflecting brightly off the snow? If anyone at all was out there, surely this would attract their attention? The killer hadn't thought of that. It was a mistake, one that just might save her. Perhaps there was hope after all.

What she had to do now was stay awake. It was so tempting to sleep. She needed to keep her eyes open and stay as warm as she could in this frozen icebox. She pulled her hood over her head and tied the strings as tight as she could. She tucked her face into the car seat to protect her nose and her cheeks from the cold. Her collar was up as high as it would go, her hands were tucked back up inside her sleeves. She curled herself into a ball, like a small animal. Her legs were cold. At least she had warm socks on and leather boots. Her feet were not too bad. She tried not to shiver, not to let her teeth chatter. She started to sing to herself. That might keep her awake

"Twinkle, twinkle, little star. How I wonder what you are…" Her daughter used to play that on the violin, years ago. Then "I see the moon, the moon sees me." Except tonight there was no moon. She kept on singing, over and over again, alone, out in the cold in the middle of nowhere, fighting off the need to close her eyes and give in to sleep.

ROXANNE DROVE OUT of the village, wondering if Margo's disappearance was linked to what Archie had told her. She shouldn't be doing this alone, but Matt was the last person she needed with her. She stopped the car and texted Izzy, then drove to the highway and turned south. Shortly after, she reached the intersection she needed and turned west again. The night was clear, moonless. The bright light of a satellite crossed the sky.

She was still two intersections away when she saw a red glow above the trees. It moved, flickered and grew brighter, redder as she drew closer. She stopped the car, stepped outside, smelled the smoke and called in a fire alarm. As she climbed back into her car she saw a burst of flame above the treetops.

She pulled in just short of the driveway, leaving it clear for the fire crews, and ran towards the house. The top part of the A-frame was ablaze. Flames had burst through the skylights and ignited the roof. Through the lower windows she could see that the centre of the ground floor was also engulfed. The front door was locked. She peered in the window of the garage. Only one car was parked there. No sign of the red Sierra truck, which meant Annie and Panda might not be trapped in the fire. No one was in the adjacent workshop either. Her ears pricked to the sound of a siren over the roar of the blaze. A fire truck was racing from the direction of Cullen Village. One from Fiskar Bay wouldn't be far behind. She turned to see Izzy's car pull up behind hers.

"Bill Gilchrist and the guys are on their way," Izzy shouted, joining her in time to witness a glass window on the ground floor explode. "Geez! How did that take hold so fast? Where's Matt's aunt? And Annie Chan?"

"I don't know," Roxanne replied. "But their truck's not here."

Izzy glanced at her. "The Sierra? It's parked down the road. I passed it on the way here."

They jumped into Izzy's car. As they retraced Izzy's route from Fiskar Bay, a fire truck raced past them, then an RCMP car. Sergeant Gilchrist raised a hand in acknowledgement from the window.

Soon, Roxanne could see the truck, off the road, on a track that led towards a forest, one used by hunters in the winter. They stopped, stepped out, switched on their flashlights and cautiously approached the vehicle. It was unlocked and empty. On the front seat was a large brown envelope. Matt's name was scrawled on the front in black marker. It was sealed.

In the back of the cab a large, painted canvas was propped up behind the seats. Izzy pulled it out and shone her flashlight on it. It was one of Annie's. It showed Angus Smith, his wiry old body torqueing down through the hole in the ice, his feet twisting into the water, his arms stretched above his head, his face distorted into a grimace of horror and outrage.

"Look at this!" Izzy gasped. "You'd think she'd actually seen it."

"She did, Izzy. She was there."

"You must be kidding!" Izzy stepped back, appalled. Her flashlight beam swung away, illuminating the back of the cab. Roxanne spotted a dark shadow behind the painting. She put down her own light, pulled the painting forward and found a large, rectangular art portfolio. When she opened it she found the original drawing of Stella and a couple of sketches, studies for the painting of Angus.

"Grab my light, Izzy, so we can see better."

Izzy had recovered from her initial shock. She held up both lights, one in each hand. It was bright enough to see another big sheet of paper, shining white in the light beams, surrounded by black shadow. It was covered with drawings, done quickly, little more than dark, curved lines. But they were explicit, and what they described was clear. A woman falling into the front seat of a car. The same car in a snowdrift in a ditch. The same woman sprawled out on the front seat of the car, a gash on her head, obviously dead. She was quite recognizably Margo Wishart.

26

MARGO LAY IN a hospital bed, the lump on her forehead swollen and red, the gash covered with tape. Her cheeks and nose were ruddy from frostbite, her fingers bandaged. She had concussion. She also had a wicked hangover.

"Did one of them hit your head on the door frame when they put you in the car?" Roxanne was sitting by her bed. Brian Donohue leaned against the windowsill.

"I don't remember. Do you think they shoved the car into the ditch with me in it?"

"It looks like they pushed it with their truck. You've got a cracked back fender. The car's being checked out for paint scrapes and for traces of blood on the frame."

"I don't think I'll be keeping it." Margo shuddered, thinking of how close she had come to dying in her little Honda. "How long was I out there?"

"Brad Andreychuk came along around nine, so it would have more than three hours."

Brad had been out on his skidoo, skimming along the ditches, heading home after a day's fishing and drinking. He'd had a few beers out on the lake then some more with his pal Billy while they gutted their catch, so he'd taken the back roads home to avoid being caught driving drunk. He had spotted the flashing red lights and gone to check them out. He had saved her life. Now he was a hero, redeemed in the eyes of the village.

"You got lucky," Roxanne said. "No one lives out on that road. You were cold, but it could have been a lot worse. It went down to minus forty-two last night. People were out looking for you by then, but it would have taken them a long time to find you, where you were."

"So would I have frozen to death?"

"You wouldn't have made it through the night."

"Then Annie's plan would have succeeded."

Margo had been hypothermic when she arrived at the hospital, and the alcohol in her system hadn't helped. But she hadn't been outside long enough to lose any fingers. She would recover.

"You think it was Annie's idea?" Roxanne asked.

"I know it was. Annie was the killer. She found a knife in my kitchen. My best boning knife, it's really sharp. She wanted to kill me with it, right away, but Panda talked her out of it. She said they needed to make it look accidental. So they taped my arms behind the back of the chair with duct tape and Panda held the brandy glass up so I could drink. I had poured myself a glass of wine. I think seeing it on the table gave them the idea of making me drink it, but Panda said they needed to get me really drunk, and faster. She found the brandy in my kitchen cupboard. I used it for cooking, at Christmas. Hardly any of it was gone. Annie said she'd stab me if I didn't drink all of it. She meant it. I knew she did."

"Why did she want you dead?"

"Can you pass me that water?" Margo gestured to a glass with a straw that was out of reach. Roxanne held it to her lips. "Rehydration." Margo sipped tentatively. "I haven't been able to hold anything down, even water, until now."

"It all started yesterday afternoon? There was a lunch at your house? Panda and Annie were there?"

"They were. That's when I realized that they'd done it. Killed Stella. I was sitting on one side of the table. Annie and Panda were opposite me. I don't think anyone noticed what happened except Panda and me. It just took a moment. Someone asked Annie a question about Brandon, what she knew about the town, and she didn't reply right away. She stalled. Avoided answering. She looked across the table at Panda. Not a look of alarm or anything, more a warning—a 'keep-your-mouth-shut' kind of look. And I saw it. Panda turned her head and looked across in my direction. She caught me looking. It all happened so quickly. I knew, instantly, that they were hiding something, and I didn't know how or why, but I was certain it was to do with the murders. Panda carried on talking like nothing had happened. I hoped she hadn't noticed, but I suppose she had.

"There was another moment. It had happened earlier. I said something about Panda knowing that something was wrong with Stella's accounting and she froze me out. She just didn't want to talk about it.

"I thought about it all through the rest of lunch. Why would Annie not want to talk about Brandon? She was a nurse, you know, before she was an artist."

Roxanne remembered Annie springing into action when Phyllis got sick at Angus Smith's funeral.

"She grew up in Virden, west of Brandon," Margo continued. "It made sense that she'd have gone to Brandon to train as a nurse. She could easily have been there when Stella had her baby. She's a few years older than Stella so she's the right age. Then she'd have known Stella's secret. Turned out I got that part right."

"Did they tell you that?"

"Panda did, while I drank the brandy. I choked if she gave me too much, so it took a while."

"It's pretty well gone."

"No wonder I feel so lousy. Anyway, Annie took off for a while into the garage. She siphoned off the gasoline in the car so it would be almost empty when they left me in it. And she took everything away that would have helped me. The survival kit in the trunk. Paper and a pen in the glove box. She came back and told me she'd removed them. They wanted to wait until it was really dark before they took me out in the car. Panda told me the rest of the story while Annie was busy. She said that Annie recognized Stella right away when they moved here, to the Interlake. Annie has a great memory for faces and Stella wasn't someone you'd forget easily, not even after all these years. She also recognized Erik. He had shown up in Brandon at the hospital, right after Stella had the baby, screaming and yelling that he wanted to see her. He was breaking things. Drunk. They had to call the police. Stella wouldn't talk to him so they made him go away. Annie hadn't forgotten."

"How did that lead to Stella being killed?"

"Panda told me all about that too, later, when she was driving me to the ditch. We were in her truck. They'd blindfolded me so I couldn't see where I was going and put tape over my mouth so I couldn't scream. Annie must have driven my car. I think Panda needed to tell someone. Once she started she couldn't stop. That's what Panda's like, she needs to talk. She said it all started as an accident. Can I have some more water?"

Roxanne held out the glass and she sipped again.

"I hope I remember this right. I was so drunk. I really had to concentrate on what she was saying, so that I would remember. She said it all happened at their house. Stella came to visit them, the day before she was supposed to leave on her trip. George Smedley had told Stella that Panda knew something was wrong with the StarFest accounts. One of Panda's clients had made a big donation and Panda had spotted that the amount in Stella's books was less than it should have been so she'd asked George about it. Stella tried to convince Panda that it was a mistake. She told her that she would never cheat, but Panda didn't believe her. Panda said the books needed a proper audit. Then Stella said that maybe Panda could audit them for her. Stella would pay her really well for doing it.

"Panda told her that she wouldn't do that. That she didn't like cheats and liars. And Stella just laughed in her face. That's when Annie got involved. She said that Stella had better listen to Panda, or she'd tell Stella's other little secret. She'd tell everyone how Stella and Erik Axelsson had a baby years ago. She said she'd bet his wife, Roberta, would like to know about that.

"Stella's face went white, Panda said. Stella stepped towards Annie and raised her hand, like she was going to hit her. Panda stepped between them and pushed Stella away. That's all it took. But Panda was strong and Stella fell backwards. She hit her head hard, on the corner of that big cast iron wood stove that they have.

"Panda said she should have called for an ambulance right away. She hadn't meant to hurt Stella. It was an accident. She'd tried to defend Annie. But Stella wasn't moving. She was making this awful sound. Annie said she was in a coma. That she'd never wake up. She'd seen it happen to someone before when she was nursing, a girl who'd been thrown from a horse and hit her head. Stella was going to die and Panda would get the blame. Annie grabbed a pillow and pressed it over Stella's face until the noise stopped.

"Panda said that Annie thought Panda would get locked up and she couldn't stand that, so that's why she did it. Panda could never stop Annie doing what she wanted to do. She tried to excuse Annie, because Annie had a hard time growing up. Her dad was strict and she was the only Chinese kid for miles around. 'Annie's quiet,' she said. 'But inside she's a burning furnace. That's what makes her a great artist.'"

"She did drawings," said Roxanne. "Stella's head, then Angus. She did a big painting of him going down into the lake. Did you know that she made some drawings of you too? In the car, in the ditch. As if you were dead."

"She did? Well, that was a bit premature." A wry smile flickered across Margo's face. The dimples appeared on each frostbitten cheek. "What do they look like?" Roxanne took out her phone and showed her the photographs. The red nose wrinkled in disgust. "I was terrified."

"You had good reason to be scared," said Roxanne.

Margo shifted on her pillow. "I was mad at them too. You know, they were too clever. That was their problem, wasn't it? They tried so hard to hide Stella and Angus's bodies. It was so calculated, but it was over-complicated, too. So it made it more likely that they would make an error. Did they leave Stella's body outside to freeze? Do you know?"

"Not yet," Roxanne replied. "Her body could have been stored in an outside workshop that Panda had. It wasn't heated. Our forensic guys have been checking it for evidence." Brian nodded his head in agreement.

"Then they drove to Winnipeg," she continued, reflecting that after what Margo had been through, she deserved a complete explanation. "It looks like Annie took Stella's Toyota and left it at the airport. It was early Saturday morning by then. Panda probably drove their own truck and waited outside the parking lot to pick Annie up and bring her home. They had all of Saturday and Sunday to take Stella's body over to Angus Smith's workshop and cut it up after it was frozen."

"Ghoulish." Margo shuddered. But she was curious and dying to know. "So they must have gone to the dump that day to make sure Stella was buried in the landfill, but then it wasn't." She figured it all out aloud. "And Stella's body was found right away so their plan began to unravel almost right away. And I hardly ever go skating. Angus could have been under that ice for another two or three months if my dog hadn't spotted him that morning. Their plan to make it look like I had frozen to death didn't work either, but only because I was rescued in time."

"Annie made sure that Angus and Stella were dead," said Brian. "Why did she take a chance that you would be found alive?"

"Panda did that. I don't think she wanted me to die. They had such an argument about it. Annie would have had me dead in a minute but Panda insisted they do it this way. She left me room to survive. In a funny way, she maybe saved my life, too."

Roxanne wanted to tell Matt Stavros that. He needed to know that his aunt hadn't been entirely bad.

"How did the dog get locked out of your house?" Brian asked.

"I tried to close the door on them when they came back to my place but Panda pushed it open. The dog got between us, barking and growling. Panda threw him outside. Bob kept barking at the door. Annie wanted to kill him but Panda said that the plan wouldn't work if she did that. She said it needed to look like I lost the dog and was searching for him but he found his way home. It might explain why I was out there, driving around drunk. Annie went and opened the door. She had the knife in her hand. I was so worried for him. But all she did was kick him and he ran away. Bob's a bit of a wimp."

"And he's the reason we found out you were missing." Roxanne fed her some more water.

"I did get lucky. Twice. First, that Bob was picked up and Sasha figured out something was wrong and, second, that Bradley Andreychuk happened to come my way. Other people weren't so fortunate. Annie had a thing for knives. I could tell, just from the way she handled mine. She'd have liked to stab me like she did Angus Smith. That was scary. But they wanted it to look like I'd frozen to death, all on my own." She shivered again and pulled a blanket closer. "Annie was deadly. Panda was just an accessory. I liked Panda a lot. And I did admire Annie. Used to." It sounded like she was tiring. "It's all so sad. Did you have any idea that it was them?"

"Too late," said Roxanne. "Archie Huminski at the dump told me yesterday afternoon that Panda had visited Angus Smith's workshop not so long ago. He had helped her mend the legs of an old table she was restoring. And earlier in the winter Angus had taken her and Annie out fishing one Saturday afternoon. They knew about the workshop and where to find Angus's ice shack. So I did suspect them, but not enough to act on it right away. And it was difficult with Panda being Matt Stavros's aunt. I'd decided to wait until Sergeant Donohue got here in the morning."

"Angus went out of his way to help them and then they killed him?"

"I guess so. But they didn't succeed in killing you, and you have answered a lot of our questions. We'll go and let you get some rest."

Roxanne could see Margo's eyes beginning to droop. She rose from the bedside chair. Brian joined her. "I'll write up a statement," he said to Margo. Maybe you can sign it later?"

Margo waved her bandaged fingers. "If you can wait until these are mended I'll write it myself. Maybe a couple of days?"

"She's gutsy," said Brian, as they walked down the hospital corridor. "And she did everything right. Are you staying here for another night?"

"I don't know yet. I've got loose ends to finish up here. I need to talk to Matt and Izzy."

"How's he doing?"

"They've given him leave."

"You know you've been recommended for a commendation?"

"I have?" She stopped at the hospital door, surprised. "For what?"

"For saving the Axelsson women from that attack."

"Oh." She was stuck for words. Was that one of the things he had been doing in Winnipeg? Maybe he wasn't as self-interested as she thought.

"All the publicity you got helped. You'll probably get promoted up to sergeant after this if you apply."

"Can't think why," she said. "That woman in the hospital bed and two old guys at Cullen Village Dump figured out what had happened a lot faster than I did. I didn't solve the case in time to stop Annie and Panda from dying."

Two charred bodies had been retrieved from the burning house. The police were waiting for official identification but there was little doubt as to who they were.

"Hey," said Brian. "You were on the right track. Take the credit while you can." His car was at one end of the parking lot, hers at the other. "Why don't you come over for dinner to our place Saturday night? Sally and I will have the kids for the weekend. You could bring your boy along."

"Sure," she said. "That would be great." She'd missed calling Finn again last night. Her sister had not been pleased. "You can't let him down like that," she had said to Roxanne. "Well," she had replied. "Something came up." She'd be home tomorrow.

27

PANDA AND ANNIE'S house was shrouded in ice. The peaked roof had collapsed. The centre was a blackened maw, the sides jagged but standing. Water from the fire hoses had frozen in cascading icicles, some thin and fragile, others thick and dense, layers of them, glossy rivulets that formed arches and caverns with translucent blue green pools at the bottom. More ice piled in creamy, opaque mounds at the foot of walls and around what had once been furniture.

"It looks like something out of an old fairy tale," said Izzy.

"Yeah. There were plenty of witches in those." Matt was morose, his hands pushed deep into his pockets, his collar pulled up to his ears. "They got burned up too, didn't they?"

"I wasn't thinking of that." Izzy flicked him and Roxanne a sideways glance.

"It is pretty spectacular—an ice castle," said Roxanne, trying to sound supportive. The place really looked bleak. She remembered the letter Panda had written to Matt before she died.

Dear Matt,

I'm sorry I'm leaving you with this mess. I've checked the house insurance and suicide is covered. Don't let them tell you otherwise. You can rebuild, if you want. It's all yours. Annie left everything to me, and she died first. And I have left everything to you. The safety deposit box key is in the glove box of the truck. Number 362, Credit Union in Fiskar Bay. All the papers are there. I hope I haven't wrecked your life with the RCMP. Sorry again. But there'll be enough cash for a fresh start, if you need it. Hope not. You're a good cop.

This whole thing was so stupid. Stella never should have died. I didn't mean to hurt her. But one death led to the next. First her, then Angus. And Margo Wishart? Left lying out there in the ditch to die? That wasn't right. She was a friend. That didn't sit well with me. When we got home, Annie couldn't wait to get upstairs and start drawing her. I couldn't stand it anymore. It had all gone too far and it was time for it to stop. So I got the gun and went up there and stood behind her. I shot her through the head. She never knew a thing about it, she was so busy drawing.

I've got the pictures she did. Evidence, that's what you guys need, right? They kind of tell the story. I'll put them in the truck and then I'll drive it down the road and leave it where it'll be safe from the fire. Where you'll find it. And then I'll walk back here and I'll set up the gun. I'll get the jerry can of gasoline that we keep for the snowblower and start a fire and hopefully I'll have enough time to shoot myself.

When Stella was lying in a coma and Annie smothered her, she said it was because she couldn't live without me. And I can't live without her either. So that's how it's all going to end. We'll go up in smoke together, Annie and me. We won't need a funeral. This will be it.

You, my boy, are the only person left that will miss me. Don't be sad.

Love, Panda.

Matt's a good guy, Roxanne thought. He doesn't deserve this. How can he *not* be sad?

The Ident team had left but yellow tape still festooned the place. The insurance agent had taken photographs, shaken his head and gone.

"We have to stick to the edges," Izzy told Roxanne, but her eyes were following Matt, who had walked off towards the back of the ruined house. The site was unstable. Dangerous. They picked their way over broken pieces of burned timber frozen into patches of ice.

"There's nothing left worth saving." Matt kicked aside the burned frame of a chair. "The fire department wants it torn down by nightfall."

A small, blackened body had been retrieved from the centre of the house. Annie had fallen from the studio upstairs when the floor collapsed. Her oil paints and canvasses had fed the flames. And there had been a much larger body, not quite so badly burned but still beyond recognition, lying just beyond the heart of the fire. The heads of both bodies had been blown half off.

A car drove slowly by, stopped, then drove on again. Gawkers.

Roxanne walked past the garage, which had been doused to save it from the blaze and now formed an icy box. Annie's car was still inside it. A hole had been hacked into the wall of the adjacent workshop, where Panda had refinished furniture. The RCMP had retrieved a laptop from a cupboard, and a cellphone. They were checking to see if they belonged to Stella Magnusson. And they had found fibres that led them to believe that Stella's body had been stored there after she had been killed.

Matt was peering inside a freezer that had survived the fire. Izzy stepped next to Roxanne.

"We'll be all right, you know, me and Matt," she said with grim determination. "I just hope he doesn't get transferred out after this."

"He'll have to leave this area. He could apply for the Major Crimes Unit." Roxanne had already thought about that. If he did, he'd still be close enough to Izzy. He could work out of the city, as Roxanne did. "He'd be good at it." She hesitated before continuing. "It's not easy," she warned, "being a couple, with both of you in the Force. There's always the risk of something going wrong."

"Like you and that guy you were married to? The one that got shot?"

Roxanne regarded Izzy with surprise. "You knew?"

"Hey, Corporal. Kathy Isfeld and I found the whole story online first day, before you ever got to Fiskar Bay. 'Course we all know." She started to pick her way over the burned, icy rubble towards Matt, then turned back to Roxanne.

"You know, there's danger everywhere. Truck drivers die on icy roads. Farm kids fall into grain bins and suffocate. Women get beaten to death. Bad stuff happens. You can't avoid it. That's what we're here for, isn't it?"

"You know, Izzy," said Roxanne, "you'd be good in the MCU too. I'd recommend you in a minute."

"I dunno," said Izzy. "I want to have a life too. Know what I mean?" She went back to stand beside Matt.

That's me told, thought Roxanne. This work eats you up. But this case will be wrapped up soon. I'll get home to my boy, for a while.

"Who would ever want to live where something like this happened? What am I supposed to do with it?" she heard Matt say as she approached. "I still can't believe that Panda and Annie were the killers. Annie was always different. She was quiet, but I just put that down to her being an artist. I never thought of Panda as dangerous."

"Your aunt really wasn't the murderer. It's because of her that Margo Wishart is still alive." It was small consolation and Roxanne knew it.

"Yeah. But Panda ended up dead too." Matt cast her a wry glance, then turned to Izzy. "Want to go with me to the credit union? I should find out what's in that safety deposit box."

"Okay," Izzy said. "You sure you're done here?"

But Matt had already turned and walked away. He didn't look back, didn't lift his eyes off the ground as he walked to the car. Another truckload of sightseers cruised by.

"Creeps," said Izzy.

As Roxanne turned to open the car door, the sun came out. Crystal light was reflected from the ice-covered house. The icicles resembled the huge, shining teeth of a dark, prehistoric beast. Sooner they bulldoze it the better, Roxanne thought as she started up the engine and drove away.

VISITING HOURS STARTED at 2:00 pm. At 1:50, Margo heard voices and feet coming down the long, polished corridor. No one stopped them.

"I'm only supposed to have two of you in here at a time," she said.

"Forget that," said Sasha. "I'm going to go get another chair." She left a bunch of wrapped flowers on Margo's side table.

"We brought lunch and dinner for later so you don't have to eat hospital food." Roberta pulled a thermos and plastic containers out of a bag. "One of us will stop by and help you with it until your hands are better."

Margo had already told them by phone that the hospital staff was good and attentive, but they had made up their minds. "Please don't open that," she said, as Roberta began to peel off a lid. "I can't stand the smell of food right now. And I've got concussion, which means I can only have Tylenol for my headache. Can you talk quietly?"

Sasha returned, lugging a chair. "I charged up your iPad. Will you be able to use it?"

"Don't think so." Margo waved her wrapped fingers in the air. There was a TV monitor up on the wall. She might be stuck with that for now. The staff would turn it on and off for her. She wished she could hold a book. Sasha was peeling back the paper from the flowers. They were daffodils, with yellow petals just beginning to pop out from green buds.

"Probably shipped all the way from California," she said, "but smell them." She held them under Margo's nose. "Spring, right?"

"I'll go get a vase." Phyllis went off to find one.

Roberta inspected the swelling on Margo's forehead. "Bet you're going to have two black eyes. You're going to look worse than me." She had discarded the eye shield. Her eye was still swollen and was turning into shades of purple and green, edged with bilious yellow. "Is it true Brad Andreychuk found you? "

Margo rolled her eyes. "Who told you?"

Sasha laughed. "Me. It's the talk of Cullen Village. Jack Sawatsky says Brad was out fishing all afternoon. He brags all the time about how he knows how not to get caught drinking and driving. Takes the back roads home. So he's your knight in shining armour. On his trusty Ski-Doo."

Phyllis had returned. She put the daffodils in water and placed them on the windowsill in the sun.

"I owe him," Margo said. "Maybe I'll take him a bottle of rye or something when I get out of here."

"That's a waste," Sasha said. A nurse stuck her head around the door and frowned when she saw the crowd, all seated, coats off. Sasha grinned at her and waved a hand. The nurse departed. "Buy him some beer instead. Did you really drink all that brandy, neat?"

"I didn't have much choice."

They all fell silent, thinking of Margo seated at her table, being forced to swallow glass after glass. They had peeled off their coats and pulled the chairs up to the bed. Roberta opened a flask of tea and began pouring.

"It was Panda made you drink it?"

"Yes, but it was Annie's idea. She was going to kill me with a kitchen knife if I didn't swallow it."

"So scary!" said Phyllis

"There was always something a bit off about Annie," said Roberta.

"Oh, come off it, Roberta," Sasha protested. "Annie was just different."

"And intense," added Margo.

"Well, yeah. That too. But she was a genius. Wasn't she? Weren't we all a bit impressed that she was our friend? The famous Annie Chan. Wonder what will happen to her paintings now? Will they tank?"

"Or become collector's items, for rich people with specialized tastes. If you can put something in that tea to cool it maybe I could drink it though a straw. Corporal Calloway showed me photos on her phone of the drawings Annie did. My car in the ditch on its side and me, lying in it like it was going to be my coffin. That was spooky. There was a painting of Angus going down under the ice. She stabbed him, you know. And she wanted to stab me too. I could tell, the way she handled my boning knife, standing there at the table. I don't think I'll ever forget that. I wonder why she was so full of hate."

"Was she?" asked Roberta.

"Yes. You should have seen her. Her eyes glittered with it, from the moment I opened the door and saw them standing there. She was so still and so, well, concentrated. That evening, she loathed me. Or someone like me. Who knows. Annie came with a lot of baggage. She hid it well. We thought we knew her but we didn't even get close. Wasn't it all so ingenious? The whole plan to make it look like I had ditched the car and frozen to death out there in the cold? Look at how they tried to hide all the other bodies. Annie thought all that up. That took some imagination."

"They're saying Panda and Annie were both burned past recognition," said Roberta. Again, the room went quiet for a second. "I did like Panda," she continued. "She wasn't mean. She just loved Annie too much."

"We all liked her." Margo turned her head slowly to look at all of them. "She was fun."

"Well," Sasha said, "she might have sent a text to that nephew of hers to tell him where to find you, before she offed herself. She could have made sure you were found in time."

"I suppose. But I would have definitely been dead if Annie had had her way. Panda persuaded her to make it look like I'd frozen accidentally. That gave me a chance. And I'm sorry she's gone."

"So am I." Roberta leaned forward. "But listen to this. I got a phone call this morning from Mo. She calls herself Magnusson now. She wants to buy out my share of the farm."

"Really? For her dad?"

"No. She's going to move in herself. Her and her boyfriend Keenan. She's going to turn it into an animal shelter."

"Does she know anything about animals?"

"Sure. She worked in a pet shop. She loves them."

"Why your place?" asked Sasha. "She's got Stella's, right?"

"She's selling it. To Leo Isbister. He's got plans to develop the land."

"Into what?"

"Dunno. She wants to have possession of the farm by the end of April. I'll maybe have enough to buy a little place of my own out here. Maybe I won't have to leave after all."

They all smiled, relieved. Some good news was welcome.

"So there's just the four of us left. In the book club." Roberta held out a mug of tea with a straw. "I think this is cool enough for you to drink."

"Not the same, is it?" Margo sipped. It didn't taste too bad. She realized she was beginning to feel slightly better. "I'll be out of here soon. I'm not sure how I feel about going back into my house after what happened there."

"Tell us when and we'll come and get you," said Phyllis.

"We'll stock up your fridge so you don't have to cook for a while." Roberta poured her more tea. "Sleep over if you need company."

"Bob'll be glad to go home." Sasha grinned. "We can do another lunch. Start over. And we still have the book we were going to read. We haven't talked about that yet."

"Let's choose a new one." Margo said. "We should start fresh."

The daffodils were opening up on the windowsill. Outside, high up on the eavestrough, was an ice dam, a slab of ice that had built up on the edge of the roof during the long winter months. The February sun was just warm enough for it to begin to thaw. It began to drip, drop by drop by drop.

Acknowledgements

SPECIAL THANKS TO Nancy Hall, who was an ardent supporter of this book from the beginning, and to my literary daughter, Kirstin Macdonald, who edited the first draft and made it much better.

THE FOLLOWING PEOPLE have lent their expertise and encouragement when I have needed it:

Andrew Minor and David D'Andrea, who corrected all my false assumptions on how the RCMP operates. Any further errors in this book are all mine.

Patricia Sanders, who took the time to read my manuscript and gave me good advice and encouragement just when I needed it.

Faye Sierhuis, who told me how the financial world works (and sometimes doesn't).

Jackie Goodman, with whom I spent a delightful afternoon discussing how you could dispose of a dead body in a Canadian winter.

I AM SO grateful that Signature Editions agreed to publish "And We Shall Have Snow." Thanks to Karen Haughian and Doug Whiteway for shepherding me through the whole publishing business, and especially to Doug, for his thorough and patient editing of the final manuscript.

I first worked with Doowah Design back in the 1980s, when they were the graphic designers for Prairie Theatre Exchange, where I then worked. I am so pleased that Terry Gallagher of Doowah is the cover designer for my first crime novel.

About the Author

RAYE ANDERSON IS a Scots Canadian who spent many enjoyable years running Theatre Schools and delivering creative learning programs for arts organizations, in Winnipeg, notably at Prairie Theatre Exchange, and in Ottawa and Calgary. Her work has taken her across Canada, coast to coast, and up north as far as Churchill and Yellowknife. She's also worked as far afield as the West Indies and her native Scotland. She has two daughters and one granddaughter.

Now, she lives in Manitoba's beautiful Interlake and is part of a thriving arts community. *And We Shall Have Snow* is her first crime novel.

Eco-Audit
Printing this book using Rolland Enviro100 Book
instead of virgin fibres paper saved the following resources:

Trees	Water	Air Emissions
4	2,044 L	292 kg